# A Fistful of Dust

# A Fistful
# of
# Dust

NASSER HASHMI

Matador
9 Priory Business Park,
Wistow Road, Kibworth Beauchamp,
Leicestershire. LE8 0RX
Tel: 0116 279 2299
Email: books@troubador.co.uk
Web: www.troubador.co.uk/matador
Twitter: @matadorbooks

ISBN 978 1784625 009

British Library Cataloguing in Publication Data.
A catalogue record for this book is available from the British Library.

Printed and bound in the UK by TJ International, Padstow, Cornwall
Typeset in 11pt Palatino by Troubador Publishing Ltd, Leicester, UK

Matador is an imprint of Troubador Publishing Ltd

MIX
Paper from
responsible sources
FSC
www.fsc.org
FSC® C013604

*...To those Golden Oldies*
*Who fought their Jihad*
*By taking a giant leap...*
*...To the West*

# PART ONE

*Oh boy, make me breathe again…*

# 1.

Doctor Howarth leaned back in his seat, straightened his tie and told me I had a few black spots on my right lung. He was about half my age so I ignored him and played with my wife's butterfly hair clip. Fareeda had been dead for five years and had warned me about Turner Brothers for a lot longer. I didn't listen and now had asbestosis, according to the gloomiest man in the whole infirmary.

I pictured Fareeda sitting a few feet away from me with her hair flowing down the back of the chair. I would have reached over and tied her hair, caressing the strands between my fingers. It was the least I could do. She had been sweeping the wet, yellow leaves off our doorstep on that cruel morning. I had been yards away, watching the listless sun peep through the gasworks to create an enticing glow on her forehead. Seconds later, her body was lying on the pavement, her eyes at peace and her mouth kissing leaves. Her heart had stopped. The ambulance came but she was dead by the time we arrived at the infirmary. I only remembered taking home the hair clip: the rest was a blur.

Dr Howarth told me not to worry as mine wasn't an advanced case and the pleural plaques, whatever they were, were quite localised. He waffled on about medication and finally asked if I had any questions.

Thousands, but all the mill bosses were probably dead by now. He rose from his chair and offered his hand across the table.

'Good luck, Mr Shah,' he said.

'Er, Shah's my first name.'

'Of course…'

I left the room and ambled down the corridor, unaware the hair clip had snapped in my hand. I walked out into the car park and couldn't remember where I'd parked my Proton. It took me at least 10 minutes to find. I got in and drove home but my mouth was so dry I felt I was suffocating. I had hidden all this from Nadia, my daughter, but it was time to come clean about the rough breathing patterns, the wearing of gloves in bed and the occasional need for a coat while sitting in the living room. I dreaded the conversation because I knew how she would react. She would be adamant that I had no choice but to move in with her family in Edmund Street. She had wanted me to do precisely that since Fareeda died but I had resisted. I didn't feel it was genuine after Fareeda's passing because the house in Edmund Street was full – there was my son–in–law Salim, my 22–year–old grandson Wasim and my 14–year–old granddaughter Elisha – put simply, there was no room for me. But now there were two things in Nadia's favour: the first being that I was ill (and she would say, lonely) and secondly that Wasim had gone to Kashmir in 2005 to help out with the devastating earthquake and had not returned. There was now a spare bedroom. But why should I leave 'Mucky' Maple Street as she called it?

I liked the gasworks, the soldier–like assurance of the red–brick chimneys and the tight back alleyways. I had warmed to them after 39 years of comfort and liked the people too, even when my neighbour's rowdy son, Danny Langley, used the back alley as his personal play area for his provocative group of friends. If it was good enough for my wife to die here then it was good enough for me. But Nadia did have point: how many more slightly burnt naans, cold beans and undercooked gherkins could I consume from the same sea blue plate while watching North West Tonight on my old Hitachi 28 inch? Until I was fit and well, of course, but Dr Howarth's brutal verdict suggested I was far from that.

I phoned her as soon as I got home and she came over immediately. I thought I was under strain but her saggy, shredded eyes, made me feel like an amateur. She had a bunch of ghastly, bright–coloured clothes under her arm which she threw onto my dark brown settee and then followed that up by throwing her blue folder on top of them. She was a mature student doing a Fashion and Textile Retailing degree and my house was regularly cluttered up with her oddball designs, university handouts and ink–drenched stationery. But in the last few months, she had visited less frequently and I missed her tender smile and magical cooking. I put this down to the fact that she was in the third year of her degree in Huddersfield and was simply too busy.

Nadia made me bitter melon and mince meat for dinner and then filled up a steel bowl of hot water for my twice daily steam inhalation. I had dreadful trouble with my sinuses – my throat was jammed with mucus and the left ear popped regularly – but it was something I had got used to along with the fluctuating smells of stale onion soup, cigarette ash and burning rubber. Nadia walked in after doing the dishes. She started doing her studies on the settee while I lowered my head above the steaming bowl of water. She took pictures of the strange–looking clothes with a mobile phone and I instantly remembered the photos I took of her arm in arm with Fareeda on lazy Sundays at Hollingworth Lake. She used to wear a little orange sun hat, which was carefully pushed right back to show off her metronomic fringe and smooth forehead. Even then, at the age of ten or so, she had a sense of style and distinctiveness. I now looked at her and couldn't wait to be in her graduation photo. I wanted to see her make a career of it after all those years of secondary citizenship to that layabout husband Salim. I felt much more hopeful than I did after seeing Dr Howarth.

'We've finally got a diagnosis,' I said, raising my sweaty face from the bowl.

'What a surprise,' she said, picking up the white mini–skirt. 'So it wasn't a panic attack?'

'Asbestosis…nineteen years after my last shift at that fucking factory.'

Nadia looked at the image in her phone and flung her shawl over her shoulder. She put the white mini–skirt down, got up and walked towards me. She picked up the hand towel off my shoulder and gently wiped my damp face. She sighed and moved her face closer to mine until our heads were touching.

'I'm putting this house on the market tomorrow,' she said. 'You're coming to live with us in Edmund Street.'

A Ukranian family bought the two–bed terrace for a generous £73,000 after only three weeks on the market. Saskia and Andrei were the second set of people to view the house but I was lying down in my bedroom when they came. I forgot to rinse out my mouth after I'd inhaled my morning medication and I was sure I'd picked up a painful mouth infection because my ulcers were never that big. So I stayed in bed while the letterbox rattled and, after a few minutes, the sound petered out. Nadia later had to apologise to Keystone estate agents for the botched viewing but it was rearranged (with Nadia at home to show Saskia and Andrei around the home) and a deal was done. I was relieved the mini–soap opera of selling a home was over – so many phone calls and thick pieces of paper to consider – but leaving a house I'd occupied for more than half of my life was still going to be a wrench, even though a buying price of £125 in 1967 had now turned into a tidy profit.

Nadia had organised a removal company to clear the house and I couldn't bear to look at it now. She had the vacuum cleaner on downstairs and the noise was unbearable. So I walked into our cold, empty bedroom and opened the door of the only fitted shelf. Fareeda's bright red jewellery box was still there packed full of luxurious gold necklaces, earrings and broaches. I picked it up and felt the gorgeous

7

red felt in my hands. She hadn't worn or touched the jewellery since our wedding day 42 years ago. Nor had I. We married relatively late, in community terms, because my father sent me off to work in a textile mill in Faisalabad to provide food for the family and I didn't return to my small village in Kashmir until I was in my late twenties. He had always had his eye on Fareeda for me but she was four years older – and there was talk in the village that there was something wrong with her because she was still unmarried into her thirties. But the ceremony finally took place when she was 33 and I was so happy that I had a wife – and a prospective family – before I took the intimidating journey to England a year later. That gave me immense strength. The only regret I had later was that Fareeda could not bear me more one child, partly because of her age, but more because she developed Type One diabetes in her third year in England. I wanted more children but the constant injections, fatigue and general monitoring of her condition meant she lost interest in going into hospital again, perhaps for another caesarean. But, at least, I still had the jewellery box. I opened it up and looked down at the snake–like, spaghetti junction of items. I hadn't known there was so many. I picked up her necklace and felt it between my fingers. Father told me brides never looked up because they were weighed down by so much jewellery – but Fareeda did. As we finally sat down side by side to carry out our marriage vows, she touched her necklace and glanced up at me. It was a wonderful, shocking moment but no–one else noticed it. That was what I liked about Fareeda. She was poised and self-assured in awkward moments and tense situations. She would know exactly what to do now.

I walked down the corridor to the bathroom and placed the jewellery box on the edge of the sink. I looked into the mirror and lowered my head to look at my shock of white M–shaped hair. It was stupid but the only word I could think of was Mesothelioma. I had to snap out of it. I rushed out of the bathroom and headed downstairs towards Nadia. She didn't notice me so I stopped halfway down the stairs and looked at her. She looked so radiant and stylish in her thick red pullover and jet–black trousers. There was a lot of Fareeda in her. I walked down into living room and stopped by her side. She kicked a button on the vacuum cleaner to make it stop. She looked up at me and shook her head.

'See Daddy, that's why you need to come with me,' she said, stepping forward. 'Come on, raise your arms.'

I realised I had put my grey jumper on back to front. It was easily done. There was no tag on either side so it was difficult to tell at times. I wasn't embarrassed: it was an easy mistake to make. I put my arms up in the air and Nadia took off my jumper. I felt incredibly cold and exposed in my flimsy short–sleeved shirt but Nadia's soft breath warmed me up like no amount of clothing ever could. She pulled the jumper over my head the right way and then patted it down with her hands. She hesitated a moment and then looked up into my eyes.

'All your stuff's in the Proton now,' she said. 'You

get going, I've just got make some final calls to make sure everything's shut down.'

She gave me a quick hug and I walked towards the front door. I was going ask her about Wasim but thought better of it. She had her hands full and it would probably spoil the cordial atmosphere anyway. I stopped by the door and suddenly remembered that I'd left the jewellery box balancing on the sink. I told Nadia and she said she'd get it. I was annoyed that, after the jumper episode, I'd forgotten something else so soon. I was relieved that Nadia was the only person here to experience it. I stepped out of the front door and a gust of wind nearly blew me across the street. My Proton was parked a few yards away halfway up the pavement, almost touching Mr Pitkethley's front door. I took short steps in my cherry brown slip–on shoes and savoured every last stride. I got in and looked over my shoulder at the brown boxes and carrier bags in the back seat. Apart from the clothes and other necessities, the other items felt worthless: the Mukesh and Roger Whittaker cassettes; the unread biographies of Dickie Bird and Gamal Abdel Nasser; the VHS recordings of *Love Thy Neighbour* and Roses Matches; the World of Sport annuals and the 30–year album of Hollingworth Lake photos. I felt I couldn't enjoy them anymore because the pleasure was draining away from life. My narrowing, murmuring chest was denying me a long, wholesome breath and my cul–de–sac throat rarely listened to instructions. I hoped Dr Howarth's medication would ease the symptoms, particularly my night time coughing benders, but I was sceptical.

I drove carefully away from Maple Street for the last time. I looked in the rear–view mirror and could still see the exact spot where Fareeda had fallen. It would never leave me. I turned left into Manchester Road and drove past the high, hulking College Bank flats known as the Seven Sisters. These greyish brown, multi–storey concrete blocks dominated the town centre skyline and I still couldn't forget the five months I spent in Underwood block when I first arrived in Rochdale in 1967. I paid four pounds and one shilling for a one–bed flat and had to cook a very basic meal of bread and lentil curry after my first shift at Turner Brothers. On the odd occasion, I had to get my food from the chip shop on Spotland Road because I ran out of lentils but the stench of vinegar was too strong and made me sneeze repeatedly. I was thankful that Fareeda finally arrived from Kashmir six months later. She got me healthy again.

I drove up Spotland Road and missed the turning to get to Edmund Street. I had visited Nadia many, many times before but somehow drove too far down the road and had to put the brakes on quickly. I pulled into Holmes Street and knew what had happened: my mind had wandered to the derelict Turners Brothers site which was further down the road, beyond Spotland Bridge and up Rooley Moor Road. It did not exist anymore but I could not escape its towering presence. The biggest asbestos factory in the world had given me money, work and prestige but it was now haunting and intimidating me with its toxic legacy. I had not been there since I left in 1988. I did not dare go as far down as Spotland Bridge because I knew I would be sucked into the giant, charismatic site which had employed about 3,000 people at its powerful, freewheeling best. It was now being primed for housing and there was a campaign against any development on the site because of pollution. I had read an article about it in the *Observer*. I did not want to know any more or become involved in the campaign. It was simple fear on my part, nothing else. I did not want to read about any asbestosis or Mesothelioma sufferers. It brought back memories of my 21 years of service and the repeated evidence that these kind of illnesses can raise their ugly heads 20, 30 or 40 years later. In my calculation, it had been 19 years since I'd left and almost 40 years since my first shift at the factory. I did not want to read, hear or see anything more about it. Even the *Observer* report had made me dizzy and light–headed and I hadn't been diagnosed at that stage. Now, it would be a total blackout. The strain of trying to get compensation would make me seriously ill, I was sure of it.

I tried to put these thoughts out of my head so I stopped the car and tried to take a few deep breaths. But it was no good because I still couldn't understand how I'd got ill. We were told we did not need face masks because we were in the rubber department helping make motorway signs and brake pads. The real protection was given to workers in the textile and spinning departments along with blue overalls and steel toe–capped boots. I remembered my blue overalls were flimsier – they had no arms – but there was a certain logic to it because, in our department, asbestos fibres weren't escaping and fizzing up into the atmosphere. We were working with solid pipes and small pieces of metal and, besides, even some of those for whom masks were necessary took a liberal attitude to having their faces covered, particularly the work–shy Charlie Hassett who took great pleasure in doing the opposite of what was requested. So was the whole factory polluted? Or did I catch it from another worker in the canteen during our merciful hour–long breaks? And to think, I was one of the few workers who always clocked in to work about half an hour before the start time – at 6pm or 6am for 12–hour shifts – but what good did that do me now? I walked all the way from Maple Street with my tartan drawstring back over my shoulder and gave that company the best years of my life. They had now taken something from me. With silence and stealth, they reached in with their giant, grubby hand and placed a poison arrow against my chest.

Suddenly, there was a thud on my back window and I looked over my shoulder. A burly man in a brown Gola tracksuit top was eating what looked like a chip muffin drenched in ketchup. He ran round to the driver's side and asked me to open the window. I reluctantly opened it and he introduced himself as Paul. He asked if I needed some help in reversing the car out of Holmes Street because I had stopped the car in a tight little spot, perilously close to the main road. I said I was okay and he shook my hand. I noticed him moving up very close to me and listening intently as I talked. I knew my voice was getting softer by the day. Paul said he was bored and needed something to do. He also said if I ever needed anything I could visit him in the Atherstone block of Falinge flats. I wound down the window and drove off. As I headed up Spotland Road again, it occurred to me there was a connection, however tenuous, between Paul and a devouring employer like Turner Brothers. Paul was probably unemployed and Turners gobbled up workers and spat them out with ferocious regularity. But what did he do now? Where was the work? What I saw around me in the town wasn't pleasant – and what was happening to me was even more unpleasant – but Paul had got into my head and got me thinking about something bigger than myself. It was an unpalatable thought but perhaps Turner Brothers had offered something to the town after all: employment.

After a few minutes, I got into the top end of Edmund Street and drove past Spotland Primary School – the place where Wasim spent his early years. I couldn't help but think of my grandson now. Paul had got me thinking about him plus the dreaded realisation I was going to sleep in his bed. I felt guilty about taking over his room: what if he came back tomorrow? Nadia said he was doing well in Kashmir and wrote letters or phoned most months to tell of his latest tour to a village or fundraising drive. His picture had even appeared in a national newspaper along with the aid agency he was travelling with. In his last call, he told his mother he had been translating for the agency – and that they had even offered him a job as a freelance translator. He said he was thinking of taking up the offer. That was the last update we'd had from him. He was doing good work out there but I wondered if Nadia was punishing him for not coming back? I chose to believe she genuinely wanted me there because I was unwell and needed help.

I drove past Silver Street chapel, which was opposite the school yard, and headed towards my new home. Thankfully, as it was mid–afternoon, there was plenty of room to park my car and that was a massive relief. I pulled in outside the pebble–dash terrace with the Georgian windows and could already see Mrs Gleeson, two doors down, looking out from her front window. I got out of my car and walked up the path towards the front door. I glanced at the front garden – which had a two foot brick wall around it – and pulled out a set of extremely long keys Nadia had given me. She had pointed out the front door key to me but as I aimed for the tiny keyhole in the lime green door, I was so tense that I nearly choked on my saliva which naturally set off a dry, painful round of coughing. I was worried about the neighbours – particularly Mrs Gleeson – seeing me fiddling about so I gathered myself and concentrated harder. Eventually, I got in after three attempts and a surge of relief fizzed through my body. I stepped in and closed the door. I rested my back against it and, even though my bags and boxes were still in the car, I didn't want to go out there again, at least until

Nadia came home. I tried to take a deep breath and looked down into the hallway. Yes, it was familiar but had to become more than that: it had to become my home. I walked past the empty coat hooks and looked at the shiny wooden cabinet to my right with its beige touch–button telephone propped up by two Yellow Pages directories. Nadia had already scoured its pages for solicitors' firms. I had asked her not to bother: it wasn't worth the trouble. I headed for the stairs and grabbed the brown handrail while sliding the palm of my other hand across the cool dark blue wall on the other side. After a few steps, a sudden rush of sleepiness hit me and there was only one solution. Every day at this time – about 1.30pm to two – I felt the same tugging so I headed across the landing to Wasim's bedroom and opened the door. I walked in and sat down on the slightly hard double bed. I took off my shoes and socks and rubbed the soles of my feet into the bushy maroon carpet. I glanced round the sparse room and wondered if I'd ever get to sleep in it. There was a small set of dumbbells, a pair of ripped Reebok trainers and a black Head bag in one corner near the white dressing table. A swivel chair and small desk were hastily arranged next to the dressing table but looked empty without a computer or laptop. I figured Wasim probably took it with him. A map, about the size of windscreen, was displayed right across the cream–painted wall above the bed rest. It said 'The Ummah' in big white letters and it was a map of the world with all the Islamic countries shaded in red; all other countries with sizeable

Islamic populations were partially shaded in red and the rest of the countries without Islamic populations were left white. I looked at the UK: it was partially shaded in red. I had never seen the map before, probably because I'd never been in the room before. I deduced Wasim was another lost boy in a town full of them. It made me feel even more tired. So I got up and did my final preparations for sleep: windmills of my arms and a few neck rolls. I then stripped down to my white vest and underpants and slipped in to the cold bed: I couldn't be bothered getting my pyjamas from the car. I pulled the bed covers over my shivering body and sorrowfully looked up at the ceiling. Turner Brothers had taken my house, my health and my dignity. I wondered if my grandson had any dignity left after abandoning his parents. It didn't matter now: his noble adventure had cost him. This bed was mine.

# 2.

Seven weeks had passed but I couldn't get settled. Nadia did everything for me: filled in my disability benefit forms, cooked potato pancakes for me in the morning, washed my clothes, served my inhaled medication, helped me change GP's but she could not give me the thing I wanted most – time. I missed her dearly when she walked out each weekday morning to get into her Citroen to drive to the wrong side of the Pennines and watched the late afternoon minutes tick by until she returned. Salim, on the other hand, was not missed at all. It occurred to me that he was not comfortable with me moving in but Nadia had twisted his arm to ensure he didn't upset me. He had not spent more than five minutes in my company and hadn't asked me once about my condition and how I was coping with it. I was so relieved when he walked out of the front door, a few minutes after Nadia, and headed to Carphone Warehouse in Yorkshire Street where he worked. As for my granddaughter Elisha, I simply didn't see enough of her. She walked to Oulder Hill School with her friends and when she came back, she was either upstairs listening to some dreadful racket on her stereo or in the front room hunched over the computer late into the evening. We got on fine when we did speak. We had one long conversation about the difference between religion and culture while eating Pringles and drinking warm, flat Lucozade but that was about it. I wanted to spend more time with her.

Throughout this period, Wasim was hardly mentioned. Nadia said he had recently phoned her about five weeks ago but she didn't elaborate. Instead, she changed to the subject to Len, one of the umpires at the local cricket club at Redbrook, who had contacted her and said he wanted to speak to me. I was an occasional umpire there, too, but hadn't stood in the middle since the illness flared up. He had heard I had moved to Edmund Street and wanted to visit to see how I was doing. I could not face him. It was too much, at this stage. He would ask me about my condition and then the whole sordid tale of Turner Brothers would have to be dredged up once more. I wasn't ready for that. Len had become a friend in later years, perhaps the only one. I didn't have any real friends after Fareeda died. He was annoyed that the cricket club had to share its facilities with lacrosse and squash but decided not to make a fuss. He had introduced me to umpiring after I had met him during a local election campaign in which he was standing as the candidate in the Brimrod and Deeplish ward. Fareeda had contacted him direct and asked him why he wasn't doing enough about Danny Langley's mob who were drinking and smoking joints round our back alley and generally causing a lot of grief for residents in our area. To our surprise, he turned up on our doorstep and pledged to 'clean up our streets' of anti–social behaviour. It didn't quite happen, because even though – on Len's advice – we started keeping a diary and eventually had to call the police because one boy had threatened to kill another, the group carried on being unruly after they had been warned. Len made a passing comment that 'these boys needed a good clean game' to keep them off the streets and that's how our conversation about cricket developed. He said he was an umpire for the Central Lancashire League and asked if I liked the game. Did I like it? We got talking about the Roses Match and how we missed the likes of Jack Simmons, Harry Pilling and Frank Hayes: real characters that brightened up our lives and knew the value of sportsmanship and good humour. We even spoke about our grudging admiration for some Yorkshire players, although Len noticeably winced when I mentioned the all–round quality of Ray Illingworth. To my surprise, Len then asked me if I'd ever considered being an umpire. I hadn't – I thought I was too old. I was 56 at the time and still coming to terms with being made redundant at Turner Brothers two years previous in 1988. He suggested an umpiring course, which I took, and eventually passed. I spent the next few years travelling to games in Royton, Bury, Oldham, Werneth and many others. I felt alive again. As for Len, he wasn't elected as a councillor but never complained. We were quite close in the early days but since Fareeda died, I really wasn't close to anyone, except my daughter.

So on the 49th miserable day in Edmund Street I had no intention of meeting Len. But he was there in spirit. He liked having six peanuts in his pyjama pocket at bedtime and then eating them one by one. It helped him with concentration levels while on umpiring duty, he said. I chose not to go that far but the counting habit in bed was just as obsessive. Overnight, Paul and Wasim had somehow penetrated my defences and joined up to serve up a nasty dream. I couldn't really remember it, which was just as well, but I woke up counting the number of mills, derelict or otherwise, in and around Rochdale: State Mill, Mars Mill, Warwick Mill, Crawford Mill, Moss Mill, Arrow Mill. Instead of stopping at six I carried on counting. Crimble Mill, Albert Mill, Grove Mill, Fieldhouse Mill, Marland Mill, Dicken Green Mill. I couldn't remember many more: Fieldhouse Mill, Victoria Mill, Jennings Mill, Buckley Mill. I didn't know whether these buildings were still standing or if they ever employed a great number of people but that was a sizeable number of factories and mills – and they were the only ones I knew. Throw in the incendiary Turner Brothers and the chimney–loving landscape was complete. Somehow, all this was merging together to create a set of ambivalent feelings that I was extremely uncomfortable with so I got out of bed, picked up my inhaler and tried to snap myself out of it. But the feelings remained. I kept thinking about how little our young people had in terms of work prospects in this town yet I also realised that I had been scarred terribly by my brutish 21–year service at Turners. Which choice was right? Work and get ill or no work at all. It wasn't much of a choice.

I took the cap off my inhaler and took a pathetic, wimpy breath. It was utterly pointless. Sometimes, the medication made me more breathless than the illness itself. I went downstairs feeling extremely low. I glanced at the front door and could a see a few envelopes lying below on the bushy green mat. I thought about ignoring them because I desperately needed some fuel to get my body going but one of the envelopes caught my attention. So I walked to the front door and picked it up. It was a white airmail envelope with a blue and red border and it was addressed to 'Salim and Nadia Rafeeq'. It had a partially torn, black and white stamp in the top corner showing a city I didn't recognise with the date '1920' written underneath. I looked on the back of the envelope and it made me shudder: there was no address – apart from a sorting office stamp which said 'International Service Centre, Baghdad International Airport' and there was a tiny red, white and black flag on the bottom which left me in no doubt over its origin. I could feel my jaw shaking as I clasped the envelope in my hand. Stress lurked like a snake on my shoulder. I raised my inhaler to my mouth but it was no use: I could not get my lips properly around the mouthpiece.

I went to make breakfast and left the envelope on the wonky dinner table in the living room. After I'd dipped my cake rusk into my tea and been reinvigorated by the cardamom and caffeine, I paced around the living room for a few minutes wondering what to do. But there was no dilemma: I was the head of the family and needed to know what was going on this house. So I sat down on the sturdy metal chair by the table and tore open the envelope. Inside were three folded–up pages of lined white paper – marked 1, 2 and 3 at the top corner of each page – and I spread them across the table. My eye was drawn to the number at the top – 786 – and I instantly knew whose handiwork it was. The red handwriting was tall and angular with big, flourishing circles over the 'i's' and extremely wide verticals crossing the 't's'. It was neater than I expected; I didn't know he could write that well.

786
*Salaam Amee and Abujee*

*What a mission! Allah–thallah has rewarded me to come to this great land and I'm enjoying every moment of it. It is hot, at times, yes, and I don't get as much roti and dhal as I'd like but there are more important things than food and I'm here to make those things happen. My brothers in the Iraqi Khalifa Brigade are taking care of me and I will repay their faith.*

*It's important for you to understand how I got here because I couldn't help but think of the Prophet's (PBUH) journey and how he spread his message. First, I left the earthquake zone in September 2006 and stayed at crazy Chacha Manzoor's house in Muzaffarabad for a few months. Then, I travelled to Quetta and stayed there for about two weeks and then onto Peshawar where I met a man who* thought I could be useful in Iraq. But that was the easy part! Getting there was another mission. We had to go through some hairy parts of Iran (and you know I love my Shia brothers!) and it took nearly four weeks in the end. Now I'm settled and live in the house of one of Khalifa brothers, so there really isn't a problem.

I know you'll be wondering exactly where I am. I'm sorry but I can't tell you that because the kufr Annans will be on to you like Cyril Smith on a sofa! They won't waste a second in shopping me, you and our family so I'd advise that you keep this all to yourselves. Their agents are everywhere.

So please, please don't worry about me. I'm in good health and being looked after by a good family. I will be back when the mission is completed. I've heard there is a surge going on in the country by the invaders but I don't see many of them around here. They don't know if they're coming or going.

I do miss home but hanging around the Wheatsheaf and playing football on Lenny Barn can't really compare to this. I had to leave and do something else, something more worthwhile. There's too much suffering going on of our people and someone had to take a stand. Now, I've found the right path and, I hope, with your blessing, that I will succeed in this critical mission.

Of course, it's much warmer here too which helps!

Allah Hafiz

Wasim

To calm down a bit, I watched one of my VHS copies of the Roses Match and relished the sparse Old Trafford crowd, the comforting drizzle and the spirited cricketers. The umpires too, had the total respect of the players and knew how to diffuse a vigorous appeal with a smile or a wink. Wasim could learn from these matches, I thought. He could learn about teamwork, discipline and tolerance; he could learn about the power of personality and language to get your message across rather than physical confrontation.

The Roses Match took me up to noon and Nadia had left me a plate of brown rice and keema for lunch but I could only eat a few spoonfuls because its taste was dry and metallic. So I decided to fold up Wasim's letter, put it in my beige trouser pocket and lie down for a couple of hours – until Elisha came home. I rested my head for a matter of minutes when the doorbell rang. I wasn't going to answer it but caught sight of Len walking away down the street through the front window. The orange flat cap, knitted burgundy cardigan and brown corduroy trousers were unmistakable. On balance, it was better to speak to him now. I opened the door and called him back but it was obvious he still hadn't invested in a hearing aid. His stubbornness was admirable but it had practical drawbacks. I stepped out and picked up a tiny stone from the front garden and flung it over his head. It landed a few yards ahead of him. He turned and smiled.

'I've rang many a time. Are you poorly?'

'Come in, it's too cold out here.'

He walked towards me and took his cap off. He stubbed out his Woodbine on the muddy part of the garden wall and placed it in a tiny pouch within his flat cap. Same old Len, I thought, his umpire's coat was full of these terrible little stubs. He hated litter and got depressed by the state of modern pavements and roads which should have been like the square on a cricket pitch. He even railed at his fellow smokers for not getting 'rid of their dirty work' and, peculiarly, never once sounded hypocritical about it. He grabbed my hand and shook it vigorously. I followed him in and he sat down at the dinner table in the living room. He placed his cap and the Woodbines on the edge of the table. He folded his arms and looked at me as I sat on the sofa. There was an uncomfortable silence between us and I knew I had to come clean. It was as though my illness had become a secondary consideration to the bombshell of my grandson's letter.

'It's asbestos–related,' I said, clearing my throat. 'Got it from Turners. Had some symptoms out in the middle a few month ago: choking and chest pains. Not sure if I'll be able to umpire again.'

Len shook his head and sighed. He picked out another Woodbine and lit up with his silver Zippo lighter which had his three daughter's names engraved on it like a set of wickets. He rubbed the extravagant letters softly with his index finger and looked up at me. A strand of his neat silver hair had dropped onto his forehead and I was surprised he didn't reach into his back pocket for his comb as usual. As a former barber, of 26 years experience, he liked to be immaculately groomed up top. He used to run a shop in the town centre but it closed when business began to dry up after the opening of the Wheatsheaf Centre. He claimed it was simply because the old people, who were his clients, had passed away and the younger ones didn't want to have their hair styled by an old codger like him. He heard all the local gripes and opinions in his barber's chair, however, and used the experience to run as a candidate in the local elections after his shop was forced to close. He only missed out being elected by 26 votes in the end but it didn't stop him taking part in local affairs because he joined the National Trust immediately and started fundraising to protect sites and buildings in the area. On non–umpiring days, he liked to take leisurely walks and contemplate why his marriage to Sylvia hadn't worked out.

'Young Briley's still crying about that lbw decision you gave him,' he said, slipping the comb in his back pocket. 'Too many people in this town have suffered at the hands of Turners. I had a few people come up to me when I were standing as a councillor asking for help. Lord knows what happened to them…I don't want to pry too much but what are doctors saying?'

'Didn't really understand him but he said it wasn't too bad.'

'Good, so you can come back and do some umpiring then. Getting back in the middle'll do you good.'

'Don't think so. I'll get anxious if I go out there again.'

Len raised one his side of his mouth as he was prone to do when he was doubtful about something he had heard. He got up and slowly walked towards me. He stopped inches away and nodded. He took off his cap and placed it on my head. It was too big for me and I could hardly feel it. He sat down next to me and put his hand on my shoulder.

'How about a charity match then?' he said.

'Look Len, I'm grateful for you coming round but I'm not sure I'm ready for all this yet…'

Len slowly sat back on the sofa. He looked at his lighter again and then, to my surprise, handed it over to me.

'You know how proud I am of my girls…but what you probably don't know is that my youngest daughter, Alice, trained for two years as a copper but then got breast cancer. She didn't tell anyone outside the family. Anyhow, somehow the police found out and she was suspended for letting a pub brawl get out of hand because she was poorly. She was even sent emails from a former boyfriend at the station about breast enlargement and things like that. Nasty, spiteful stuff. Anyhow, she had chemotherapy and didn't give up. She battled on and, thankfully, got better. She's back out on the streets now…'

I looked at her name on the lighter and handed it back to Len. I was about to reply but the front door opened and closed. The living room door opened and Elisha walked in with the headphones of her

Creative Zen MP3 player in her ears – a device she'd been telling me about for weeks. She had her black v–neck sweater tied over her shoulders so its floppy arms created a nice window at the front where her white shirt and black tie could look their best. Her sleeves were rolled up to show off two wristbands: one blue, one white. She smiled at both of us and walked straight through the living room towards the kitchen.

'They're lovely when they're that age,' said Len, with a smile. 'Anyhow, I've got to get going. I've travelling up to Gawthorpe Hall this after…' He got up and walked to the door. I got up and followed him. He opened the door but suddenly turned and put his fingertips on his forehead. 'Oh, before I forget, Alice were telling me the force are desperate for new recruits. They're after more people from the community, that kind of thing. There's so much going on, terrorism, gangs, drugs…they're a bit short on that front. I told her I'd put a good word in, see if you know anyone.'

'Trust is a problem, as you know…'

Len opened and the door and smiled. 'Bring the young Turks along with me for a walk. There's only one Trust that matters and that's the National one.'

Len popped a Fisherman's Friend into his mouth and left the room.

I walked into the kitchen and could see Elisha dabbing down a piece of brown bread to complete her cheese and pickle sandwich. She squashed it down so hard that the pickle came bursting out of the sides. She ran her fingers round the crust to scoop up the tangy brown stuff and then licked her index fingers.

'I'm so happy you're here, nana jee,' she said. 'Hope the big I am never comes back.'

She picked up the plate and breezed past me before I had a chance to reply. As I turned to follow her, there were four quick breaths followed by fuzzy, light-headed feeling at the front of my brain. I stumbled and felt a volcanic shot of pain in my chest. I sat down again immediately and reached into my pocket for my inhaler. I was going to call Elisha for help but thought better of it: I could see her rummaging through her maroon gym bag with the sandwich hanging from her mouth. A few shots of the inhaler steadied me but the chemical fumes went up my nose and set me off on a familiar coughing bender which, this time, had the added discomfort of the sickly mucus remaining in place rather than being ejected by my throat. I managed to stumble back into the living room but Elisha saw me and rushed over. She put her soft arm around my shoulder and ushered me across the sofa, where I sat down.

'I've never heard you talk about Wasim like that before,' I said.

'So what,' she said, straightening her wristbands. 'He bought a hijab for me as an Eid gift but I didn't wear it. He got a cob on from then on so I just played my music a bit louder. He then came into my bedroom one afternoon and cleared out all my CDs. Why should I want him back?'

'Do you know where he is?'

'Preaching somewhere, probably. I don't care. I'm much happier you're in his bed.'

It was nice to feel wanted although I got the impression Elisha would have welcomed anyone into the house as long as it wasn't Wasim. I pictured her pale, plump face ripened by a bright hijab but felt it would drain the life from her sparky eyes and straggly, shoulder–length hair. She was a mere schoolgirl: religious utopia could wait. I wanted to press her further on the bouts with Wasim but realised I might be heading down a blind alley because it was difficult to tell how serious a brother and sister altercation really was. I was in no doubt, however, about the letter in my trouser pocket. It was like a second erection waiting to make a devastating impact.

The dinner table was never big enough for all the food so Nadia used the window–ledge to place the jug of water or odd plate of fruit. The water melons received that dubious honour for our evening meal and I was annoyed because I would have needed a tennis player's agility to reach the elusive plate of juicy pyramids. But there was more than enough food to be going on with like the plucky pakoras, the luscious mangoes and the towering plate of salad which was crucial to neutralise the zippy taste of the steaming meatballs. In a way, I thought Nadia overdid it – and she had been doing this since I moved in to Edmund Street. She made too much food and she knew it. It was as though she expected a famished Wasim to magically turn up for his evening meal and wipe the table clean in one of his legendary binges. She always made that bit extra for him: an extra chapatti, a few more potatoes with the lamb; a bigger bowl of trifle but now I was in his chair and there was no way I could measure up. It was true I had a weakness for things like pakoras, kebabs and samosas and Fareeda used to fry me the odd treat every week but despite me constantly pointing out to Nadia that she didn't need to do the same, she always did: every week.

I watched her as she finally sat down at the table to eat her meal. She looked tired and distressed; her unbuttoned light green cardigan needing a constant waft of the hand to stop it slipping off her shoulders. Elisha was sat next to me, dabbing unenthusiastically at the quarter meatball with a sorry piece of chapatti. Salim finally breezed in 20 minutes late, which was an improvement. Some weeks, he was gone for two or three days at a time, usually to Manchester with his old school friends, and Nadia watched him slump into bed in the early hours reeking of cannabis and tobacco. She confronted him regularly and he nearly always agreed with her but after a few days or weeks he did the same things again. In recent years, he had become overweight too: a sign of his lunchtime trips to Ali's Chippy in Yorkshire Street, which was only a few yards away from where he worked. When he married Nadia at the town hall, he was six three and as lean as an upright wicket and everybody was blown away by his elegant butterfly–collar, red bow tie and pinstripe suit at the reception which was just as well because the huge venue was far too big for a group of 60 guests. But that was his style: pay for the best and take it on the chin if it doesn't come off. I knew an arranged marriage would have been better for Nadia. Now she was lumbered with that oaf.

I cringed when I thought about how Salim would deal with Wasim now. One time, when Fareeda and I came round for Eid, I saw Salim pin his then 11–year–old son to the wall because he'd been wearing ripped jeans and an Oldham Athletic top all day – old, regular clothes rather than the shiny, colourful ones expected of good Muslims on this specific day of celebration. He grabbed him by the neck and told him that if ever wore 'that filthy gear' again on Eid he would 'disown' him. Wasim cried and we could hear him, in his bedroom, kicking the football in anger against the wall. He eventually came downstairs again for his evening meal because he was hungry but, ultimately, I sensed no connection at all between father and son. It was a practical relationship.

Salim walked up to the table, took off his dark brown leather jacket and placed it on his cushioned chair. He sat down and rolled his shirt sleeves up, straightening his silver wrist chain in the process. Despite my sinus problems, I could not escape the whiff of deodorant.

'Sorry, I leathered it here,' he said, picking up a pakora and dipping it in the chutney. 'There were an RTA in Middleton.'

The first time he said 'RTA' I had to ask a friend

at the cricket club what it meant and I felt genuinely enlightened when he told me it was a Road Traffic Accident. I had learnt something. But Salim continued to use it whenever he saw a motorway pile–up on the TV news or when there was a report of a local crash in the *Observer*. That was the kind of man he was: he liked to use terms that people in authority or institutions used. So police used RTA, journalists used 'bosses or chiefs' and banks used 'ISAs, PEPs and TESSAs'. Salim used all these terms and more. I could and should have let it all pass – after all it was harmless – but a couple of weeks after I'd moved in, he went too far. Generally, he had been helpful and sympathetic about my condition but when I was speculating about how and when I might have caught the disease, he shortened Turner Brothers to TBA – its correct title (Turner Brothers Asbestos). He continued to refer to them as TBA like some creep employee who knew them so well he had a job for life. It infuriated me but I was too weak and cowardly to say or do anything about it. I left it at that. But now, the RTA line had driven me over the edge. He would be punished for it. He would not know his son had sent him a letter.

I went upstairs that night feeling sad, frustrated and lonely. I desperately wanted to speak to Nadia but she was busy with the dishes and then had a friend round the house to complete a university project they were working on. She said she'd speak to me later that night but never got round to it. It was understandable but it didn't help my mood. The letter was still burning a hole in my pocket and the options about what to do with it were narrowing. I felt no–one was interested in me or the letter. I also suffered the added annoyance of having to get my steam inhalation bowl myself. As I got down to the bottom of the stairs, I was surprised to hear Salim and Nadia talking in the living room. I thought Salim had gone out but obviously not.

'Why didn't you put the old bastard in an old people's home?' asked Salim.

'Don't be stupid,' replied Nadia.

'Lots of Asian families are doing that nowadays.'

I felt my knees were about to crumple beneath me. Even by Salim's standards, this was a breathtaking escalation. I forgot all about the steam inhalation bowl. I went back up the stairs and lay in bed looking up at Wasim's Islamic map on the wall. The house was alive but I wasn't. I scoured the map and looked at all the countries. Where had I been? Where was my sense of adventure? Perhaps Salim was right: I was washed up and needed constant attention. I was 73–years–old but the only places I'd been to were Faisalabad, Karachi, Mirpur, Maidenhead, High Wycombe and Rochdale. That was it. Why hadn't I been to London yet (apart from Heathrow in 67)? I didn't include the odd summer outing to Blackpool kindly laid on by Turner Brothers. That was their doing. Yes, there were trips around Lancashire for umpiring duty but those, again, were part of work. Fareeda and I had organised a trip to the Lake District one summer but we had to cancel because Fareeda suffered a hyperglycemic attack two days before we were about to leave. Hollingworth Lake was as far as we got.

I also thought about Wasim and how on earth he'd ended up Iraq. Did he loathe his family? Did the town not treat him well? There were hundreds of boys (and girls) like him in Rochdale and I shuddered at the thought of their unoccupied, underemployed minds being polluted by some frustrated preacher who dazzled them with nicely–scented books and utopian dreams. I comforted myself by imagining what I would do to one of these know–it–alls if I ever met him: a cricket bat slap bang on his backside would be an appropriate starter. But surely Wasim's lifestyle didn't warrant that kind of attention? As far as I could remember, he occasionally went to Boundary Park to watch Oldham Athletic play, he liked a musician called 50 Cent and had a long obsession with films starring Laurence Fishburne. He was a regular Rochdale boy: cheeky, brash and hospitable. So how did he get his head turned? All these thoughts were making me angry rather than helping me sleep. Salim's 'old people' jibe had got under my skin more than I thought. Why wasn't there more for young people in the town? What were the councillors and politicians doing? Had I not done everything to bring this family to this land and settle them in? Did I not sweat blood at Turner Brothers and provide a future for us? Here I was lying in Wasim's bed – sick, isolated and resigned to my fate and there he was thousands of miles away on a deluded mission which would only end in tears. I started to sweat profusely and my involuntary cough began to stir up again. It was making me depressed. I looked up at the map again and, suddenly, a bolt of clarity shot into my forehead. I sat up in bed and looked at my trousers lying across the dumbbells in the corner of the room. They looked tiny and flimsy against the powerful slabs of weight. I got out of bed, reached into the trouser pocket and grabbed Wasim's letter. I sat down again and reread it. Strangely, I started to think how much money I had in my Skipton Building Society account. The sale of Maple Street – and my savings – had bumped it up to a healthy £57,423,42p. I wanted to give more of that to Nadia but she wouldn't take a penny. It was time to do something with that money. I looked up at the map and made a decision. I would go to Iraq and get my grandson. I wanted to feel alive again. No–one could stop me.

The thrill of going to Iraq had to be put on hold in the early hours. I ended up over the bathroom sink coughing up filthy lime green drops of mucus. Some of them missed the sink and ended up on the mat below. I rubbed them in with my sandals. But I wouldn't be denied. My tiny bathroom in Maple Street was always the best place for clarity of thought and although the substitute was too big, it still provided calm and sustenance. I figured I had about two months supply of inhaled medication (more if I used it sparingly) and it would be enough to see me through the early part of the trip. I didn't think the stuff was really working anyway but it would be reckless not to take anything. The steroids wouldn't be missed: they made me irritable and prone to overeating. I left the bathroom feeling better about the early preparations for the trip.

I woke up the next morning and walked into the front room after breakfast. I sat in front of Nadia's computer carefully following the scrawled instructions on the yellow Post–it note about how – if ever – I wanted to browse the internet. The orange curtains hadn't been drawn and the room got darker throughout the morning as each raindrop pelted against the window. I eventually got onto a search engine – as Nadia had instructed – and typed in 'British Airways flights to Iraq'. What a fool I'd been for thinking it would be that easy. They had no UK flights to Iraq. It was understandable but I was so frustrated that I left the room and came back after consuming a small bowl of cashew nuts. This time, I searched for all 'UK flights to Iraq' and, again, the results came back negative. I was beginning think my idea was far–fetched and delusional. After all, how would I actually find Wasim? Where was he? Baghdad, Basra, Mosul? And even if I did track him down, would he be pleased to see his granddad giving him grief about his so–called noble deeds? Would he take kindly to an old man clipping him round the ear and dragging him home to Britain? The doubts were increasing by the minute and, at noon, I was ready to pack it all in and let Salim and Nadia take responsibility for their wayward son. But then I caught sight of a link saying 'Austria to begin flights to Iraq' and couldn't resist exploring further. Yes, it was true: Austrian Airlines were offering two flights a week to Erbil and the time it took – roughly four hours give or take the time difference – wasn't too hard to manage either. I was excited again. I got up from the computer and started planning my route. I drew the curtains but didn't wait to look outside. Instead I walked over to the shelves by the computer and picked out a Collins World Atlas. I looked up 'Erbil' and found that it was in Kurdistan. That wasn't such a bad thing, I thought, because I'd heard a few reports that Kurdistan was much less volatile than the rest of Iraq. I pulled my finger down the page and tried to work out how far Erbil was from Baghdad. It didn't look too far, perhaps 200 miles but obviously it would be a little more challenging than a sleepy journey down the M1 to London, not that I'd ever made that trip. The momentum was now pushing me forward at an alarming rate. I managed to log into the Austrian Airlines website and licked my cold blue lips as it offered the chance to book flights immediately. I didn't wait and booked a single flight to Iraq. I then checked for flights to Vienna from Manchester and found there was no problem: there were plenty of airlines offering cheap fares. Checking the visa arrangements, however, wore me out and made me hungry. There was conflicting evidence but most of the correspondence said the same thing: that I could get a visa stamp on my passport in Erbil. Never had a bout of clicking raised my blood pressure so much. I decided to book it all there and then. I had to act before Wasim did any more harm.

After having spinach and lentils for lunch, which Nadia had kindly left for me to warm up, I drove my Proton to the town centre. The rain had eased off and it had turned into a brash and breezy spring day. The bold, white clouds had gobbled up the grimy ones and fragments of clear blue sky were breaking out an alarming rate. As I looked out of the windscreen onto Spotland Road, I almost wanted to stop the car and grab my umpire's coat from the boot and call for the start of play. It was that kind of zippy, zesty afternoon: a seam bowler would have loved to run in and extracted some joy from the pitch. But I was more distracted by the two teenagers standing outside Lucky Fish Bar, shovelling chips and gravy into their mouths from their mountainous plastic white trays. One was also consuming a can of Fosters while pivoting the tray of chips into his mouth with the other hand. Opposite them, on the other side of Spotland Road, there were three young worshippers on their way to the Golden Mosque, for afternoon prayers. One of them couldn't control his wavy grey shalwar kameez and nearly took off like an elderly comrade on the seafront. All these wandering boys had one thing in common: they weren't attending school, college or work. I glanced in the rear–view mirror, out of curiosity, and imagined the chip–eating boys having flasks in their hands while heading down to Turner Brothers for a shift. Equally, I hoped the Muslim boys had somehow morphed into fashion designers with nifty sunglasses, shiny shoes and colourful shirts. Alas, none of it came true and instead I saw the Fosters can flying across the road to the other side – in whose direction, I wasn't sure.

I got into the town centre and parked my Proton opposite the library. I walked up Yorkshire Street with four targets in mind: money, a new pair of sandals, a couple of books and a shoulder bag. It was a good test for the harsh, rugged terrain of Iraq. I knew Skipton Building Society was right at the top of the slope so getting there and back would give me a good indication of my strength, stamina and quality of breathing. As expected, getting there wasn't a problem but the trip back down was more challenging: the feet hit the ground hard and I gasped for breath just outside Littlewoods. This may have been more to do with the strenuous task of showing multiple ID to a woman at Skipton Building Society who eventually let me withdraw £30,000 but not without some funny looks and a devastating line. 'You're doing well,' she said, 'but that's the saddest face I've ever seen'. She was pleasant enough – a short, stumpy woman with long brown hair and an orange hair clip – but her words stung. Had I become so gloomy and sad that other people were now clocking it too? Why didn't Nadia tell me? Yes, my health was failing and I didn't have any friends or pastimes to speak of but I prided myself on perking up whenever I was involved in any community interaction. The Skipton woman was wrong. She wound me up so much that I couldn't wait to get out of the town centre. When I got back in the car again, I examined my face in the rear–view mirror and came to the conclusion that it wasn't as sad as she was making out. It was the corrosive curse of Turner Brothers.

I needed cheering up so I drove all the way to Newhey and walked into Romida Sports shop for a little treat. After a short, afternoon browse, I bought a white Slazenger sun hat, a Kwik Cricket set with plastic blue wickets, a blue cricket bat and a rubber red ball. As I handed over the money, my mind wandered to the Gunn and Moore cricket bat I'd bought for Wasim which he hardly ever used but ended up as an exhibit in a court case. One of Wasim's friends had used it to attack a taunting teenager on Lenny Barn and the flashing blade was never seen again. I wondered if the court kept hold of those things. Perhaps, the judge took it home with him and played with it on his lawn.

It had been a productive afternoon and I felt an incredible sense of achievement when I got home: I had bought everything I needed – plus a few goodies – and managed to nip back in before Elisha came back from school. I went straight upstairs into Wasim's bedroom and got changed. I looked at his Islamic map on the wall and felt a curious sense of envy that he'd already travelled to a country like Iraq at the age of 22. At a similar age, I was drinking lassi from a metal cup in a Faisalabad chapatti hut as I failed to come to terms with the news my father had died of pneumonia after a particularly harsh Kashmiri winter. I travelled home immediately but my mother blamed me for leaving home in the first place. The quest for work always comes at a price. England too, was a difficult decision for her to take but the right one. Now, I had to take another leap of faith – into a different country and a different world. I walked up to the map and slowly took it off the wall. One of the pieces of Blu–Tack was stuck to the back corner of the map and wouldn't come off so I left it. I folded up the map and put it neatly into my new bag. I got into bed and prepared for my afternoon nap. I felt hopeful and relaxed for the first time in five years. I felt Fareeda was by my side. Goodbye asbestosis; goodbye Turner Brothers.

# 3.

I only started thinking about the words about half an hour into the Austrian Airlines flight to Erbil. I had been locked in the toilet for most of that time because my throat–clearing mechanism since take–off from Vienna had failed and become an embarrassing vocal tic. The throat–clearing was a persistent problem and it became one part of the Bermuda Triangle, as I like to put it, with swallowing and hushed breathing making up the other points. If I didn't swallow enough, I breathed too fast; if I breathed too fast, I couldn't clear my throat and so on until all three disciplines were so out of synch that there was a 'trapped' feeling from which there was no escape. But as I stooped over the tiny sink, with the grinding whirr of the engines popping and piercing my ears, I had second thoughts about the note to Nadia. Was it the right thing to do? Did I choose the right words? I had left the note in a white envelope in her bedroom before walking to the bus station to catch the bus into Manchester. I could have taken a taxi straight to the airport but some drivers knew me so it was better not to take the risk. But it was the tone of the note that was literally hurting my head. Was it too arrogant? Was it too short, too long? Was a search party already out looking for me? Were they on this plane dressed like

US air marshals looking for an Al-Qaida operative? I came to the conclusion the words were all wrong: I should have written more. I should have been more upfront with the daughter who'd done so much for me.

*Nadia, don't worry about me. I'll be back soon – with Wasim.*

I poured water over my face and wondered how I'd become so wound up in a matter of minutes. The words were puny compared to the size of the task. I took hours over the note and rewrote it a couple of times. Everything before then had gone so smoothly: the knockdown sale of my Proton to Mushy Khan at his garage in Primrose Street; the nostalgic conversation with the cab driver, Frank, from the bus station to the airport about his daughter's tour of Afghanistan; the quick, efficient check–in at the airport in Vienna; the short, soothing wait at the airport lounge with its extraordinary giant red flowers painted on the sky–blue walls; the colourful interior of the plane with its yellow, red and white serviettes draped over the back of the dark green seats; and finally and most beautifully, the elegant stewardesses in their all red suits and red shoes adding a touch of style with their snappy neck scarfs. It was all so easy and relaxed, I thought, and I'd be sleeping in my Kurdistan hotel in no time. But as I undid the lock and walked back down the tight aisle, my breathing was reaching a rapid rate and the lack of mucus from my throat was always an indication I was in for a rough ride. I had to get busy and try to do something. So I awkwardly took my seat and reached into my shoulder bag for my Parker pen and hardback A5 notebook. A fresh note to Nadia would keep me occupied as well as purge the guilt I was feeling. I looked around before I opened the notebook and acknowledged the extremely slim man across the aisle who had spoken to me as we boarded. He had dimples, curtain–style hair and was wearing brown corduroy trousers that were slightly too big for him. He told me he was a Kurd and he was going back home after attending the London Kurdish Film Festival. He was a camera operator and decided to stay in London for a few months afterwards to 'shoot some cute stuff'. He winked at me while doing a 'click–click' sound through the side of his mouth and I nodded in acknowledgement. Somehow, the man's Polaroid moment loosened my throat and led to an extremely important ball of mucus emptying into the sick bag. I felt so much better. It didn't help my writing, however. A few minutes later all I had done was click the top of the blue–halved Parker a few times rather than get anything onto the page. I looked up over my seat and saw a stewardess walking down the aisle. I lowered my head, expecting her to walk past, but she stopped right by my side.

'Entschuldigung…' she whispered, bending down with surprising agility despite her red tights and her tightly–worn blue neck scarf.

'Sorry, I speak English…'

'My apologies,' she said, smiling and looking over

her shoulder as a passenger brushed past her. She looked at me again with a more downbeat expression. 'Have you taken a drink, sir? The walk back to your seat was a little shaky.'

'No, I have a condition. I'd rather not go into it.'

'You have pills?'

I shook my head. I didn't say anything else because I had a strange thought I could be bundled off the plane and quarantined in some extraordinary rendition procedure where US soldiers poked my lungs with a baseball bat.

The stewardess nodded and stood upright again. 'I understand sir, if you need help, just give me a call. Don't be shy.'

I nodded and she eventually walked away. I felt slighted. I'd never had a drink in my life and she had the audacity to say I'd been tippling when I had asbestosis? I took it as a sign of the times: everyone poked into everyone else's business. The last time I got on a plane, in 1967, no–one hassled me from Islamabad to Heathrow: I was the one asking all the questions. To be fair, the point about drinking might not have been technically true because I did sit in the Woolpack Inn five years later when Pete Blacker and Colin Shawclough urged me to join them after work – and I did try a half pint of Guinness after a lot of persuading. But I didn't like it and felt I was being pushed into it. Len also repeatedly tried to get me down to the Owd Betts, in Edenfield Road, after a match but, again, I declined. I never felt part of that world.

I picked up my pen and prepared to start writing

again but kept my eye on the nitpicking stewardess who was chatting to a well–dressed gentleman at the front of the plane. If I was slighted by what she'd said how would I cope if insurgents or Americans waved a gun in my face? They wouldn't think twice about knocking off an old–timer roaming their territory. I had to try to put my illness in perspective because I was going to a place where almost everyone was ill. I looked down at the blank page and decided there was nothing to say. Nadia would do the right thing. I placed the notebook on the empty seat next to me and crossed my hands. Half an hour went by and I eventually fell asleep. I didn't wake up again until we reached Iraqi Kurdistan.

I looked at my watch as soon as I stepped out of the airport. It was nearly 3pm and there was a sense of exhilaration of being somewhere important even if the low, flat airport building was smaller than I expected. The red, green and white Kurdistani flag flew proudly from the top of the brown and white building while a brash, scorching sun burst through the three colours to compensate for the hazy one trying to break out of the silver blue sky. I stood outside for five minutes not knowing what to do. There were no fleet of taxis waiting to take passengers away and I was getting some strange looks from the security men who may have been Pashmerga soldiers, policemen or just plain security heavies who liked gawping at foreigners. But how did they know I was a foreigner? I thought I blended in well. I could have passed for Kurdish or Iraqi easily – as long as I didn't open my mouth too much. Eventually, a man in a snappy black suit, embedded sunglasses and an earpiece approached and wanted to see my ID and visa which I provided. He asked me a few questions about the 'nature' of my business and then directed me to 'a free bus' which would take me to a fleet of taxis in about five minutes. Even though it was nerve–racking, I felt better for the exchange. It gave me confidence that I would blend into the surroundings and not stand out too much – as long as I could keep my coughing under control. Within ten minutes, my luggage was being put in a taxi driver's boot and I was on my way, hopefully to stay in a luxurious hotel bed for the first time in my life. The taxi driver, called Azaad, was wearing a baggy black t–shirt, dark blue Tacchini tracksuit bottoms and brown sandals but may have regretted his flimsy attire because my Kwik Cricket gear bulged out of the suitcase and grazed his knee. But he shrugged it off admirably and wanted to get going as quick as possible. His white taxi with a dash of orange on its wings had a dent on its bonnet which spoiled it somewhat. I got in the car and Azaad had his car radio on very loud indeed. The fuzzy reception pierced through my head for that mild, sickly feeling that always preceded a migraine. There was a small household generator plonked on the fur–covered back seat and I leaned on it with my elbow. I tried to tell him where I was heading but he raised his hand, asking me to wait. The cheeky bugger, I thought, hadn't he heard of the 'customer is always right' line? To compound matters, he started to move off.

'I'm going to the Erbil International Hotel,' I said.

He raised his hand again and listened to the radio more intently.

'Are you listening?'

There was a pause in the radio broadcast. Azaad turned down the radio and grabbed his t–shirt delicately with his forefinger and thumb, blowing down it for some much–needed air. He then glanced over his shoulder and smiled.

'It's my son, sir, I'm sorry, I get very emotional. It's his first broadcast on Radio Lawan. It's our first youth radio station in Kurdistan. Where did you say? The International, yes?'

I nodded. I was pleased that he'd turned the radio down because I knew at some stage I would have to make some contact with people who knew their way around. I looked out of the window at the swathes of bare green grass dissected by criss–crossing dirt tracks and was surprised to see the sheer number of scaffolding and high–rise buildings under construction. I had to pinch myself to think I was in Erbil and not Dubai (even though I'd never been there). But there was no point in looking out of the window thinking about the future, now was the time to capitalise on the cabbie's emotions.

'I need to go to Baghdad,' I said. 'How much do you need?'

I watched him blow his cheeks and rub the back of his neck. He looked astonished. I pulled out Wasim's letter from my trouser pocket and reminded myself about the name of his group. 'I need to find a group called the…Iraqi Khalifa Brigades. Will you help me? My grandson is with them. As a father, I'm sure you'll understand…'

I regretted letting it out so early. I felt like a kerb–crawler demanding a service for any price. And worse, my chest became painful every time I felt exasperated or was involved in a feisty exchange of views. So I stopped and chose to stay quiet for a few minutes. The car was slowing down as we approached a checkpoint and I could see Azaad staring at me in his rear–view mirror. His arresting green eyes and coal–black stubble put the wind up me. What did he think of me? Did he think I was a naïve old fart for entering a war zone thinking I could find my grandson with a click of the fingers? I didn't think I created a great impression. My elbow slipped off the harsh metal generator so I crossed my hands. I watched him as he wound down the window and talked to the guard at the checkpoint. They spoke for a few seconds and then the guard waved us through. Azaad drove off and looked at me intensely again in the rear–view mirror.

'You're breathing fast,' he said. 'Are you ill? You need a doctor?'

I felt paralysed by the question. I wanted so much to tell him but I didn't know him well enough at this stage. The doctors, over here, probably had enough on their plate.

'I'm fine,' I said, clearing my throat. 'What about you and your family? Do you have other children?'

He nodded. He was hesitant at first but then said he had a teenage girl who he didn't really want to talk about. He claimed he was only driving taxis because he couldn't afford to keep his electronics shop running in the town centre: the rent had jumped up from $400 to more than $600 in a year and he had to shut it down (I wondered why he kept talking dollars rather than dinars but later realised dollars were accepted here too). But he didn't want to talk about his old shop too much. Instead, he wanted to tell me about Sayid's involvement in Radio Lawan. He was a sound editor and helped build the radio station in just 25 days. It was a joint project with a Swedish radio station. The only down side for Azaad was that his son wanted to go to Stockholm and study there. It was out of the question, said Azaad, he wanted his 22–year–old son to stay in Kurdistan and help build the institutions and infrastructure. Azaad was on a roll and I was happy to let him talk until we got to the hotel. I could feel myself nodding off anyway.

He got to the hotel quicker than I expected. I was pleased that he'd finally warmed to me but I wondered if that was more to do with my condition or age. I looked out of the window and felt energised by the shimmering Erbil International Hotel with its ten–storey steel and glass building plonked on top of a solid brown structure. I knew it had a pool, a sauna, tennis court and a gym. It was a long way from the Seven Sisters in Rochdale, I thought. Azaad kept the engine running and asked if I had any dollars. I didn't so he asked for 5,000 dinars which I thought was pretty cheap. He got out of the taxi and ran towards the boot. I waited for a moment and eyed up the front entrance of the hotel: it looked intimidating and daunting. There was a class of people going in there I wasn't used to: suited men in expensive ties, stylish women in scarves, clean–shaven men in flip–flops and shades; I felt underdressed in my blue short–sleeved shirt, white woolly sweater and beige trousers. Would I stand out? Would they laugh at what I was wearing? And when I began coughing and spluttering, what then? Surely they'd gang up on me and have me carted out on the grounds of being a nuisance and a sick old man. I was mulling over these issues when Azaad abruptly flung open the back door. He had a mobile to his ear and stepped back a little, shifting the suitcase away from the door with his foot. I stepped out of the car and prepared for the short walk to the hotel. Azaad raised his hand, ordering me to wait. He carried on talking so I looked around at the people in the streets: the boy in a luminous yellow Barcelona shirt; the ancient man in the tweed blazer and flowing robe; the pale–faced woman smoking with a rolled–up magazine under her arm and the diplomat getting out of his blacked–out limousine followed by his granite–jawed bodyguards. But, in particular, a family, probably from South Korea (I remember watching the 2002 football World Cup) caught my eye. They were dressed in 'traditional' Muslim clothing and had their toddler between them taking painfully slow steps. The man was in a brown robe, white hat and black v–neck sweater while the

woman was in a light blue jilbab and wore thick–
rimmed glasses. Very traditional – but what was the
boy wearing? A grey baseball jersey with Detroit
splashed across the front and sunglasses which were
falling off his nose. It was comforting to discover the
generation gap wasn't solely confined to Rochdale.

Azaad ended the call and slid his mobile into his
tracksuit bottoms.

'I've called a man who will take you to Baghdad,'
he said. 'I will take you to him tomorrow. Then it's
your problem.'

'Good result,' I said. 'Thanks for everything
you've done.'

He picked up my suitcase and headed towards
the hotel. He looked over his shoulder. 'Are you sure
you don't need a doctor?'

I shook my head and followed Azaad to the hotel.
My left knee creaked and I heard it click as I took
the first few steps. I took out my inhaler and smiled
before wrapping my dry lips round it. I took a long,
lingering breath and felt a good slab of warm air enter
my lungs. I couldn't wait to slump onto my luxurious
hotel bed and sleep for a very, very long time.

I phoned room service for supper. It had been a
frustrating few hours because even the gorgeous,
inviting bed couldn't deactivate my brain to provide
some sleep. I wondered if the hotel room was too grand
for me: the red sofa, the giant mirror, the seductive bed,
the attractive lampshades, the immaculate towels and
the stylish James Gent shampoos and showers gels.

There was no other explanation. I had slept about four hours a night for a week before I travelled and I had a two–hour nap on the plane, that meant I was ready for my big 10–hour marathon which usually came after a seven or ten–day insomniac–stretch. But after my seventeenth roll to the left – and an increasingly desperate count of how many lbw dismissals I'd given in my final season at Redbrook – I gave up and went to have a shower. After a bit of difficulty getting the hot water on, I came out feeling extremely sleepy and phoned down for a plate of grilled fish, a salad and a cup of tea. I couldn't finish the food and the tea tasted sourer than ever. The liquid sloshed around in my mouth for a while as I tried to extract something, anything but it tasted more like urine than a pleasurable hot drink. It had probably started back at Edmund Street with my early morning cuppa when I noticed my sense of taste going south. No food was affected – and still wasn't – but it was agonising to lose the sensation of a warm, sweet beverage which had been my companion for so long. I wanted to get it back one day.

I didn't finish the tea and lay on the bed trying, without much success, to switch the TV channels with the remote control. About half an hour passed and I knew I was in the right mode for a serious bout of sleep. But then I was startled by the sound of the phone and the remote fell out my hand. Oh Lord, I thought, have I been rumbled by Nadia? Was she here in Iraq looking for me? Yes, old man, hunched, 73, white hair, white woolly jumper, extremely pale, breathing problems, is he here? Of course, madam, he just ordered room service. Can I phone him, what's his number? The back of my neck was sweating and I wondered if I should answer it. After the fifth ring, I got off the bed and decided to pick it up.

'Hello mister, you need to be ready tomorrow,' said Azaad, speaking extremely quickly. 'Ibrahim will take you to Baghdad. He can't go Friday, okay? I pick you up at 10 in the morning.'

'Er, hold on there,' I said, switching the receiver to my stronger right hand. 'I've got a reservation for two nights here, why can't he do Friday?'

'More trouble on Jummah. You want more danger?'

I hesitated and thought about the Golden Mosque back in Rochdale and how Friday was always a day of calm and compromise. Now, I imagined hordes of Muslims gathering in Lower Sheriff Street with their bombs, weapons and luxurious beards. It wasn't true, of course, but was that the kind of thing Azaad was getting at? Was Friday in Iraq a write–off left to insurgents, American soldiers and religious zealots to battle it out on the streets? How could I have been so naïve? There was a surge going on and it was obvious that civilians, of which I was now one, had to be extremely careful. Perhaps, I didn't think it was as dangerous as everyone said.

'Look, this call is costing me lots,' said Azaad. 'Ibrahim is a good person. I pick you up at 10 and take you to him.'

'Why can't you come? I don't know this…Ibrahim.'

'I have two big jobs to Sulaymaniyah tomorrow. I can come next week.'

I knew I couldn't afford to stay in the hotel for that long; I needed to have enough money for the journey to Baghdad and beyond.

'Okay, but I want to talk to this Ibrahim for a few minutes before we go...'

'You're the boss...'

'Er, just one last question...'

'Yes...'

'How did you get this number?'

'Things work differently here, we know everyone...'

Azaad had a lot of difficulty squeezing his car past the street vendors in the centre of Erbil. They were blocking his way and lined the edge of the road to sell their flat–bread, cheap DVDs and colourful second–hand gifts. I was constipated by this stage – probably as result of the succulent grilled fish – so I wasn't as enthusiastic as the night before. But I had no option but to grin and bear it because I sensed Baghdad was close, probably about four hours away, and that meant Wasim's world was tantalisingly within reach. Azaad finally found a small gap to park the car and we both walked towards the cramped tea hut to meet Ibrahim. He was a big man, about six four, with a moustache, no neck and a meaty, filled–out face, and was sat on a tiny red table drinking water and reading a newspaper. He greeted me warmly by almost massaging my shoulder with one hand while giving me a handshake with the other. But after that, he said little and listened to Azaad's instructions about the trip to Baghdad. I wasn't sure what to make of him but I sensed a restrained geniality about him because after Azaad told him about my 'illness' – even though he didn't actually know what it was – he said 'I can go and get my grandmother to come with us'. It was a nice touch and he looked like the sort of person who'd play with a straight bat. But even if he didn't, I had enough experience of dodgy cabbies or drivers – particularly at Islamabad airport in 67 when a man tried to smuggle me into a cab and made a pass at me – that I wasn't unduly worried. I'd gone beyond that stage. We spoke for about 20 minutes by which time Azaad said he had to go to Sulaymaniyah to drop off an American couple who were thinking about settling in Kurdistan. After Azaad had gone, Ibrahim and I walked towards his car and I was surprised because it didn't have the four corners of orange like all the other taxis I'd seen in the town so far. Was he actually a cabbie? Had I got him wrong? I sat in the back seat of the white Toyota Corolla with the black roof and got so worked up about it that I could feel my body weakening and, inevitably, a dry cough developing once more rather than the messy mucus one I'd experienced for the flight in. Perhaps I should have been scared. Perhaps he was a kidnapper, killer or a frustrated Baath Party member looking for some revenge on a British subject? It didn't matter now, I was in his hands.

The interior of the car was a sparse, scruffy affair. The back of the passenger seat was ripped and I could see a bit of foam sticking out while some fluffy orange bits were clearly visible underneath the seat. The gear box had obviously been changed because the needle–like gear stick was the thinnest I'd seen. There was also an unzipped brown holdall on the back seat which had bulky, silver–foiled items bulging out of it as well as four unappealing bottles of water. But what caught my eye most was a strange cube – about the size of that Rubik monstrosity – hanging down from the rear–view mirror which changed colours and complexion by the minute. It was intriguing and dazzling. First, I could see that all the six sides were the colours of the Kurdish flag. Then it changed to America's stars and stripes. Then it changed to the Iraqi flag. Then it changed to an all green affair with La–illaha–Mohammed–ul–rassulalah written in Arabic on all six sides. I wondered how the hell this was happening and, more importantly, why? I waited until we were on the outskirts of Erbil to put it to Ibrahim. He looked in the rear–view mirror but didn't smile.

'This many checkpoints,' he said, taking his hands off the steering wheel for a few seconds and almost signalling a wide. 'When we see American soldiers, we have American flag.' He pointed to the cube as it changed to the stars and stripes. 'When we go near Iraqi security, we have Iraqi flag.' The cube changed to red, white and black with tiny green writing. 'When we go near Ansar–e–Islam boys or Al–Qaida, we have Islamic flag…'

'Hold on…how are you doing that?' I asked, moving forward to get a better look.

He glanced over his shoulder and then gestured to his right hand which was in his right trouser pocket. I looked through the gap between the driver's seat and window and watched him pull a remote control out of his pocket. He pressed a button and the flag on the cube changed again. He handed me the remote. 'You want a go?'

Lord help me, I thought, I've ended up in the car of a James Bond fanatic who's probably got wings on the side of the car to take us up into paradise. I admired his innovation and courage but my enthusiasm for the cube was diminishing.

'Isn't that dangerous,' I asked, sitting back. 'Won't they be suspicious if they see a remote–controlled device?'

'It's not fantasy; it's survival. You have to be good with your hands where I come from.'

I wanted to ask him a bit more about his background but I could feel my jaw muscles tensing up each time I tried to speak. I knew I wasn't ready for a long conversation so I settled back and looked out of the window. The green–tinged valleys of Iraqi Kurdistan were gradually disappearing and snatches of bare, brown desert were coming into view. The grinding wheels of a Toyota pick–up truck had been behind us almost all of the way and I wanted Ibrahim to let him past – or put his foot down – because my ears were suffering. But he was content to go at about 50 miles an hour because he said 'Pashmerga and Americans have their eyes everywhere' which didn't fill me with confidence. But I couldn't see them, where were these warriors? So to divert my attention from these phantoms, I unzipped my shoulder bag and pulled out a Lata Mangeshkar cassette which Fareeda liked listening to in the evenings while rolling out the chapattis in the kitchen. I wanted to hear it so badly that I hadn't noticed there was no cassette or CD player in the car, just a radio. It was a crushing blow. It was going to be a long journey.

After a few minutes, however, Ibrahim started talking about his family and I managed to calm down. His languid, drawn–out delivery ate up the time. He said he lived in a remote, but beautiful, village in the mountains but developers were circling because they wanted to build a small guesthouse in the area. He was sick of the attitude of the 'town bosses' and said villages were being crippled because local produce was being replaced by Iranian, Syrian and Turkish goods. His family had been self–sufficient – they grew their own crops and had a tiny store which the villagers could reach on foot – but now the future was uncertain. The developers had already paid off some villagers but others weren't prepared to go so easily. That's why Ibrahim was going to Baghdad, he said, to meet his 'great friend' Gulzar, a lawyer, who helped them so much with his 'patience and advice'. They had met by chance when Gulzar temporarily fled north after the bombing of Baghdad in 2003 and Ibrahim had picked him up in his cab outside the Citadel. It was at that point that Ibrahim stopped talking. He wouldn't say anything else and raised his hand as if to apologise. I wanted to know more but Ibrahim didn't speak again for the rest of the journey. The image of a Baghdad lawyer cowering outside the giant caramel fort was difficult to get out of my mind.

# 4.

I was woken by the sound of banging on the car window. An old man with a tall, ancient tea–pot and a tiny silver cup offered me a drink but I didn't know where I was never mind feeling thirsty. I felt like I'd been asleep forever but it was clear we'd arrived because I could see a few damaged palm trees, a row of stubby army vehicles and the odd burnt–out building in amongst the proud, solemn ones. It had become a scorching afternoon with the sun now fizzing through the window making my eyes sting and my skin crumble. Ibrahim had slowed the car down, mainly because he didn't want to run the old man over or break his arm, but the man was incredibly resourceful and kept up with us, particularly when we stopped at some non–working traffic lights or were questioned by a bored Iraqi soldier in beige t–shirt and ripped army bottoms.

The traffic got worse as we drove along and, at one set of lights, I was sure I saw a round of bullet holes sprayed into the orange traffic light pole but thankfully, I didn't have time to work out how the dispute might have developed. The biggest thing that struck me, however, was the lack of people milling around. Apart from the odd street seller, Iraqi security and a few young boys in t–shirts and sandals throwing stones into a ditch, there was no–one else around in the streets. Most of the people I could see were tucked safely in their cars, probably thinking the sanctuary of their own vehicle was better than taking a chance on foot. It all felt lopsided and I had a strange urge to get out of the car and disturb the bare, peaceful landscape because it was being neglected.

But romantic notions of tiptoeing across the landscape didn't last long. I was looking at a wonky telegraph pole, with its hanging wires almost disappearing into the small bush below, when the blast was heard. Then it was followed by a smaller one. Then it was followed by one that sounded like a firecracker. It was extremely difficult to pinpoint where the sounds were coming from; my ears had enough problems with TV sounds, kettles and doorbells never mind bombs. There was no smoke coming from any of the buildings, no screams were heard and all the cars continued sedately down the road. I wondered if anything had actually happened but Ibrahim, thankfully, confirmed I hadn't been hearing things. He simply shook his head and pressed his remote control to change the cube to the 'Islamic' flag. I wasn't sure why he did it because all I saw in front of me was an army of blue–sleeved Iraqi police in their flak jackets carrying rifles and looking extremely bored. Perhaps there was a zealot or two among them.

Ibrahim knew I had different ideas in terms of the type of hotel I wanted to stay in because I'd told him so at the start of the journey. I wanted to try the Adam

Hotel first in Sadoun Street and then the Andalus Palace Hotel or the Khayam Hotel in the same area as back–ups if there was no space at the Adam. I considered the Erbil International Hotel as a once–in–a–lifetime experience but now I wanted something less glitzy and more down to earth. Ibrahim, however, had other ideas. I thought he was taking me to the Adam Hotel but he shook his head when I repeated my request.

'You have a death wish?' he said. 'There are high concrete security barriers in that area near Abu Nawaz market. They go on for half a mile.'

'I'm old enough not to worry about those things,' I said. 'I just need a toilet and a mirror.'

'You'll have nothing if you go down there.'

Perhaps Ibrahim was right. I was a stranger in this country and had no idea how dangerous it was. But in my eyes that was a good thing. It was a good thing that my condition was so corrosive I couldn't feel anything outside my 'sphere'. Without the internal struggle, I wouldn't have been able to step on the plane, never mind come to Baghdad. Now I was here, I felt calm and composed. It was as though the turmoil of the city offered a comfort blanket. It was a companion, a partner in strife.

'I can take you where there's plenty of room,' said Ibrahim.

'No, no I couldn't possibly do that,' I said. 'You've done enough for me. Just take me to the Adam and that will be fine.' I reached for my wallet in my trouser pocket. 'How much do I owe you anyway?'

Ibrahim saw me taking out my wallet and raised his hand. He looked over his shoulder. 'Put that away, old man, you owe me nothing. I'm not taking any dinars off you.'

I put the wallet back in my pocket and sat back to relax. But as I did, I felt a scent of rubber in my nostrils and a sick feeling in my stomach. I reached into my trouser pocket and picked out my emergency sick bag (a scrunched–up carrier bag from Lidl in Spotland Road) in order to release some of the locked–down liquid from my lungs and throat. But when I bent down and launched into a mighty heave to get rid of the sorry substance, nothing came out. All I had for my troubles was a few colourful drops of saliva, a bitter taste in my mouth and unbearable pain in my chest and stomach. Ibrahim asked me if I was okay so I lied and gave him the thumbs–up.

'Are there any mills or factories here?' I asked.

'Not now,' said Ibrahim, 'They're used for other things like killing…'

'Must have learnt from Turners,' I said, under my breath.

'What's Turners?'

I didn't reply but I was satisfied with my quick–witted response. It told me that I still had some intellectual range even if parts of my body were failing.

'So are you kidnapping me or taking me to the Hanging Gardens of Babylon?' I asked.

Ibrahim smiled and took out a mobile phone from his inside pocket. He glanced left and right out of both windows before tapping in a number and putting it to his ear. 'You have to be careful with phones over here; stupid police think something's being blown up.'

'Who are you calling?'

'Gulzar, he's expecting you.'

I tried to leave the Lidl carrier bag in the car but Ibrahim was watching so I had to pick it up and take it with me. I wanted Gulzar's house to be a few yards away but each time we walked past a gate or an entrance to the tight, sprawling neighbourhood, we soldiered on to the next building. The baking heat had a slight impact on my breathing patterns but I hardly noticed because I desperately needed the toilet. But there was the odd distraction to keep me going; in particular, a staring, overweight man in a black t–shirt and tight jeans whose face was horribly disfigured by what I presumed was some sort of blast or bomb. His dark face had white blotches on one side and one of his eyes was missing. His other eye made me shudder; he didn't look away once. I wanted to touch him when I walked past but didn't have the courage to do so. I wanted to tell him that I understood how everyday people were left on the scrapheap while companies, governments and other authorities carried out their dirty deeds. But when a barefooted old beggar in a grey robe suddenly stood by my side and snatched my Lidl bag all my noble thoughts turned to dust. Good luck with the empty carrier bag, I thought. Maybe the poor codger would use it to put it over someone's head.

There were other distractions too but none as memorable and disturbing as the staring man. A woman in a burka was telling off her son as he sat on a tricycle, three American soldiers were surrounding a teenager with one checking his pockets and one man was lying face down by the wheel of a motorcycle surrounded by a heap of rubbish, a ripped sofa and a dog sniffing his feet. It was a lot to take in and the atmosphere wasn't pleasant. I was relieved when Ibrahim finally stopped by a cream–coloured, two storey house with a black gate and black bars across the windows. He waited for me to catch up and then pushed open the gate. I walked in to the small front yard behind Ibrahim and had to carefully sidestep a stack of cardboard boxes full of clothes, picture frames, jewellery and magazines. I could see a man sat on the doorstep in the shade with a home–made fan in his hand. He got up and walked towards Ibrahim. He playfully wafted the straw fan in Ibrahim's face.

'Power's totally fucked again,' said Gulzar, embracing Ibrahim but looking over his shoulder in the process. 'Now, who's this Englishman you've brought me?' Gulzar let go Ibrahim and walked towards me. 'Ibrahim says you've made a great many sacrifices to be here. You're here to find your grandson, yes?'

'Yes, but can we talk later? Sorry I just need the toilet…'

'It's on the upper floor, first left. Are you in good health? I hope no war criminal has fired on you…'

I shook my head and entered the house.

'Be careful,' said Gulzar. 'It's extremely hot in there; the walls are like flames.'

I walked in and saw the curving staircase immediately. I wondered what the toilet would be like because I couldn't really manage a hole in the floor right now. I was too tired and inflexible. It wasn't as though I'd never done it like that before – in fact, for the first 19 years in Kashmir the hole in the floor didn't exist and the woods with all their prickly, bottom–grazing pleasures had to suffice – but the journey from Erbil had taken more out of me than I thought and I needed every advantage or luxury I could get. I walked in to the bathroom and thankfully the slim yellow bowl was waiting for me. The sweat was pouring off my hands as I undid my trousers and I just made in terms of sitting down in time before the dam burst; incontinence in Baghdad wouldn't have been a good start in terms of first impressions.

After that fantastic relief, I headed back downstairs and could see Gulzar and Ibrahim still standing outside. Gulzar spotted me and came inside. He was a smart, lean man with high cheekbones and a neat moustache. His pinstriped shirt with gold–coloured buttons, grey trousers and shiny black shoes gave him a certain poise and authority The only blemish was a set of stitches beneath his bottom lip which reminded me of the haphazard needle and thread surgery I had to carry out when wicketkeeper Giles Cooper was struck on the chin in Royton during an under 18s match in the early 90s. Gulzar wanted me to join him upstairs on the balcony, where it was cooler. I agreed but wondered where all this was heading. What did he want with an old man like me? Why did he invite me here? What was the nature of his relationship with Ibrahim? I wasn't worried about his intentions because I had grown to trust Ibrahim but he still looked like a man you wouldn't quickly say 'no' to. I walked out onto the balcony and sat down on the small crimson sofa next to Gulzar. I noticed the far side of the green balcony railing was missing. The hole wasn't big enough to get a human through but it still looked highly dangerous.

'It's the green zone,' said Gulzar, with a sly laugh. 'Avoid at all costs.'

Gulzar clasped a yellow cushion tightly to his stomach and rested his head back on the sofa. He didn't say anything for a couple of minutes so I tried to look out into the city but the scorching beige and blue landscape was difficult to absorb. The River Tigris was visible, cutting across the bunched–up caramel buildings, the odd high–rise hotel and the minaret of a sturdy mosque. There were a couple of moving black spots in the blue sky and I wondered if these were Apache helicopters or simply my failing eyes giving me the runaround. My vision was impeded by the neighbours' clothes lines outside the balcony so it may have been the latter.

'You're grandson's in Sadr City,' said Gulzar, putting the cushion down on the sofa. 'The Khalifa Brigades are having a few problems.'

'How do you know all this?'

'In this city...' he said, folding his arms and looking out. 'It pays to know everything. You have to take any sort of employment you can get.'

My imagination started to run wild. Was Gulzar part of the Khalifa Brigades? Was he a smuggler or a terrorist? Would he use me as bait? I wanted to know more and I hoped he would talk because I could feel another embarrassing throat–clearing marathon coming on. He agreed to tell me everything but only when Ibrahim came upstairs with a bowl of the biggest peaches I'd ever seen. He said he needed the fruit to neutralise the pain. Ibrahim, who took an eternity to come back, placed the fruit on the small wooden table and then sat next to me on the wonky arm of the sofa. Gulzar picked up two peaches and handed me one. I took an awkward bite and was grateful to get some liquid in my mouth although the flat, watery taste was less enjoyable than I expected. Gulzar got through his peach incredibly quickly and then looked up at me and smiled.

'You have lung issues?'

Some of the liquid dribbled down onto my chin. 'Er yes, how did you know?' I said, trying to wipe my chin but only succeeding in getting my fingers sticky.

'Your swollen fingers. My father–in–law had a stroke before he died. He was in a ward with a man who had fingers like yours. He wanted to hire me because he had lung problems after working at his tiling company. He died before I got back to him.'

Gulzar paused and looked out into the city. There was an excruciating long silence. He started to pick the stitches on his chin.

'But that was a long time ago,' he said, finally breaking the silence. 'My father–in–law always said we should never leave Baghdad no matter how bad it gets. I thought he was wrong because in 2003, two houses in our neighbourhood were obliterated and I felt we had to leave. So I took my family: three children, my grandfather and my wife and squeezed them in to a small Mitsubishi. Most people were escaping to Syria or Jordan but I had some friends in Kurdistan and in Turkey and I thought it was a good tactic. But just as we passed Kirkuk, a stationary car directly in front of me exploded and I put on the brakes as fast as I could. It must have been a roadside bomb, or something, but I couldn't stop the front of the car hitting the side of the burning one. Our car flipped over a couple of times…'

He sighed and picked up another peach. He wiped the side of his mouth and put it down again.

'My father–in–law had his seat belt on, so did I, but the children, my wife and my grandfather were in the back…'

He got up from the sofa and walked across the balcony. He stopped by the 'green zone' and bent down. He looked through the hole out into the city.

'They were all dead, apart from my grandfather who was badly injured. The car was drivable and I tried to take him to Erbil hospital but he died on the way there…' He got up and folded his arms. He walked back towards the sofa and sat down.

'I don't know how but I ended up sleeping somewhere in the Citadel that night. That's where Ibrahim picked me up the next morning.'

My mind wandered to the day after Fareeda died and the sense of confusion I felt when I woke and heard the sound of the whistling kettle in the kitchen. It had to be Fareeda, I thought, or there was no point in getting out of bed. She was still with me, serving up my shortbread and cardamom tea. But two minutes later, I knew it wasn't my wife but my daughter Nadia who'd come to stay with me for a few days. It was a devastating, horrific feeling because those two minutes were the cruellest I'd ever suffered. But what was my suffering compared to Gulzar's? His whole family had been wiped out and he still managed to look calm and composed. I couldn't imagine what was going through his head but I had to admit I was starting to feel some kind of connection or kinship with him. Yes, Ibrahim and Azaad were nice people who had helped me greatly but I felt Gulzar knew where I was coming from and understood me.

'You will stay with us tonight,' said Gulzar, putting his hand on my knee. 'There's more than enough room.'

Gulzar had prepared lamb and rice for dinner but it was so rich and succulent that I could only eat about half a plate. There was also some fruit mixed in with the hot lamb which I'd never experienced before so that gave me an excuse to bail out quickly. After dinner, the three of us sat in Gulzar's front room drinking tea from glass cups and, although I was tempted by the accompanying stuffed dates, I knew I would have problems getting them past my sticky throat. Instead, I enjoyed rubbing the soles of my feet into the giant blue and orange rug which covered nearly the whole floor. I could tell the room wasn't used very often; the light yellow curtains hadn't been drawn, the arm of the brown sofa emitted a waft of dust and the TV had a white blanket over it. It wasn't a surprise when Gulzar said he'd been trying to sell the house for nearly two years because it looked like a place in limbo. But he feared its plummeting value would mean he would eventually have to take it off the market. I perked up when Gulzar started talking about Ibrahim's family and how they had helped him recover from his tragedy. He said he had never lived in a quiet, remote mud–shack before and his tedious family lawyer duties in Baghdad were put starkly into perspective. Ibrahim then asked him if he could advise the family in terms of planning and land issues but even though he had no experience in that field, he was desperate to help and began expanding his limited lawyerly knowledge. He was now ready for a battle with developers, he said, and 'wouldn't give them an inch'. I began thinking about the battle back home between the developers at the old Turner Brothers' site and campaigners who were worried that the whole area was contaminated and needed to be made safe. I had only read one article on the subject – through choice – but shouldn't I have read more? There was plenty of publicity about the campaign so why had I ignored it? As the night wore on, Gulzar asked me about my background and how England had reacted to foreigners in the Sixties. I felt flattered that he wanted to know so much about me and I couldn't resist the temptation to tell him everything about my illness and how it had come about. He also told me he knew a relatively well–off Iraqi friend in Derbyshire who ran a solicitor's firm and could help me with my problem.

'Why haven't you tried for compensation?' he asked. 'I'd take them for everything.'

I didn't have an answer and chose not to provide the simple one: fear. I didn't want to go through the strain of being asked detailed questions about my symptoms from solicitors on their daily rounds. They would delve deep and aim to uncover things that weren't relevant. Some would manipulate and twist the facts. It was an ordeal I could do without at this stage in my life. Gulzar sensed I was uncomfortable talking about it and didn't press home the point. He also misinterpreted my reticence as tiredness.

'You can sleep in Rashid's room,' he said. 'Ibrahim will show you where it is.'

'No, I'm fine really.'

'I insist. We have a lot to talk about tomorrow, particularly your grandson. We will go to Sadr City and get him for you. If you want to stay here, that's not a problem.'

'I'd prefer to go myself and see him. It's really a private matter between us. I'm grateful for everything you're doing for me but I'd like to do it that way really.'

Gulzar smiled and looked at Ibrahim. 'Private matters in Iraq, hey Ibsy?' Gulzar turned to look at me again. 'There's not much that's private over here. There are holes in every wall.' He sighed and picked up a date. 'But it's not a problem; I respect your decision totally. I was simply thinking about your safety and health. Sadr City is not as dangerous as last year because of the surge but it's still got big problems.' He put the date into his mouth. 'But what about seeing a doctor? They're very good round here – they have to be. I know a very good one who saved my father–in–law after his stroke. He can give you good medication.'

'Thanks, but I'm only thinking about Wasim at the moment.'

Gulzar nodded and spat out the seed in his hand. 'Pity, he's not thinking about you.'

Gulzar wanted me to relax at his house for a few days, particularly after I told him about my umpiring background and how I could bring the game to Iraq, but I didn't want to waste any more time because I was desperate to know what Wasim was up to. So he decided to drive me to Sadr City himself, in Ibrahim's car, but admitted he was only doing it because of my stubbornness and his respect for elders. It wasn't that it was too dangerous, he said, although that was a problem, it was more that he didn't want 'a tourist' like me to see this part of Iraq because it created a bad impression. I felt he was overdoing it but the deeper we got into eastern Baghdad, I started to understand what he meant. As we stopped at the fourth checkpoint, an Iraqi guard with a brown handkerchief tied round his face, checked the boot of our car but I couldn't stop looking at the massive 12–foot concrete barrier behind him. It stretched down the road as far as I could see, on both sides, and I wondered how the cordoned–off people in this place actually got around. The guard eventually gave us the all–clear and we drove down into a more populated part of the town. I looked out and could see two young boys daring each other to touch the barbed wire as a niqab–wearing mother tried to usher them away. A battle tank and two Humvees were stationed by a burnt–out car with three American soldiers examining the damage; they obviously weren't concerned about the group of boys on the other side of the car who were running away with one of the wheels. Most of the crumbling, impoverished buildings I could see were still in one piece but the odd one was completely sliced off or disfigured and I wondered if anyone actually lived there. Outside one of these shattered buildings, a young boy was attending to an old man in the back of a wheelbarrow navigated by a donkey. Three women, in multi–coloured headscarfs, were a few yards away from him waiting to be ushered across the road by another Iraqi guard. It was a lot to take in but, ultimately, I felt the opposite of what Gulzar had said. I didn't think the place created a bad impression at all. In fact, it was strangely comforting and invigorating. I felt better than I had for days.

Gulzar drove into a narrow street and hadn't said anything for about 15 minutes. He obviously knew the place well because he turned briskly into every corner and even acknowledged a beggar by name. Eventually, he stopped by a market area and said we couldn't go any further in the car. There was less security in this area but I still spotted two American soldiers with their helmets off, sitting on an empty market stall talking to a man in traditional Arab headdress and robe. There were stalls left and right but hardly any customers. Where was everyone? Was there a curfew? We walked down the bumpy dirt–track and Gulzar immediately put his hand over his nose. A few yards ahead, the dirt–track was full of water and muck and we had to walk on tiptoe across the edge to get past. I didn't look down at the sewage because I didn't want to feel sick – but it wasn't as though I hadn't smelt a lot of that lately.

After a few minutes of deep concentration and delicate walking, I suddenly felt a poke in my back. I turned round to see one of American soldiers looking down on me with his rifle by his side. His tightened the chin strap on his loose helmet and then touched his shades.

'What's in the bag, snow white?' said the American soldier.

I smirked but regretted it instantly. It was enough to tickle my throat and set off a mild bout of coughing. I managed to reduce it by swallowing repeatedly. I gathered myself and looked at Gulzar who nodded. I took my bag off my shoulder and unzipped it. I pulled out the plastic blue stumps and plastic bat. The soldier moved closer and prodded his rifle into the stumps as though the three plastic wickets might suddenly grow teeth and attack. I told him it was a sport and he asked me demonstrate. I pulled out the plastic ball and told him that someone bowls it to a batsman and tries to get him out. They have to try and hit the wicket with the ball, I said. He placed the rifle over his shoulder and took the bat and ball off me.

'So someone just pitches you the ball and you slam it as far as you can?' he said, pushing the ball against the bat. 'Sounds a bit weasly.' He eventually handed me the bat after turning it into an imaginary guitar for a few seconds. He squeezed the ball in his hand and looked up. 'Aren't you a bit old for this shit?'

'I want to spread the game. It's the best game in the world.'

'...And that's the nature of your business here?'

I nodded. He handed me the ball and then looked at Gulzar.

'And you, Mr Aviator, are you the old timer's guide?'

'I live here,' said Gulzar. 'I'm showing him around.'

'Here in Sadr?'

'...In Baghdad.'

The soldier then asked me to provide my documents and, after a bit of fiddling, I did. He glanced at the picture in my passport and looked up at me.

'So you were born in Faisalabad...in Pakistan, right?'

'It was in India then but...yes.'

The soldier looked over his shoulder. He was distracted by the sound of a car failing to start. 'So do the Pakistanis dig their cricket? Or are they more into IEDs these days?'

Gulzar stepped forward and put his arm across me. 'We're going now. All our papers are in order. So you have no reason to keep us.'

The soldier wasn't listening and was still looking over his shoulder. The sound of a car being driven extremely fast was heard. The soldier shook his head and threw the passport back to me. 'Baseball rules, bro,' he said. 'And get a doc to see to that coughing shit. It don't look good.' He ran quickly and skilfully right down the side of the sewage–laden dirt–track towards his colleague near the stall. I took a deep breath as I heard the screeching of tyres. I expected the sound of an explosion but it didn't come. Instead, there was a thudding sound as though the car had hit something harder than expected. I looked at Gulzar but he still had his eyes on the scampering solider. It was a cold, harsh stare. It took him a long time to avert his gaze. He finally turned around and put his hand on my shoulder. He started walking again and I tried to keep up but he had quickened his pace considerably.

Eventually, after an agonising 10–minute walk, we turned into a wide, deserted road and Gulzar stopped near an ageing shoe seller who was sitting in the shade repairing the base of a sandal. In the cramped jewellery store next to him, another man was kneeling down and praying on a rug which wasn't big enough to cover his head; he looked like he'd dyed his hair because of the dusty mark on his fringe. Gulzar stood with his hand on his hips and waited for me to catch up. But I was out on my feet: the exchange with the American soldier left me exhausted. I needed a flat bed and a darkened room. I bent down and put my hands on my thighs to catch my breath. Gulzar patted me on the back and then approached the shoe seller, speaking to him in Arabic. They had a conversation for about two minutes and then the shoe seller got up and walked through a small gap behind the stall which led to a back alley and some stairs. Gulzar walked in behind and asked me join him. I wanted to ask him what was going on but didn't have the energy to do so: I needed a seat. So I followed the two men up the steep stairs and we eventually stopped by a flimsy door which had a couple of dirty football shirts wedged beneath it, presumably to stop any draught coming through. I waited by the door as Gulzar and the shoe seller walked in. There was absolutely nothing to commend the dark, tiny room: a hole in the floor for a toilet, a cracked sink, crumbling blue walls, a dangerous stony floor and a sorry excuse for a mattress. The only thing worthy of a normal sleeping area, or bedroom, was the matching lime green pillow and bed cover.

'This is where Wasim stays,' said Gulzar, blowing his cheeks. 'But he's only here for one day a week – and he won't be here for another four days.'

I nodded but didn't answer. I looked around the room and knew there was only one solution. I would have to stay here until Wasim returned.

# 5.

I didn't want to take my cricket jumper off because I had my standards to keep up but even I had to admit defeat after lying on the rock–hard mattress for 20 minutes. My armpits were drenched and the wool was sticking to the back of my neck so there was no option but to fold the jumper up and use it as a source of air conditioning; it was thick and bulky enough to do a passable job as a substitute fan.

I persuaded Gulzar to go home and he was naturally reluctant because he was worried about my health but I told him there was no way I would budge. He eventually agreed although he insisted he would pay for the so–called room. But he did fill me in about the shoe seller who was a bachelor, comfortably over 80–years–old and had a droopy left eye which only half–opened. Everyone called him Bilu: he had no family to speak of and had lived in the same place for at least 65 years. I wondered how someone like Wasim got to know someone like Bilu. Wasim couldn't speak Arabic so how did they communicate? It was obviously down to the middlemen or jihadi networks; Wasim never did anything for himself.

After sitting up and wafting my jumper about for 10 minutes, I grabbed my inhaler and breathed in repeatedly. It had little impact but at least the reassuring little blue toy was by my side; we had come a long way. The sound of a distant Azaan faded as Bilu walked in with a tray of food and placed it on the floor by my side. I examined him in more detail than before. He was a short, slim man with pointy shoulders, generous eyes and a closely–cropped beard. He wore a tight grey robe, dark blue blazer and cream–coloured sandals. Surely, the stories of him being eighty odd were a lie? He looked no more than sixty. He'd cooked a watery lentil curry for me with brittle, crumbly naans even though I wasn't very hungry. After watching me tear off the first piece of naan and dip it into the coriander–heavy curry, he disappeared for a couple of hours only to return with a silver portable TV, a Snakes and Ladders board game and some dubious DVD titles. Bilu began to set up the all–in–one TV and DVD player by the sink with the help of a small, noisy generator. I was truly grateful for his hospitality but told him I didn't want to watch a film and simply needed some sleep and a bit of privacy. He obviously didn't understand and went back downstairs to get a wooden shoe rack which he used as a box office seat next to my mattress. His 'home cinema' viewing didn't last too long, however, because he noticed my deep, snorty breathing and curiously looked over his shoulder. I looked into his static eyes and realised I'd never felt so tired and so weak. My head was like a steel football which needed puncturing. The trip had finally caught up with me: the flying, the anxiety, the illness and, of course, Wasim. He had caused all this and I would make sure he knew about it all when I got hold of him.

Bilu pulled away the shoe rack and put his knees on the mattress close to my body. He was arched over me and I wondered what on earth he was doing. He raised his hand and rested it harshly against my chest. He took an extremely deep breath to demonstrate and asked me to do the same. I took the longest breath I could and he pushed down on my chest so hard that it was almost painful. He looked down at my abdomen and nodded. He asked me do it again which I did a number of times. Slowly but surely, I could feel the length and quality of my breathing improve. I could feel tiny waves of energy swimming in from God knows where to temporarily give my depleted body a boost. Was it as simple as that? Why didn't anyone tell me that breathing through the abdomen rather than the chest area was better for someone with respiratory problems? Bilu then stopped and smiled. I didn't want him to stop. I was ready to throw my inhaler away. He then surprised me by raising his rough, yellow–tinged finger towards my chin like a wicked umpire giving a vindictive decision. Again, it felt as though some dormant bulbs had been switched on – but this time it was more uncomfortable because an area at the front of my brain was aroused. Had I been depressed? I must have been because the difference was startling. Bilu then slipped his hand round my neck. He took much longer to find the specific area he was looking for. He eventually pressed down, with three fingers, on a soft area at the back of my neck and, again, there was an immediate impact. There was a glorious rush of energy at the front of my face, particularly my nose, as though my nostrils were about to be unblocked. How could such a small workout make so much difference? At one moment, I even thought I had a new set of lungs and had never set foot in Turner Brothers. Bilu continued with some more procedures: pushing down on my belly–button, clinching my toes with his hands and pinching my wrists but none of it could be compared to the earlier breathing and neck–pressing exercises. There was a certain magic in his bony fingers.

Bilu had done something amazing. He had driven my illness so far underground that I now felt like a buzzing, energetic individual ready to take on some activity rather than lie flat on the mattress all evening. It wasn't enough for me to watch a film – that needed too much concentration – but it was enough for me to play Snakes and Ladders with Bilu on the mattress. We must have played till midnight at least.

I felt so good in the morning that I was ready to take the game to the opposition. I had slept for six unbroken hours without needing the toilet and Bilu's breakfast consisting of herbal tea and potato pancakes topped off a fruitful early–morning period which made me wonder how I could be so perked up now and so crippled the day before. So I put my bag over my shoulder and headed out into Sadr City. I didn't have a clue where I was going but at least my relaxed breathing patterns helped to calm a distant, but natural, anxiety. It was a hazy, humid late morning and there were plenty of people pulling their shutters up on their stores. One man, sitting on a wooden chair with a hookah planted in his mouth, stared at me as I walked past and must have wondered why I was smiling. It was because I could; it had been a long time since that had happened. But I didn't want to get carried away and walk too far simply because I felt better. Getting lost would be extremely silly after having such a good few hours. So I decided the first group of young children I set eyes on would get the benefit of my experience.

Unfortunately, I walked on and on and on, past stalls and stores, past Iraqi soldiers and shopkeepers and eventually past the Al Rasheed bank which had a sizeable queue of about 40 people outside it. I knew I had come too far because I didn't have a clue where I was but a sacrifice had to be made to bring the real beautiful game to the masses. I could see a group of about 15 to 20 children playing football further down the road but if my eyes weren't deceiving me they were using a tennis ball. The ball kept running underneath a stationary yellow truck, which I presumed was a 'coalition' vehicle although I couldn't see any soldiers. As it was so small, there was no problem in retrieving the ball because it usually ran between the wheels and through to the other side. This was my opportunity and I felt excited that a new chapter was about to begin in this is great country's history. I wanted to find a strip of grass or playing field to demonstrate but knew the road would have to do for now. That was one good thing about Baghdad and the surrounding area, I thought, the roads were always wide enough. I walked quicker than ever towards the children and stopped a few yards away. None of them could have been more than 12–years–old. Two of them were wearing black Real Madrid football shirts, one was wearing a torn grey robe, one had a red England shirt on and another was wearing an oversized baseball cap and Adidas tracksuit bottoms. I admired one of the Madrid boy's ball controls because it wasn't easy trying to shield a tennis ball with his flimsy sandals. I watched them for a few minutes as they chased the ball from one side to the other. Where were the goals? I couldn't see any. I waited until the tall Madrid boy lost the ball, which was a long time, and stepped forward to make my move. He stood with his hands on his hips and turned to look at me. Most of the other boys chased the ball but also stopped when they realised Madrid boy was playing no more. They ran back to join him and all looked at me, wondering what I was up to. I was a couple of feet away from them all now and took a long, deep breath. Most of them folded their arms, tilted their heads and gave me the kind of stare probably reserved for a man with a gun.

'I'm the Shah of Iraq,' I said. 'You want to play a real game?'

No–one answered so I took my bag off my shoulder and started unzipping it. I pulled out the blue cricket bat, the red ball and the blue wickets. I walked to one side of the road and carefully placed the wickets near some empty boxes of cooking oil. It wasn't easy as the surface was uneven but I got an immediate rush from seeing these three blue sticks standing upright, ready to be the main attraction. Of course, Kwik Cricket wasn't Test cricket and the latter was always the deepest and most profound challenge on the planet but for the game to flourish, you had to begin somewhere and this was the perfect introduction for young people.

I took 22 short strides back from the stumps. They had to be short or I'd walk into that eyesore of a truck on the other side. I could see the children watching me and I was pleased about that. Observation was a great quality to have. Perhaps a few them could be umpires one day; we definitely needed them. I put my bag down after I'd counted 22 and then picked up the ball and bat. I walked over to Madrid boy and handed him the ball. He grimaced as he clenched the ball in his hand as though I'd just offered him a grenade. He had darker skin than the other boys and the tip of his index finger was missing. He threw the ball on the floor and used his feet to move the ball from side to side.

'You know Younis Mahmoud?' he said. 'I play like him.'

I shook my head and wondered who the hell Younis Mahmoud was: a Real Madrid footballer? I picked up the ball and demonstrated what he needed to do by adopting a subtle overarm motion. I handed him the ball and he attempted to do the same but couldn't get his arm over to the 360 degree position.

Instead, he gestured that he could throw it which I suppose was a start. Perhaps the boys had plenty of experience of chucking with American soldiers milling around? But woe betide they would throw for long; they had to learn the game the proper way and that meant bowling properly; overarm. So the Real Madrid number ten, sponsored by Siemens, held the ball in his hand while I walked back down the road with the bat to take guard. I flicked away a few stones and the odd drinks can with my bat as I approached the wickets. This was the beginning of a wonderful journey, I thought, it was the birth of a new era in this war–ravaged country. I'd already had a title: *A Maiden in Mesopotamia*. Whether it would be a book, poem or small article in the *Observer*, I didn't know, but it was the start of something special. I had the longest leg in the desert.

If only it could have been that easy. I tried to set the field but gave up when one of the boys became a Saddam–type statue and refused to budge. He was less enthusiastic than the other boys and ended up walking off to join his purple headscarf–wearing mother who had just come out of the bank. He kept looking over his shoulder though, so perhaps I hadn't lost him forever.

Rishi, the Real Madrid boy, threw down the first ball and I played a neat forward defensive. My sweaty, flimsy hands couldn't quite grip the bat satisfactorily – but I still got an immense lift by looking into the boy's eyes while taking guard.

One of them, however, a stocky boy in white shorts couldn't help laughing as soon as any action took place, no matter how slight. He let out a gasp, shriek or giggle every few seconds which sometimes developed into machine–gun laughter. It may have been overexcitement but I couldn't discount the possibility he may have been laughing at me: Bilu had done a good job but he could do nothing about my embarrassing throat–clearing tics. I varied my strokes from the next few throws so the boys could get a better understanding of the game's profound palette. I attempted a cover–drive, leg glance, on drive and lofted drive but I tired quickly, after about seven deliveries, so I handed the bat to Rishi and decided to have a bowl. I regretted it instantly. He clobbered my second lollipop delivery over the truck and high into the sky: a bright red bullet fizzing over the toffee–coloured buildings heading into another road, street or shack. Had he played the game before or was he a sporting natural? It didn't matter because I knew I could work with the boy; his grin and raising of his fist after he'd tanked the ball to kingdom come told me that. He could be my captain. But I had no ball now. I had no energy to go after it and all the boys looked stunned that he'd actually hit it so far. I shouldn't have worried, however, as Rishi nonchalantly reached into his trouser pocket and picked out the tennis ball. He rolled it down the road to me so I could have another go. Not so fast, I thought, there was no chance I'd serve up another full toss so that Rishi's eyes could light up once more. I picked up the ball and walked towards Rishi. I almost wanted to embrace him but understood it might be inappropriate. He handed me the bat and I gave him the ball. He put it in his pocket and started to walk off.

'Don't leave,' I said, holding his arm. 'You could easily play under 18s for Rochdale…'

'I have to see my father in hospital,' he said. 'And get some food also…'

'Will you come back tomorrow?'

'Only if I can keep hitting it…'

With that signal of intent, Rishi walked off and most of the other boys peeled away too. I had made my mark but had to be thorough from now on to help the boys' understanding of the game. I picked up the wickets and walked back towards my bag. I glanced up at the sky and treasured the moment: close of play had never felt so good.

For three further days, I taught the boys how to bowl, bat and field properly. It wasn't easy because an American soldier and Iraqi guard moved us on because of 'security reasons' but that was the beauty of this type of cricket gear: it could be placed any time, any place and anywhere; bad light permitting, of course. There was also the slight problem of the boys wanting to finish their game of football first so I had to wait until they'd had their fill and then turn to the real business in hand. But once they were ready I pounced and showed them how to score runs, how to get batsman out and how matches were won and lost. On the second of these days, I had to admit I got lost getting back to Bilu's – I ended up in a crowded but ghoulish area of town which had a few too many flattened buildings and donkeys for comfort but a bored street trader eventually came to my aid and set me back in the right direction. I only had to say 'Bilu' and he knew instantly who I was talking about. I had asked four people before him, as well as three Iraqi soldiers in floppy sun hats, but they must have thought I was mad because by, that time, I could only mumble because my throat was so dry. The only downside to the street trader's assistance was that he wanted me to take his slippers back to Bilu's to get them fixed. I had no choice but to grant his request.

But that was the only blip in an amazing period when I thought I was walking on air and had been gifted a new set of lungs. In the evenings, Bilu would get his spindly fingers working on my body to propel me forward to the next day where I could use the renewed energy and vitality to give the boys detailed knowledge about the game as well as scamper the odd run. It didn't stop all my symptoms but I could walk a bit faster, speak more fluently and communicate with more authority (that was important when I was trying to tell the boys about silly mid off and short leg). They did look extremely bored, at times, with their shoulders slumped and arms folded but they needed to know that fielding was one of the most important disciplines in the game. We began to attract a crowd too. On day three, a cloudier afternoon with a touch of drizzle, there must have been at least 30 people watching including a sizeable niqab brigade who were either fascinated by the game or simply ensuring their sons weren't up to mischief. It didn't give me pleasure to look at these black–uniformed women but only because it reminded me that the players they were looking at weren't in all white as they should have been. My jumper was scant compensation.

That day was so enjoyable that we went on until the sun went down. Catching practice had created the exuberance and joy I'd dreamed about and it was wonderful to see the children trying to catch the ball with all the skill of *Edward Scissorhands*. Rishi and another boy called Kazim were the best catchers but the others were just as enthusiastic and that was the most important thing. At the end of play, I expected them to get into their huddle and then trail off as usual but Rishi stayed behind and watched me as I put the bat and wickets back in the bag. I wondered what was on his mind. I knew he was a talented boy but he'd never said much in previous days. He was wearing a white Real Madrid shirt today and I wouldn't have been surprised if he'd had all their shirts for the last 10 years. He walked up to me and handed me the tennis ball. I put that in the bag too. He handed me a sweet in a green wrapper. I put it in my pocket and said I'd eat it later.

'I see you cough?' he said, putting a sweet in his mouth. 'You can't hide it.' He hesitated and kicked away a stone with his foot. 'My father is not normal too.'

Charming, I thought, but at least he's communicating. He briskly went on tell me he was

11–years–old and his father had fought in the war against Iran at the age of 15. He subsequently had mental health problems and didn't even know about the US–led invasion in 2003. Rishi desperately wanted his dad to come home but on the previous occasion he'd been allowed out of the hospital, he left his bedroom in the middle of the night and headed out to attack Iraqi soldiers. He wounded one of them at a checkpoint and had to be admitted again. Rishi said he wanted to tell me all this because I was a 'Britisher who likes sport'. Well, yes, but I didn't want to tell him how much I hated football. He then took out a tatty pack of cigarettes which had the initials 'DJ' on them. I knew what he was about to do but it still shocked me. He pulled one out and put it into his mouth.

'Can I take the bat home?' he asked.

'Yes, but the cigarettes have to go. Don't put your tender lungs in danger.'

He looked at me and put the cigarette back in the packet. 'Only for now,' he said. 'The bat, can I take it?'

I sighed as I watched him put the cigarettes away. I unzipped the bag and took out the bat. I handed it to him and he smiled. He ran his palm down the blue blade and then gripped the handle tightly in both hands. I put my bag over my shoulder and couldn't help but think about Wasim.

My immensely satisfying work with the children gave me a lift and I was looking forward to finally meeting Wasim who was scheduled to come back.

But Bilu's simple shake of the head, when I asked him about Wasim, tempered my euphoria. Bilu was haggling with a short, stocky customer at the time who was smacking the sole of the shoe against the stall to test its strength. I almost wanted to get it off him and smack it even harder so it was destroyed. Where the hell was my grandson? Why hadn't he arrived yet? The four days were almost up and there was nothing to indicate that I'd see him soon. Had I been naïve? Was I an old buffoon out of his depth? Yes, and rightly so. I was here to do good things and if I ever got my hands on him I'd show him what life was really about.

Bilu's shake of the head sent an immediate bullet of depression into my brain. I could never sustain joy, exhilaration or satisfaction because even the most mundane of news had a way of seeping through my defences and altering my mood. It swung from euphoric to passive in an instant. But as I lay on the mattress and looked up at the ceiling, I decided not to care any more. So what if he didn't turn up? He messed up the lives of people while I improved them. Who had done the better job? It wasn't hard to deduce.

Bilu came upstairs after half an hour with some pancakes, dates and milk but I wasn't hungry. I felt sick and had difficulty in moving my neck to the right. It had been clicking for a few years but now it was hardly going past 45 degrees because it hurt too much. The sound of four rapid but distant explosions didn't help either. Each time my neck jolted a little and the flimsy pivot it rested on was loosened once more. Bilu got to work on it and did improve it a little but the rest of my body was too rigid and stiff to be wholly responsive. As Bilu varied his neck–pressing techniques, I asked him if he knew why Wasim hadn't turned up yet. He instantly stopped what he was doing, got off the mattress and left the room. I hoped I hadn't insulted him, I thought, because he was crucial to my wellbeing. In fact, my strategy was to get to know Bilu better that evening; I ached for some communication about his background, family and circumstances. But what had I said to him that sent him away in such a huff? Was it the explosions? I shouldn't have worried because he returned within a couple of minutes carrying a white shoebox. A shoebox? I thought he didn't have any. The shoebox rattled as he walked towards me on the mattress and rested it by my side. There were three mobile phones in it and Bilu picked one of them up. I instantly recognised one of them as Wasim's – a Sony Ericsson which was distinctive because I remember Wasim turning it on its side and taking a picture, something which I thought was revolutionary – but that wasn't the one Bilu decided to pick up. Instead, he flicked open a Motorola and started pressing a few buttons. He then handed me the phone and I looked the display screen. It was a picture of Wasim lying on the green grass of Rochdale's Lenny Barn on a sunny afternoon with a football placed under his head like a pillow. He had his eyes closed, his hands crossed on his chest and trainers off. It was a beautiful but unsettling picture. There was almost no life in it apart from the bright colours of the sky and the grass. It wasn't the cold and crowded Lenny Barn that I knew. I looked up at Bilu and wondered why he was showing me these pictures. Did he think I was missing Wasim so much that all these pictures would cheer me up? If he was, then they hadn't done the trick. Further, it was a surprise to me that Bilu had these mobiles at all. How did he get them? Had Wasim left them here? I pressed the 'next' button on the mobile because I was intrigued by the first image: it was a part of Wasim I hadn't seen before. The second picture was similar: lying down, eyes closed, hands crossed but this time he was in front of Silver Street Chapel, only yards away from the family home. And on it went as I scrolled through the other pictures. The same pose was seen in the school yard of Spotland School, outside The Kut Hut, near Rochdale Football ground, outside the Carter's Rest and, most surprisingly, inside the Golden Mosque. I reached the 12th image but they started to give me a headache so I handed the phone back to Bilu. I needed to lie down straight away. My chest felt prickly and uncomfortable. I lay back on the mattress and tried to get the images out of my head. Did Wasim have a death wish? Was he suicidal or spiritual? I wasn't sure about anything apart from my wickets and bat. But the most uncomfortable question was practical: was he actually alive?

# 6.

I tossed and turned all night and finally got to sleep deep into the early hours. But that's when I felt the draught tingle my ankles. It was a creeping, cunning waft of air that I first dismissed as another symptom but when it continued for about half a minute, I knew it was something else. It had to be the door. I sat up instantly and looked up: the door was ajar and someone was standing there. I bit my tongue and my chin began to shake. How long had he been there? Why hadn't he spoken yet? It was still dark but the shape of his head and shoulders were familiar. I thought I knew who it was but when he didn't move forward and stayed silent I wasn't so sure. I pulled away the bed cover and prepared to get off the mattress, concentrating harder than usual because toppling over after a long sleep was always a big risk. I got onto my feet but then heard a shuffling movement and the door suddenly clamped shut. What kind of man was that, I thought? Peeping at me while I slept and then running away when he was rumbled. I awkwardly rushed to the door and opened it. The shaft of light hurt my eyes; it was closer to morning than I thought. I stood at the top of the stairs, looking down and could see the back of a man with a traditional red and white keffiyah scarf over his shoulders, a shaved head and a running style that I knew all too well. It hadn't changed since he was eight–years–old when I saw him chasing an ice–cream van on Molyneux Street with David Tanner and his frightful dog Wilbutts: his hands were up near his shoulders then and they were the same now. I ran down the steps as fast as I could but the more I pushed the more the legs turned into matchsticks, with no power in them. I got to the bottom and walked down the back alley. The muggy, early morning air wasn't helping me breath and though I was encouraged by the sound of items being unloaded onto a stall (because it could have meant someone had seen Wasim), I thought he'd probably be long gone by now. I walked to the end of the alley and looked out. A couple of yards away, near the stall, I saw Bilu standing with Wasim. My grandson had his arms folded and was looking at the ground. I took a deep breath and walked towards him. I hesitated and looked up into his eyes. He was bigger and better–built than I remembered him. His face had filled out and his lack of hair gave him a certain kind of authority. The transformation took a few seconds longer to digest. I raised my trembling hand and placed it on his shoulder.

'Have you no manners?' I asked.

'You shocked the hell out of us,' he said, rubbing the craters on his right cheek. 'What are you doing here, anyhow? I were just reading Fajr prayers and came back down here, as I usually do, and there you were like some fuckin' ghost from another world. I couldn't believe it.'

'Why didn't you carry on running?'

He looked at Bilu. 'I did but…he stopped us. He smacked us on the head with a couple of shoes. It made us think a bit.'

Bilu handed me one of the offending shoes and demonstrated how I should whack my grandson again if he stepped out of line. I politely declined because I would have no need for it; I would use my own techniques to get through to him.

'Come upstairs, so we can talk further,' I said.

'Look, nana jee whatever you've got in mind, it ain't gonna happen. I know why I'm here and what I've got to do. I'm happy you're here and all that – and that you're safe – but I've got a lot of things to take care of. Allah–thallah won't forgive me otherwise.'

'And I won't forgive you, if you don't listen to me or your parents.' I turned and started to walk off. 'So are you coming or not?'

I didn't look over my shoulder but after a few seconds I heard footsteps.

'Just remember, I listen to no man, only *Allah*…'

Bilu had made us two cups of tea but Wasim didn't want his. He said he was fasting and was still making up for the days he missed earlier in the year. It didn't come as a total surprise but I did wonder how far he'd gone in his religious rebirth. If he was making up for all the fasts he'd missed or broken, then he had a long way to go because I remembered him breaking a fast only a couple years ago when I saw him tucking into a kebab at lunchtime outside the Eastern Kebab House on Spotland Road after I'd visited Nadia. That was the only one I saw – I'm sure there were many others – but add those wayward moments to the 30–a–year–standard fasts and they'd pile up until you might end up fasting for half a year.

After I'd finished my tea, I lay down on the mattress while Wasim continued to sit on the shoe rack and look down on the stony floor. He hadn't said anything apart from the fasting explanation so I tried to soften him up a little by telling him about my journey and how I'd got here. I figured the three–part journey taking in Manchester, Vienna and Erbil would get him thinking about the type of sacrifice I'd made. I figured wrong and he continued to lower his head and examine the floor as though there was a map of hidden treasure by his feet. So it was time to change tack.

'I'm booking the flight tomorrow. You're coming home.'

Finally, I got a reaction. He sniggered and got up from the shoe rack. He walked over to the TV by the sink and picked up the DVD on top of it. He examined the DVD and then put it down. 'I see Bilu's got you into the Hollywood shite. It's polluting everyone's brain…'

'How many Laurence Fishburne films did you watch? Nadia lost count.'

'Mum exaggerates a lot…' He sighed and walked over to me on the mattress. He sat down on the edge but still had his back to me. After a few moments, he turned and grabbed hold of my right hand. 'Look, I

101

know you're not well but with Allah–thallah's help you'll get better. I'm also grateful that you've come all this way just to see me…' He softly let go of my hand and looked away. 'But there's no way I'm coming home yet. I've still got so many things to take care of over here. I have work to do and people to help. There's so much to put right here that if I leave now it will all go to pot again. I can't allow that to happen.'

'How did you know I was ill?'

'What?'

'Who told you?'

'No–one. I just thought after nani jee died, you got ill and haven't really got better yet.'

I had forgotten how insensitive Wasim was but I suppose his age was some sort of mitigation. He obviously didn't know about the Turner Brothers episode and, at this stage, I felt it was better to keep it that way. I didn't want to show him that I was even more vulnerable than he thought I was.

I slowly sat up on the mattress. Wasim got his arms round me and helped me up but it was a symbolic gesture rather than a practical one; I could still manage on my own. I awkwardly swung round so my feet were on the floor like his. I felt better that I was on his level now.

'Do you know how much your parents miss you?' I asked, putting my hand on his knee.

'Yeah, but there's a bigger picture, nana jee, you don't understand. It's about the rotten, black heart of the world which needs putting straight. There's so much blood being spilled and so many lives being lost that we can't just sit on the sidelines and watch, we've got to do something. The Ummah's taking a stand and I'm going to stand with it. I'm not going to let these bastards win.'

'And who are these *bastards*?'

He looked at me as if he was a pitcher at the Yankee Stadium and I'd walked out with pads and a cricket bat. He shook his head and got up. He walked towards the door and turned around. 'The kufr, the unbelievers, the corporations, the government, all of the thieving, money–grabbing liars that are here right now, raping and pillaging this country so they can get creamed…' He stopped and put both hands on the side of his head. '…I go ape just thinking about it.'

I had been naïve. I thought Wasim would listen to me, particularly because of the state I was in, and also because he was missing his friends and his life, if not his family. But I was wrong. I had misjudged him. He obviously wasn't as weak and flaky as I thought. I wanted to respond to his propaganda barrage but there was no point because I'd heard it all before. He might have thought I was shocked but Liam Sharples used to say worse about the British government when I was at Turners. He wanted to assassinate Ted Heath personally and used to tell me about it when we walked home on snowy, brutal evenings drinking weak tea from our flasks. He may have thought, as an immigrant, that I'd give him a sympathetic ear but most of the time, I couldn't understand him: I had the dissolution of East Pakistan and the creation of Bangladesh on my mind at the time. That war was extremely painful but I later understood I didn't live there any more and it wasn't for me to take part or decide something that I hadn't had a stake in for a number of years; I was not part of that country's problems. Wasim needed to think the same way. His religious justification was a cop–out because most or all Islamic countries had some sort or turmoil since their inception and that would mean never–ending war. To perish in those circumstances would be truly horrific. I wasn't going to let that happen.

I looked at him as he leaned against the door with his arms folded and thought about how his neck and chin resembled Nadia's. She had the same sharp chin and sturdy neck and it only felt like yesterday when I was telling her off in the same manner, usually about why she shouldn't take up fashion or design as a career: the children and her husband were more important.

'So did Dr Graham finally find out what were wrong with you?' asked Wasim.

I shook my head. Hearing my former GP's name threw me off balance. He was the last person I wanted to talk about because of his insistence I was depressed because Fareeda had passed away and, subsequently, didn't have a medical condition. He caused me a lot of physical and mental anguish. Luckily, for me he was away when one of his colleagues decided to refer me to the specialist (Dr Howarth) because of my breathing problems. One of the few benefits of moving to Edmund Street was that I could change GPs and, hopefully, never see Dr Graham again.

'I don't know why you bother with those corrupt doctors,' he said. 'They just have the same illnesses for all older Muslims: TB and diabetes.'

'Not for me...'

'What? I know an imam just outside Baghdad, he could get you cured straight away.'

'Exorcism and beads is it?'

Wasim shook his head and looked angry. He moved away from the door and walked towards the shoebox. He sat down and ran his palms slowly over his face. 'You see, nana jee, you're just not taking any of this seriously. I don't care what you think because I'm staying here. I've already helped hundreds of people and sorted out plenty of others. I totally respect you and stuff but I've made my mind up.'

'Well, wherever you go,' I said. 'I'm coming with you...until you decide you want to go home.'

It was a long time since I'd shared a bed or mattress with anyone, let alone a member of my own family. But that was the price I had to pay for finding Wasim who spend most of the day evading my questions. I wanted to know about his resistance group, his movements and why he was living one day with Bilu and rest with his evasive chums. He didn't answer any of these things satisfactorily and instead spoke at length of the work he did after the Kashmir earthquake. He told me the things he'd seen there horrified him to such an extent that he felt suicidal, impotent and worthless. The lack of help from General Musharraf's government inflamed him further. But I reminded him there was another person, much more important to him, who was also inflamed and angry. I remembered the sadness in Nadia's voice when she told me on the phone of Wasim's decision to leave England when news of the earthquake was breaking. I obviously had no idea of his movements at the time but she said he had been hanging around with a 'different crowd' for a while. They were a highly–educated, devout bunch who gathered in 'Taz's cellar' a couple of nights a week and on those particular evenings, Wasim didn't get home until 1am. After that, she noticed changes in his behaviour like clearing out his bedroom of all CDs, DVDs and video games, reading the ingredients labels on food cans and getting up in the morning for dawn prayers. I put these things to Wasim but he shocked me by saying his mother was trying to be a 'material girl at the age of forty–odd' because of her fashion degree.

That evening was spent in near–silence as Wasim and I ate our food with not so much as a glance upwards. Bilu wanted to celebrate our reunion – and had made a big bowl of halva for dessert – but I was full up and simply couldn't get any more food into my bloated stomach. As a mark of respect, I nibbled two spoonfuls and retired to lie down on the mattress. Wasim didn't find it as difficult, however, as he knocked back three helpings of the date–dominated dessert and calmly got up to do wuzu and then read namaz in the corner of the room. I wondered how he knew which way Mecca was because I didn't have the foggiest.

So an awkward evening became a harsh, lonely night as Wasim slipped in next to me in his striped boxer shorts and white t–shirt. He had offered to sleep on the floor but I couldn't let him do that so there was no option but for him to tuck up beside me on the mattress. I shouldn't have worried because he got to sleep about 10 minutes later while I continued to monitor the ceiling for cracks. He didn't snore but the way he had his arm right over his forehead made me think his brain may have hurt throughout the day because of all that certainty, vigour and righteousness. I wondered if he was suffering from a kind of sickness too: an ideological one that gripped even tighter and had even more fatal consequences. I came to the conclusion that grandfather and grandson were as sick as each other and, with that semi–pleasant thought, rolled over and got to sleep quicker than expected.

The blistering, frightening sound of an Azaan woke me up. I sat up on the mattress and looked across to the corner of the room where Wasim was reading namaz. He looked left and right and then swivelled round to pick up his mobile which was directly behind his feet. I could see that he was angry because of the way he glanced up at me before answering the call.

'Fuck, I thought you'd give us another half an hour,' he said, using the mobile to scratch his forehead. 'You're outside Bilu's now, yeah? Okay, I'm coming.'

He ended the call and cupped his hands to officially finish his prayers. He then picked up the prayer mat, folded it up a couple of times and threw it into the corner of the room. He stood up and slipped his mobile into the back pocket of his black jeans.

'I'm going now, nana jee.'

'Just a one–night stand then is it?'

'You knew that when you came. My brothers are waiting for me. I think you should go home.'

I ignored him and got off the mattress with a sense of purpose. I could feel my breathing increase rapidly as I ran through the possible scenarios in my head but I didn't care; I was going with him. It was time to see if Bilu's breathing exercises really did work when the pressure was on.

'Wait, I'll only take a minute to get ready,' I said.

'No, I've given Bilu some money to take care of you…'

'I don't need money, I need you.'

I reached over into Bilu's straw basket for my shirt and put it on as fast as I could. I could hear Wasim sighing behind me but I felt if that was the extent of his frustration then I didn't have much to worry about. After a few seconds, I could feel his breath on my neck and knew he was inching closer. Each time, I expected him to say something but each time only a sigh came out of his mouth. So I got my trousers and white woolly jumper on, picked my bag up and quickly headed to the cracked sink to have a wash.

'I'm going now…' said Wasim.

'Hold on, I'm nearly ready,' I said, my face frozen by the torrent of water crashing across my face. I turned off the tap and used the damp hand towel to wipe my face. 'Right, let's go. Have you got everything?'

Wasim looked at me but didn't say anything. He walked towards the door and opened it.

'We are coming back aren't we?' I asked.

Wasim left the door open and walked out.

The back door of the silver Hyundai was open. The wheel rims were missing, the windows were blacked out and there was a big dent in the passenger door. The engine was running and I could see two pairs of legs in the back seat, one was unmistakably Wasim's. I glanced left and right and wondered where Bilu was. Had he been paid off? Was he dead? They were silly thoughts, of course, but I could never control my brain at the crack of dawn.

'Get in, old man,' said the driver, after winding down the window. 'It's lucky I like your grandson.'

I could only see the man's eyes because his black and white–checked keffiyah was tied tightly across his face. He pulled the scarf down slightly and revved the engine. It was intimidating so I naturally stepped forward. I bent down and got into the car. It was a bit of a squeeze in the back seat because Wasim was on the far side, next to the window, and another man was in the middle. There was no–one in the front passenger seat which I couldn't understand.

'Need more room back there?'

'Er no, it's fine,' I said, crossing my hands.

The driver didn't move off as expected. Instead, he got out of the car and walked round to the back door.

He opened it and reached into his trouser pocket for a small item which was difficult to describe. But once he stretched it out, I could tell what it was.

'We can do this the easy way or the hard way, baba,' he said. 'Which is it? Because you must understand one thing: we love jihad, grandad – and we're here to stay.'

'What are you doing, Abbie?' said Wasim. 'You said you wouldn't do this…'

'I found this in the handbag of a contractor's wife,' said Abbie, looking into my eyes. 'She couldn't sleep at night because of the bombs and the noise. Her husband tried to kill us but we got to him first. The wife's gone back to Canada now but I have all her items – and this is my favourite. So what's it to be, baba?'

Abbie stretched out the fashionable pink and black sleeping blindfold and moved it closer to my face. I knew I was trapped and there was no way out ahead or behind. I looked over my shoulder at Wasim but he sat back and stared at the driver's seat ahead of him. Abbie moved forward and slowly began to place the blindfold over my head.

'Wait,' I said.

'What now?' replied Abbie. 'I don't have much time.'

'Smell it for me.'

'What?'

'Smell it or I'm not putting it on.'

Abbie rolled his eyes and looked beyond me at Wasim. 'Hmm…your grandson told me about your problems.'

Abbie raised the silk blindfold up to his nose and smelt it.

'What does it smell of?' I asked.

'Some shit perfume,' said Abbie, taking the blindfold away from his nose. 'So will you play or wrestle?'

I closed my eyes and took a deep breath through my nostrils. I thought of Fareeda and the way she used to spray her perfume on her wrist and then push it up to my nose for a verdict. I didn't care much for the perfume but liked to keep my nose on her tender wrist for as long as possible.

'Did it smell nice?' I asked.

'Yes, like a western bitch's pussy,' said Abbie. 'Put it on now.'

He carefully placed the blindfold over my head.

'If you even think about taking it off, Saad will clump you...'

He lowered the blindfold over the bridge of my nose and then straightened it. I kept my eyes closed and dreamt of a nice Canadian woman.

# 7.

I expected to feel much worse but the cosy, intimate blindfold provided the kind of refreshing sleep I hadn't experienced for years. The whirr of the Hyundai engine lasted for a few minutes but the rest of the journey was a beautiful blur: a black hole of peace and restlessness that I thought would last forever. It was a pity it had to be disrupted – and in such a brutal manner too. There I was dreaming of Wasim doing a shift in a giant mill where he was being thrown red cricket balls and had to bat them away up into a chimney when the car ground to a shuddering halt in what I presumed was a ditch. Then Abbie came running round towards the back seat and smuggled me out of the car. I tried to place my feet on the ground but my co–ordination was array; the bumpy, uneven surface left me hoping for the best. Mercifully, it wasn't as hot here as in Sadr City: the sun wasn't as penetrating and there was a light breeze blowing onto my cheeks but my face still felt like's Roddy McDowall's in *Planet of the Apes*. I remembered watching him at the ABC cinema in Rochdale in the late Sixties with Liam and Jim after a savage shift at Turners. I felt sorry for him under that mask. Not now. At least he could take his off.

Abbie quickened his step and I stumbled

across the ground until we came to a halt on an even surface. We shouldn't have stopped. The moment of relaxation – and probably the deep sleep that preceded it – led to my listless body almost crumbling in a heap. I felt Abbie's meaty fingers dig painfully into my shoulders to help me keep my balance. Then there was a moment of silence and an extraordinary bout of laughter from Abbie. I didn't hear anyone else's voice, only his. It was a high–pitched, squeaky laugh which didn't pause for breath and only stopped when he put his hand on my back again and ushered me forward.

'This is no place for you, baba,' said Abbie. 'The invaders vowed to stop terrorism but they've unleashed a hell that will last a thousand years. You need to go home because we're the real pioneers here. We'll have a state before you leave this miserable earth.'

I was about to respond but Abbie pushed me in. Why hadn't Wasim said something? Did he not want to protect his grandfather? As soon as we walked inside, I could hear the noise of a ceiling fan wafting its cool air onto my head. But that was the only soothing sensation. My mind was beginning to drift into darker territory like ransoms, hostages and even, beheadings. In another age and another place, it might have been seen as merciful to finish me off because workers with industrial disease may spill the beans at a later date about the 'source' of their condition but I wasn't sure Abbie and co wanted to delve into my background in too much detail. Whatever they had in store for me, this wasn't the place I wanted to say my final prayers. It was a long way from home.

After a short walk, someone opened a door in front of me. I walked forward a few steps and then felt Abbie's hand on my shoulder; I had got used to it. I could hear people talking – some in Arabic, some in English, some in both. It felt like a big room because I could breathe better and I sensed the ceiling and windows were high up. I felt Abbie's hand on the back of my head and sensed he was about to take off the blindfold – or sleeping aid as I preferred to think of it – but instead, he stroked the back of my neck which made me feel extremely ticklish.

'Man Friday, come here…' said Abbie.

I didn't know who he was talking to but thoughts of hostages and beheadings suddenly morphed into cannibalism. I imagined being stirred and boiled in a big black cauldron and then being eaten by the famished, keffiyah–wearing soldiers who hadn't eaten for years. Luckily, the paranoia didn't have much time to set in because the blindfold was yanked off almost immediately. Within seconds, I felt a sword of light burning through my right eye from a tiny gap in a partially–covered window. I put my hand over the eye but it was blinking rapidly – and went on doing so even when I left it shut. I eventually took my hand off my eye and looked behind me. Wasim was stood there with the blindfold in his hand.

'He made me do it, nana jee,' said Wasim.

'Did he fucking make you come to Iraq too?'

Wasim threw the blindfold onto Abbie's chest and it fell meekly onto the floor. He walked away towards a small entrance which had a green blanket hanging down from it. He flicked away the blanket and walked through. I wondered where he was going. What did he do back there?

Abbie bent down and picked up the blindfold. He smelt it and closed his eyes, relishing no doubt the scent of the Canadian woman. I used the moment of freedom to glance around the room. It wasn't as big as I'd initially thought: about the size of two cricket pitches laid next to each other. There was a giant rug underneath my feet with red and black calligraphy but it didn't quite fit the room because one end was folded up against a wall. I counted six people in the room, apart from Abbie and Saad, who was now leaning against the dark blue wall smoking an extremely long cigarette. Three tired–looking men with keffiyahs hanging loosely over their shoulders were sat down on the floor with their backs against the wall. One of them was holding a Kalashnikov rifle behind his neck and had it gripped tightly with his fists as though it was a form of exercise. He was staring at me while the other two men chatted limply and without conviction. In another corner of the room, an older man was crouched over a younger man, cutting his hair with a tiny comb but a huge pair of scissors. The black mountain of hair on the see–through plastic sheeting almost made me jealous. There was also another person in the room but I couldn't tell if it was a man or a woman because the person was bending down fiddling with the wheel of a bicycle. The short hair, pale skin and stud earring in one ear confused me because it was so different to everyone else in the room. Abbie walked up to me and put his hand on my shoulder.

'We rule here. No Sykes–Picot in these parts.' He handed me the blindfold. 'Now take this. It's a gift.'

I hesitated but then took the blindfold. 'I like face masks. If only I'd worn one for all those years...' I stuffed it into my trouser pocket with more difficulty than expected. 'Why do you call my grandson 'Man Friday'?

Abbie laughed and looked across at the person tending to the bicycle.

'Do you see her?' he asked.

I was about to answer but the woman's glance over her shoulder distracted me. She was wearing a black short–sleeved shirt, a baseball cap and tight navy blue trousers. How could I have mistaken her for a man? Her slender arms and ankle high boots completed my sense of embarrassment.

'Do you think Americans or other kufrs could relate to a sister in a burka or niqab?' asked Abbie. 'One look at her and their front tail pops up.'

'She works for you?'

'Nobody works here,' said Wasim, abruptly. 'We just do our duty.' He looked annoyed and walked towards Saad, grabbing his cigarette. He took a drag and handed it back to Saad.

'And what about Wasim? What's his duty?'

'Oh yes, Man Friday,' he said, perking up again.

'He's here because he believes in our cause. The only thing we disagree on is the subject of men and women worshipping at the same mosque. He thinks mosques should only be for men and women should stay at home. I think women should be allowed in. So I called him Man Friday.'

'Don't most of your chums think the same?'

Abbie walked back towards me. He raised his finger to my blinking eye and pressed down gently on the eyelid. 'He's more Taliban about it than the others. I was like him once but it's what we do that counts not what we think.' He raised his finger off my eye. 'Open your eye now. Is it better?'

I slowly raised the twitchy eyelid and, despite some blurred vision, my sight hadn't been affected. I could see them all clearly now. They were a dishevelled, disinterested bunch ambling around in a sparse, mediocre room which was short on colour as well as character. It reminded me of Paul back home and a few of the other bewildered, directionless boys I'd seen shuffling around the town. There was no spark, energy or organisation here; only a drab, dreary place where global fantasies were imagined and pipsqueak orders were carried out. If this was jihad then I was disappointed. Wasim had been fooled.

The woman's name was Ayesha but I didn't see her again that day. The bike had gone and so he had she. Abbie told me she was 23 years old and brought food and supplies for the 'Brigade Boys' whenever she could. Her mother cooked a special rice pudding for the boys on a Friday and Abbie couldn't wait for the day to come round so he could savour the sweet, melting taste in his parched mouth. He said he hated it when Ayesha rode in on her bike and didn't have that small white bag placed in the rectangular black basket at the back of the bike. On the rare occasions that happened, it had usually been confiscated by a hungry Iraqi soldier at a checkpoint or Ayesha's mother simply couldn't make it because of a rice shortage. It was clear to me that Ayesha was an important part of the set–up. Abbie talked about her more than Wasim.

Abbie told me all this over a hot glass of tea after I had been on one of my futile throat–clearing marathons. He insisted I didn't use the sink in the toilet but a blue plastic bowl in front of him so he could watch me cough and splutter. As I bent over, I almost had tears in my eyes because, as usual, hardly any mucus came out save for a tiny amount of sickly liquid. The front of my body, particularly my chest and stomach, throbbed with excruciating pain. Abbie patted me on the back and finally took the bowl off me. I got up and told him I was off to find Wasim – who I hadn't seen since he'd kindly taken the blindfold off my head. Abbie grabbed hold of my arm.

'He'll be back soon,' said Abbie. 'Don't worry about him. He'll just make you unhappy.'

I shook my head and looked across at the green blanket. I tried to take my first step but my left knee almost caved in. I could hear Abbie snigger over my shoulder and I wanted to turn, if I could, and clip him round the ear but I knew it would waste more energy and that was pointless. I looked down at the floor and the bright calligraphy on the rug set off my blinking eyes again. I got up to the green blanket and waved it to the side. I held it for a moment and looked in. There was a tight corridor and two rooms, one on each side. I walked in and immediately to my right there was a tiny room which was obviously a washing area and toilet. There were a couple of robes hanging down from the hooks, a half–filled kettle of water, a hole–in–the–floor toilet, two pairs of sandals and a small bar of soap.

I walked further down the corridor and on the left there was an entrance with no door. I stopped and looked inside. I could see Wasim lying on a sturdy but scruffy double bed with his hands behind his head looking up at the whirring ceiling fan. He still had his trainers on and they hung over the front edge of the bed. I hesitated and then walked into the room. I walked towards the bed and stood over it. I folded my arms and waited for Wasim to acknowledge his grandfather's strife. He didn't. He continued to look at the ghastly yellow–painted ceiling and keep his fingers locked behind his head. But what was that on his face? I looked closer and couldn't see the rampaging idealism and certainty in his eyes that I normally felt. His cheeks were puffed–up, his eyes were moist and his umbrella mouth looked as though it had been weathering the storms from high up.

'Been crying?'

He didn't answer. I sat down on the bed and crossed my hands. It felt relaxing; it was nice to sit on a comfortable surface for once.

'Come home, right now.'

'I'm not coming. I'm settling here…'

I turned and faced him. I tried to grab his extremely warm hand but he managed to move it away.

'Where are you going to live? In the desert?'

'Got my plans.'

I huffed and got up off the bed. I looked at the five x–shaped wooden Quran holders neatly stacked side by side on a dressing table but with no book of God to complement them. They were bright, polished and gleaming; unlike the rest of the room.

'Which one's yours?' I asked.

'What?'

'Which Quran holder is yours?'

'We share things over here…we don't own.'

I nodded and walked over to the Quran holders. I wiped away a bit of dust from one of them. I remembered rows and rows of them in Faisalabad in the early days after I was sent to Molvi Rasheed's for my so–called education. The swaying motion was enjoyable but I didn't have the foggiest what I was saying. Memorise or be hit was the mantra. As I rubbed my finger across the smooth, immaculate carving on one of the holders, I almost expected a bamboo stick to pop up behind it. But there were enough weapons here already.

'I'm not standing for this anymore,' I said. 'Get your things, we're going home.'

Wasim didn't answer but slowly sat up. He felt the back of his neck and then picked up the pillow behind him and laid it vertically against the bed rest. He leaned back and folded his arms.

'I'm sorry for everything that's gone down,' he said. 'It weren't my fault. When Abdullah found out you were around, he wanted to find out more about you. He were fascinated…'

'Abdullah?'

'Abbie…'

I nodded and walked back towards the bed. I sat down and touched Wasim's knee.

'Forget about Abdullah, come home and make your mother happy…'

'I can't. It's more complicated than that.'

'There's nothing complicated. Just get your bags and let's go.'

Wasim lowered his head and there was silence for a few seconds. He was about to answer but then looked over my shoulder after hearing the sound of thudding footsteps down the corridor. He looked me in the eye with a resigned, puppy–dog expression.

'I'm in love,' he said. 'I'm gonna get married.'

My head was swirling with confusion. How could this stupid boy even contemplate such a thing? Saad appeared at the door, out of breath. I looked over my shoulder and was about to tell him to get lost.

'There's firing and kufr soldiers at Shami's down the road,' said Saad. 'Abbie wants us all down there now.'

Wasim got up instantly and straightened his hair with his hands.

'You're not going,' I said. 'It's too dangerous.'

'You can't tell me what to do. This is what I'm here for.'

An image of Wasim tooled up with bullets and a rifle came into my head. Matching his conviction was the only way to gain respect.

'I'm coming too,' I said. 'I go where he goes.'

'No old man,' said Saad. 'Abbie says you stay. You'll be safe here.'

I got up off the bed but nearly fell over. There was a lack of co–ordination and the vocal tics began again. I held my throat and took a deep breath. 'Over my dead body,' I said, in a slurred voice.

We drove away at speed and I glanced across at the caramel–brick building with its incongruous blue door and realised it was much smaller than I thought. There were a lot of wet patches underneath the two tiny windows and I imagined they were persistent splashes of water where wuzu had been carried out before prayers. Outside, the sandy grass was dissected by the pebble–laden path – which had done its damage to the soles of my feet – and there was a clothes line hung in semi–circle formation across the front of the house. But my creaking neck didn't allow me look over my shoulder for too long. Abbie was like a man possessed, screeching down on the accelerator as though his life depended on it – and it did. We got to Shami's in under five minutes and already the sound of rapid gunfire could be heard. Abbie's car skidded to a halt on a side road outside

Shami's house. Saad and Wasim were in the back with me, with rifles in their laps and keffiyahs round their faces. The front seat was again unoccupied. The black gate was already open and everybody got out.

'Stay in the car, nana jee,' said Wasim. 'The trouble's out back. You'll be fine here.'

'I'm with you all the way now.'

Abbie was already a few yards ahead of us but stopped and turned when he heard us talking. He ran towards Wasim and pulled him away.

'I told you not to bring him,' said Abbie. 'He talks too much. An imam will straighten him out this evening.'

'You're the one who needs straightening out,' I said.

Abbie ignored me and ran through the open gate. Wasim and Saad ran in a few yards behind him. Wasim looked over his shoulder.

'Come on, nana jee,' he shouted. 'Stay close to me.'

I had less fear than I expected. I wanted to see why so many people wanted to do harm to each other. I didn't understand it. What did it achieve? There was actually shooting going on? I wanted to see if this was really happening. Why hurt so many people in one go? I could hear explosions now as well as gunfire; they helped me get a move on. I managed to run towards Wasim and it was easier than I thought: the pain and stiffness was drastically reduced. Wasim looked over his shoulder but he needn't have worried: I was almost floating now. I sprinted past the black gate and ran into the house. I followed the others down the sparkling, clean corridor and through an immaculate room with framed paintings of Mecca, Medina and the Al–Aqsa mosque on the sky blue walls. It was the most glittering room I'd seen since I'd been in the country but, unfortunately, I would only see it for a few seconds. I could see Abbie up ahead open a back door and, suddenly, even with my decaying ears, the crackling sound of gunshots, rifles and explosions was too close for comfort. I followed the others into the open area at the back of the house – you couldn't call it a garden – and the picture was vivid and terrifying. I stopped at the door and squinted as the scorching afternoon sun beat down on the dirty golden landscape. Abbie, Saad and Wasim joined Shami on the ground behind a concrete wall. Shami continued to fire his rifle over the wall despite trying to stop the bleeding from a shoulder wound which had defaced the upper part of his white robe. In the distance, about 10 cricket pitches away, I could see a small mud hut which was popping relentless fire across the crystal blue sky towards Shami's house. Bullets were whistling into the walls, the back door, the wheelbarrow and the arched windows at the back of the house. I stayed by the door, uncertain and riddled with doubt. I had been ready for anything a few moments ago but now I wasn't so sure. I hadn't expected to see bullets flying past my nose so soon. I watched Wasim as he crouched down by Shami and prepared his rifle for combat. I realised now it had been a terrible mistake to allow him to come here. He had so many years left – and I would be responsible for him wasting them. I also realised that my desire for experience was misguided. These people would continue shooting at each other irrespective of what I thought or did. There wasn't much room for a Q&A session here. I should have stayed in the safe house and demanded Wasim did the same. I decided I had only one option. First, I tried to take some deep breaths using Bilu's techniques but his methods were demolished by a crushing anxiety. So I picked out my inhaler and took a few insignificant puffs. I then stepped out into the long grass and ran as fast as my legs could take me towards the brick wall where the boys were haphazardly firing their rifles. A bullet pinged against the wheelbarrow to my left but I got there quicker than expected and cowered by the side of the wall. I looked up at Wasim who was bobbing up and down gripping his rifle tightly. He had a rage in his face that I'd never seen before: it was unpleasant and unnerving. His rifle technique was better than I expected and I shuddered each time he sprung up and emptied another round. This wasn't my grandson: it was a teenage boy lost in the haze between madness and belief.

'Who do you want to get married to?' I asked.

'WHAT?'

'What's her name?'

'GO HOME. IT'S TOO DANGEROUS.'

Wasim glanced down at me as though as I was a worm. The speed of his firing slowed down. He turned around to face me and slid his back down the wall. He sat down but held his AK–47 as tightly as ever.

'Nana jee, please go home, You're causing major aggro.'

'Is she Iraqi?'

Wasim was enraged and got up. The scowling and conviction was back again and he started firing more wildly than ever. The horrific noise of the multiple gun fire was almost unbearable: my ears were popping and I thought I was about to go deaf. Everything was vibrating: my body, the wall and the ground.

'WHAT ARE YOU DOING?' shouted Abbie. 'FIRE AT THE KUFR'S, NOT THE TREES.'

'I AM! STOP SHOUTING AT ME.'

I looked at the four desperate men in a row – all willing to lay down their lives for a cause I didn't understand – and realised, I too, would have to do something desperate to make any sort of impact. So I got up and wiped the blades of warm grass off my numb backside. The wall was about four feet high so I could comfortably see over it – or even climb over it and head towards 'the enemy'. But I decided that it would be a bit of an escalation so I simply raised my arms and gave a criss–crossing gesture to the people who were shooting at us.

'WHAT THE HELL ARE YOU DOING?' shouted Wasim, grabbing me and pulling me down to the ground.

'GET THAT OLD BASTARD OUT OF HERE,' screamed Abbie. 'HE'LL GET US ALL KILLED.'

I fell over and my nose squashed against the long grass. I turned around and got up. I was prepared to do the same again but Wasim held me down.

'Go back, both of you,' said Abbie, ripping off his keffiyah and throwing it behind him. 'You're no good to me here…'

'But I want to stay,' said Wasim.

'YOU'RE NOT STAYING.'

'Give us the car keys then?' I asked.

Abbie looked astonished and I almost felt he was about to turn his rifle on me. 'Can't you see we have a wounded man? Now get lost!'

'But I want to fight,' said Wasim.

'YES, BUT YOU'RE ALREADY FIGHTING HIM. GO NOW BEFORE I GET ANGRY.'

'NO, I'M STAYING.'

Abbie stopped firing and pointed his rifle at Wasim. I grabbed hold of Wasim and tried to usher him away. He stood for a moment – I could tell there was a lot of pride in the boy – but he reluctantly and eventually turned my way.

It would have been nice to have the car but it was out of our hands. In the end, it took about 45 minutes to get back to the so-called safe house and most of it was spent in silence. As Wasim and I walked the long road home, the sound of rifles and explosions faded into the distance. But that sense of relief was tempered by the fact my walking pattern was deteriorating with every stride. My hips and toes were under so much strain that I felt I was waddling along like a penguin.

I tried to make conversation with Wasim but he strode a few yards ahead of me, kicking the odd stone and ensuring I suffered the maximum distress for taking him away from a potentially life–threatening situation. I didn't expect him to grateful. He had left his rifle down there too so that wasn't improving his mood either. At least he couldn't shoot me with it, I thought.

The journey took us past an elderly farmer grazing his sheep, a couple of hastily–built, white–plastered homes and three boys playing marbles near an anorexic palm tree. The boys walked towards us but Wasim gave them a cold stare and they backed off. After seeing those boys running back across the grass, I decided to walk on the green stuff rather than the extremely wide, potholed road even though it took more time. It was less painful on my feet. Wasim continued to walk right down the middle, perhaps sadistically, and revelled in putting his feet in the biggest and deepest of holes.

The relief when I spotted Abbie's shabby, insignificant building was incredible. I watched Wasim go in first, about six cricket pitches ahead of me, as the late afternoon sun thankfully lost its brutal authority. I trudged in about five minutes later, breathing heavily while trying to repress my whispering cough and a bout of drooling. I glanced over my shoulder at the swathes of barren beige land with the odd mud huts dotted on the hillside and relished the total, therapeutic silence. It was a world away from the carnage I had just experienced.

I groggily walked in to the main room and it was empty. Where had all those men gone? They weren't with us at Shami's house so had they chickened out? Perhaps, Abbie asked them to scamper down to Shami's after we had left. I didn't care anyway: all I wanted was a drink of water and a lie down.

I walked to the end of the main room and hesitated as I came to the green blanket hanging from the door. I didn't really want any confrontation with Wasim, as I was exhausted, but knew it couldn't be avoided because there was nowhere else to go in this cramped, claustrophobic excuse for a home. I pulled away the green blanket and walked down the corridor. The toilet door was locked so I guessed Wasim was in there. That gave me a boost and I walked down towards the bedroom, half–expecting that it would be empty. I turned left and walked into the bedroom. To my surprise, Wasim was getting changed into a set of Umbro tracksuit bottoms and a white t–shirt. He didn't look at me and lay on the bed once he'd finished. After a couple of minutes of excruciating silence, with only the murmurs of the ceiling fan seeping into my ears, I heard the toilet door outside open and close. I imagined it was one of the men and expected the person to head for the main room, or somewhere else, but the footsteps got louder. Wasim looked up at me for the first time. The door opened and I turned around. It was a woman wearing a dark green silk headscarf, navy blue trousers and an elegant red v–neck sweater. It was Ayesha.

# 8.

How could have I been so stupid not to see it? As if I needed confirmation, Ayesha left the room almost as soon as she had walked in. She didn't give me a chance to probe further because – like a good woman in this neck of the woods – she obediently disappeared just as I was about to pop some difficult questions her way. The most pressing of these queries was how did a beautiful girl like her hook up with that brainwashed grandson of mine? It was bewildering to me that any of this had been going on because I felt Abbie was running a tight jihadi ship with all the crew concentrating on the war in hand. Obviously that wasn't the case. Did Abbie know about this? What did he think about it? All these questions were running through my head as I listened to Ayesha's footsteps fade away down the corridor. I immediately turned to Wasim, who continued to lie on the bed with his eyes fixed on the ceiling fan. I walked towards the bed and sat down. I reached out and tried to touch his hand but he moved it away.

'I'm going to marry her, whatever you say.'

The definitive tone in his voice was wearing me out. My mind wandered to a 14–year–old lad I once knew called Cammy Eastwell, who was a real prospect in the Under–18 side as a raw fast bowler.

He used to appeal for leg before nearly every over – and I rejected his appeal the same amount of times. On one occasion, he confronted me in the pavilion after the match and said I was a 'daft codger' and, worse, that I didn't understand young people. It really stung so I offered him a lift home one night which he rejected. The friction, on his side, continued until I deliberately brought in a batch of John Player League match programmes from the late seventies and eighties and browsed through them at change of innings and close of play. Cammy only had one ambition, to play for Lancashire as a quick, and he finally approached me to ask why the players weren't wearing coloured clothing for a limited overs game? It was a great feeling when I realised I was getting through to him. He was a broody, reclusive boy but his eyes widened and his face lit up. There was warmth and respect between us. Somehow, I knew Wasim wouldn't buckle so easily.

'How long have you known her?' I asked.

'Go away, I'm knackered. I need some sleep.'

He rolled over to his right side so his back was facing me. He curled up tight and slipped his hand between his thighs. I watched him try to get comfortable and then crossed my hands on my lap to get in a similar mode.

'I'm not going away; we were nearly killed out there.' I said. 'Why is a woman here anyway? I thought you lot didn't like women...'

I heard a heavy sigh and he readjusted his head on the bulky black pillow.

'…What does Abbie think about this arrangement anyway? Does he know? Have you told him?'

Wasim raised his head and smacked it down on the pillow again.

'So was it love at first sight or did it take a while?'

Wasim grabbed the pillow from under his head and flung it across the room. He pivoted around and gave me a vicious look. He brushed me to the side and sprung up off the bed like a gymnast. He tucked his t–shirt into his tracksuit bottoms and then bent down to grab his Puma trainers from under the bed.

'Have you met her parents?'

Wasim slowed down his frantic movements. He glanced up at me as he eased the trainers towards him from under the bed. He sighed and looked up at the ceiling.

'I've known her for a couple of months, okay? Abbie helped out her parents after their house had been flattened. Her uncle and brother–in–law were injured so she wanted to do something about it. So she joined up with us. Satisfied now?'

'And you think two months is long enough to propose marriage, do you?'

'FUCKIN' HELL! LEAVE ME ALONE.'

He haphazardly slipped on his trainers without doing the laces up and walked to the door. He stopped for a moment as though he'd remembered something.

'Mum says you got married to nani jee when she was 33. I don't want to wait that long.'

He whizzed out of the room before I could answer. I digested what he'd said for a moment and then got up off the bed to pick up the pillow he'd thrown across the room. I carefully placed it on the bed and lay down, resting my heavy, throbbing head on it as delicately as possible. I placed my hands on my chest and thought of the 21 years I had known Fareeda until we actually got married. I met her for the first time sitting beside a tiny stream as she battered the wet clothes violently on the black rock to dry them. She was only 12 and I didn't have the courage to approach her. We did eventually develop a friendship, through sheer adolescent loneliness and sharing of work duties including pumping water, wood gathering and fruit–picking, but it was put on hold because I was sent to Faisalabad to work. I thought of marriage there and then – I was 16 and she was 20 – but it felt too rushed and too soon, even though I was desperate to get back at my father who was sending me away. Luckily, I came back and things worked out for me – and Fareeda. Wasim, however, had only known Ayesha for two months. In my eyes, that wasn't enough time to hold hands. I had a duty to ensure my grandson didn't throw his life away by getting into something he may regret for the rest of his life. He had already been indoctrinated once: another head–over–heels belief would be a step too far.

The distant sound of water splashing off someone's face onto the floor woke me up. I looked at my watch and realised I had slept for a stunning seven and a half hours. I got up and waited for a few moments until I knew the bathroom was empty. Washing my face was a big problem because there was no mirror and the tiny, damp towel was inadequate to do any sort of drying. In the end, the sleeves on my jumper did an emergency wiping job and I had to wait five minutes before my itchy face returned to normal. When I did leave, however, I sensed the mood of the 'house' had been transformed. I walked down the corridor and could already hear loud voices, jovial banter and wild laughing. What on earth was going on? Weren't these people involved in a vicious firefight earlier on in the day? I took a deep breath as I looked at the green blanket in front of me. I tried to clear my throat but it was impossible so I offered a tiddly, sorry excuse for a cough. I pulled the blanket to one side and walked through into the main room. There was complete silence and the gawping faces of the people sat on the floor with their dark, piercing eyes sent a shudder up my spine and, inevitably, set me off on a rapid round of vocal tics. The tics, throat–clearing and coughing were now in full swing and I thought about turning back because of the embarrassment. But my eyes caught sight of the bewildering amount of food on the floor and, eventually, the annoying tics eased off. The colourful bounty strewn across the hastily–laid blue blanket had soothed my cough and had a therapeutic effect. I counted at least five dishes, all lying on miniature versions of Wimbledon's silver salvers; pity there weren't any women in the room to share them. There was a lamb salad number, a curious chick–pea and potato concoction, a ghastly–looking aubergine and tomato dish, a mince meat and vegetable mountain and, finally, a blood–red chicken pile–up with walnuts. Five exotic dishes and all I could smell was dried mint! The dishes had steaming plates of white rice by the side of them as well as side bowls of pomegranates, mangoes and water melons. Only the plastic red glasses and huge jug of water let the side down in terms of scale and impression. I looked up again and most of the people had got back to filling their bellies rather than staring at me. I spotted Abbie with his back against the wall laughing and chatting to another man, who was wearing a neat black turban and a tent–like white robe. I thought about leaving the room but it didn't matter because Abbie spotted me and ushered me over. I slipped off my shoes and placed them along with a few others in one corner. I walked forward tentatively, carefully sidestepping the dishes and praying I didn't crush a pomegranate under foot. I stopped in front of Abbie and expected him to look up at me but he didn't, he continued to talk to the man next to him. I glanced around the room, looking and feeling embarrassed. I had decided at that moment that Wasim and I would leave as soon as possible. I wasn't going to take this anymore and if Wasim didn't like it then, tough, I was his grandfather and he had to listen. Where the hell was he anyway? Everyone else was in the room, even Shami whose arm was in a sling and Saad who was slumped against the wall, looking dazed and distant. Ayesha, of course, was in her 'own space', the poor girl. After a couple of minutes of humiliation, Abbie finally looked me in the eye again. I could have moved away in that time but the harsh fact of an empty stomach kept me where I was.

'Grandfather, you're here,' he said, checking his ear for an imaginary wound. 'This is Doctor Al–Brahmi. I brought him here especially for you. Come on, sit down here and join us. You hungry?'

I couldn't lie. The dish closest to me was the mince meat and vegetable mountain and I had been eyeing it up since Abbie's initial snub. So I sat down awkwardly between the doctor and Abbie. My crooked back was uncomfortable resting against the wall but once I tucked into the food it no longer mattered. It took about ten minutes to finish the meal although the accompanying naan breads were so rich and tangy that I wanted to carry on.

'Doctor Al–Brahmi will cure you tonight,' said Abbie.

'There's nothing wrong with me,' I said, leaning back and enjoying a succulent slice of mango. 'He's wasting his time.'

Abbie looked at Doctor Al–Brahmi and smiled. He picked up a handful of pistachio nuts from a bowl. He cracked open one of the nuts and threw it into his mouth. He then turned towards me and handed me a couple of nuts. I took them but wasn't going to eat them: they would interfere with the mangoes.

'You cough a lot and can't get that shit out of your lungs. He will help you.'

'Some things can't be cured…'

'If Allah wills it, anything is possible.'

I examined Abbie's face in a little more detail; it was the first time I'd seen him without the keffiyah wrapped around his face. He may have been older than I first thought and his full cheeks, moustache and firm chin gave him an experience and authority that I hadn't fully absorbed. He was extremely relaxed too, slightly slumped against the wall with his left foot perched on his right thigh. It was a big change from the screaming brute I'd suffered earlier in the day.

Abbie lowered his hand into the bowl and picked up another few pistachio nuts. He showed me the palm of his hand. 'His pills were this big and they still killed him.'

'Sorry, who are you talking about?'

'About three years ago, my father hired a solicitor to help with the sale of our house because he didn't want to live in Baghdad anymore,' said Abbie. 'This solicitor took pills for everything and said he couldn't live without them. One morning, after coming out of the toilet, he had such a bad reaction that his face had turned blue and he wasn't responding. So my father drove him as fast as he could to hospital to get him some emergency attention. But when he got to the hospital, there was no room for him because it was overflowing with Shaheed victims and other civilian casualties. He died there and then. Where was his medical help? Where were the people he believed in?'

'Each case is different.'

'Only if you have no faith,' he said. 'Enough of

kufr solicitors anyway. Dr Al–Brahmi will now take over and solve your problems.'

'…Just got to go the bathroom.'

Abbie laughed and grabbed hold of my shoulder. 'You've just been.'

'I have to go every hour on some days.'

Abbie moved closer towards me and now had both of his hands on my shoulders. He looked at me directly and the relaxed, slightly jovial, demeanour changed into a harsher, abrasive one.

'Do you want to get better?'

'Yes.'

'Get up then.'

I got up with difficulty because my stomach was bloated. I knew I had eaten too fast which was something I found hard to control in the last few years.

'Stand there,' said Abbie, pointing to a few feet in front of Dr Al–Brahmi.

I did what I was told. What was the worst that could happen? That some crackpot cleric chanted a few verses and tried to 'cleanse my soul'? It might even be fun.

Abbie asked Dr Al–Brahmi to get up too. He was a small man, barely over five three, but the stature came from the thin spectacles, well–groomed beard and pale, creamy features. He had a shiny black beaded necklace in his hand and his fingers were flicking over the beads like an anxious shopkeeper counting his notes. He walked up to me and stopped less than a foot away. He examined my face and then nodded as though he'd found the secret to my tortured existence. He put the beaded necklace away in his pocket and cupped his hands to say a prayer. He closed his eyes and recited a few familiar verses from the Quran; I watched his supple lips move in extraordinary ways as the textured, twangy words rocketed from his mouth. Slowly but surely, I began to feel queasy, although this may have been more to do with the richness of the lamb dish than the good doctor's initiation. He stopped reciting and opened his eyes. He walked up to me and looked into my eyes. He blew across my face three times. It was pleasant enough: I always needed reminding I was still around. But then he moved his mouth closer to my ear and I felt a little more uncomfortable. He recited the same verses but with more aggression and fervour. The sound of his voice pierced through my ears and increased the trembling in my shoulders. He then glanced to his left and right and ushered someone to help him. Abbie grabbed one of my shoulders and, another man – a tall, skinny fellow with a pointy chin – grabbed the other.

'He's carrying the weight of a thousand people,' said Dr Al–Brahmi. 'Get him down.'

I tried to resist but the tall man's sharp fingernails were digging painfully into the back of the neck: I had to go down to relieve the pressure. Two more men came rushing over, as if they were disappointed to be left out, and pinned my legs down. One of the blighters had his mouth inches away from my nose and, for a second, I thought his garlic breath had revived my blocked sinuses. The doctor moved closer and stopped with his feet inches away from my head. He towered over me giving the impression his head was almost touching the ceiling. He reached into the side pocket and pulled out a tiny bottle. What was in it? Sand? He poured it onto the palm of his hand – and clenched his fist.

'This fistful of dust,' he said, sprinkling it over my head. 'Comes straight from the holy land…'

'I've got a lifetime of dust in here already,' I said, thumping my chest.

Dr Al–Brahmi sprinkled the whole bottle over me – but he was only warming up. He threw away that bottle and took another small green one out of his pocket. He opened it and sniffed it – it had a small amount of water in it. He closed his eyes as he revelled in the scent.

'This is the tonic for the djinn,' said Abbie, with a smile.

'GET OFF ME NOW, YOU ANIMALS! I DON'T HAVE ANY OF YOUR STUPID DJINN.'

'That's what they all say,' said Abbie.

Dr Al–Brahmi opened his eyes after his lengthy bottle–sniffing exercise. He looked at me and then crouched down with the bottle raised in his hand. He started talking faster, repeating the same line.

'Prophet's peace be upon you…Prophet's peace be upon you…'

He raised the bottle as high as his arm would go and then sprinkled it rapidly across my body and face. I closed my eyes but felt the splashes on my lips and ears.

'LEAVE ME ALONE! YOU DON'T KNOW WHAT YOU'RE DOING…'

A splash from the bottle stung my eyeball but I made a mistake in shouting so loud. It set off a coughing spree which rapidly escalated into a rough, tortuous burst that was impossible to stop. I gasped for air and felt as though my lungs were about to burst. I flailed my arms and legs with all the power I could summon but it was futile: the men were too powerful. Even worse, I could feel my attention–seeking bladder giving way at any moment and moistening my trousers with some poor decoration. That would have been hard to take so I tried to hold on for as long as possible. After 94 seconds, I got a reprieve. The sprinkling stopped and Dr Al–Brahmi stopped talking. Was it over? I opened my eyes slowly and saw Dr Al–Brahmi's face up close to mine. He examined me for a moment and then, suddenly, slapped me across the face with his short, stubby hand.

'Is Allah within you?'

'Er, what?'

'Is Allah within you?'

He drew back his hand, a bit higher, and slapped me again with more ferocity. My eyes watered as the tip of my nose caught part of the blow.

'Is Allah within you?'

I tried to answer but my energy levels were depleting by the second. He hit me again but I hardly felt it because a terrible warmth accelerated throughout my body. I could feel the front of my trousers moistening and the trickle down my right thigh became a glorious flood. The relief was incredible and immediate. I hadn't suffered a fly slip for 66 years: this was something worth waiting for.

The tall man, who had hold of my legs, instantly took his hands off me and stood up. He held his nose and checked his hands for urine. He gave Abbie a startled look and then raced haphazardly towards the toilet. He nearly barged into a distant figure coming into the room with a huge tray of teacups. I strained to try and see who it was but I couldn't turn my neck any further. I smiled at Abbie as he let go of my shoulder.

'Dirty British like to piss on our land,' he said.

Dr Al–Brahmi moved back and looked down at my trousers. He shook his head and then offered Abbie a handshake. Abbie looked surprised by his gesture but accepted. Dr Al–Brahmi gave me a final disapproving glance and walked off hurriedly. As he disappeared, the white teacups with gold rims came into view. The soft hands carrying them were Ayesha's. She stopped by my side as the steam from the cups illuminated her face.

'What's going on here?' she asked. 'Who was that man?'

'A good man,' said Abbie, getting up and picking up one of the teacups from the tray. 'Great food, Ashi, you did a top job.' He took a sip, got up and started to walk away. 'How does your mother cook so much?'

Ayesha sighed and put the tray down on the floor next to me. She looked at Abbie and then bent down by my side. My coughing had been reduced to murmuring levels but I still felt a tingling discomfort across my neck and chest. She kneeled over me and put her hand behind my neck to help me up. I put my hand on her shoulder and eventually got up and looked around. She stroked my back and then reached across to pick up a teacup. She slowly handed it to me and I took it with both hands. I raised it up to my trembling jaw and took a sip. It was the most beautiful cup of tea I'd ever tasted.

I spent at least an half an hour cleaning myself up in the toilet. I panicked when I realised I only had three clean pairs of Burton checked trunks left and knew I had to use them sparingly if I was to get through the rest of the trip. The thought of asking Ayesha about my washing did cross my mind but I figured I wouldn't be here much longer so it wasn't worthwhile. I didn't feel embarrassed by my incontinence; far from it. It had saved me from a prolonged session with the good doctor and his assistants. If I told them straight that I had asbestosis would it have changed their behaviour? Probably not because the vocal tics and throat–clearing were unusual and could be seen as part of a different kind of illness; more psychological and, in their eyes, demonic.

Ayesha had helped me to the toilet but now I could hear her soft, measured voice, in the nearby bedroom. She was trying to mediate while Wasim and Abbie argued in a vociferous, unfocused manner. Their disturbing conversation quickened my heart rate and got my bladder aggravated again, which was annoying. So I quickly stuffed the three–pack of Burton underwear back in my bag and did a few windmills of my arms to unstiffen my shoulders. I zipped up my bag and left the toilet. I stood in the corridor for a few minutes and hesitated, listening to Abbie giving Wasim a fearful lecture about 'teamwork and sacrifice'. But I'd heard enough – these youngsters needed an old head to put them straight – so I walked down the corridor and breezed into the bedroom without giving it a second thought. They stopped talking as soon as I walked in. Ayesha was sat on the bed, Abbie was lying on it and Wasim was standing up a few yards away. Abbie and Ayesha stared at me but Wasim turned his back.

'We're going home now,' I said. 'Come on Wasim.'

'Get him out of my country,' said Abbie. 'He's failed the group.'

Wasim turned and gave Abbie a fearful, scowling look. 'You're the one's who failed, you twat. She wants to marry me, not you.'

Abbie sprung up off the bed and headed towards Wasim. He whipped off his keffiyah and gripped it tightly in his hand. Ayesha tried to stop him but he shrugged her off. Abbie stopped a couple of feet away from Wasim and flicked the keffiyah into his face. Wasim flinched but managed to avoid it.

'Stop it, you idiots,' I said, walking briskly towards the two men. 'This is not the solution.'

Abbie laughed and stepped back. He placed the keffiyah round his neck and sat down next to Ayesha who was looking down at the floor. He tried to prop her chin up with his hand but she brushed him off and continued to look down.

'I would get him out of here quickly,' said Abbie. 'If the men find out about his dirty intentions, they will not spare him.'

'You're the dirty bastard,' said Wasim, aggressively trying to push me away and get at Abbie. 'And I'm not going anywhere without her.'

Ayesha tutted and suddenly got up. She headed for the door and walked out of the room.

'He was in the kitchen with her while we were eating,' said Abbie. 'Ask him, old man! He was doing all kinds of things.'

Wasim was incensed and managed to push me away. He launched at Abdullah and pushed him back onto the bed. Both men grappled with each other and Abudullah was nearly pushed off the side of the bed as Wasim gained a slight advantage. I watched on in horror, confused about my next move. I didn't have the strength to intervene and wondered whether I should chase after Ayesha and bring her back. But then it hit me. I looked down at my bag and unzipped it as fast as my trembling hands would allow. I pulled out the Kwik Cricket bat and held it in my hands to get a good grip. I took a deep breath and looked at the two boys rolling around on the bed. I raised my bat as far back as possible over the shoulders – like the best golfer – and headed towards the idiots with all my might.

'STOP OR I'LL HIT YOU FOR SIX.'

Abdullah saw me coming from the corner of his eye and pushed Wasim away. Wasim fell onto the floor and his head nearly hit the wall. Abdullah raised his palms but I continued to hold my bat over my head: it was the only follow through of the day that really mattered. I wanted to hit his grinning face but gradually my sense of cordiality and compromise took over and I slowly withdrew the plastic bat. I knew, at that moment, there was only one way to solve all these issues: by stepping outside and being a force for good.

# 9.

Two bloaty pancakes and a cup of extra strong tea gave me stomach cramps in the morning but the food was a necessary sacrifice to get the group indoctrinated. After the greasy breakfast, I stood up and demonstrated a few cover drives in the main room while Wasim delivered the ball underarm. Wasim hadn't spoken to me since I had threatened carnage with the bat but I didn't care: I had to do what was best for him and for the wider community irrespective of his stroppy behaviour. Abbie was sat in the room with his five lackeys and, to my surprise, had been more accommodating since my bat–wielding exploits. He hadn't said anything about his relationship with Ayesha, who had disappeared again after delivering breakfast. Perhaps the subject was too sensitive for him although I suspected he thought the grandfather of his love rival could never be neutral. He obviously didn't know me well enough: that was my job. But what he did want to talk about was the cricket bat, wickets and ball and why I'd been travelling around with them in my bag. So I told him and he wanted to know more. I tried to teach him to grip the bat – and take guard – but he found it difficult to keep his balance. Instead, he spent most of the time wafting the bat at his friends' heads, something I didn't approve of. There was a time and place for that and a peaceful morning akin to net practice wasn't it. It was true, I hadn't forgiven him for his 'exorcism episode' and never would but this was a time for pragmatism not conflict.

I recognised early in the day, however, that Wasim wasn't going to take part. There was plenty of time for that to change back home but the people here didn't have that luxury so they needed to be schooled immediately. So I strode out of the back entrance with the bat, ball and wickets at a few minutes past seven ahead of five lazy men and an enthusiastic Abbie. I envied those professional umpires with their light meters because a fuzzy, early morning haze was covering the black hills in the distance and all my blurry eyes could see was a dilapidated shed, a ditch and the sandy green fields. But there was nothing to worry about: the light was good enough for everyone to have a knock. We walked past a rolled–up rug resting vertically against the shed and took a small, two–foot jump over the ditch. As I stepped over it, I realised there was all manner of stuff lying in the dirty, C–shaped eyesore: mud–soaked jewellery, a football, sandals, cans of Pepsi, dinars and even a rifle. It set off a small bout of coughing but it had its beneficial aspect too: it would be the boundary for my imaginary pitch.

I started counting out the paces from the ditch and rested the blue stumps down when I got to sixty. It was a bare piece of grass on a slight slope but it was good enough for me. I bent down and looked at the three plastic stumps, putting my fingers through the gaps to ensure they were the right distance between one another. I patted them on the top, trying to comfort them without their beloved bails. I smiled as I got up. I turned around and walked 22 paces. I put the other set of stumps down and threw the ball towards Abbie. He crossed his hands awkwardly but couldn't catch it; he was obviously more nimble with a grenade. Then I spent a few minutes organising the five lackeys in the field: Shami still had his arm in a sling so I put him at slip where the ball was unlikely to go when I was batting; Saad was at point; Amir at extra cover; Hashim at square leg and Rahul at mid on. I examined the field one last time, picked up the bat and strode down the wicket to take guard. I asked Abbie to pick the ball up and prepare to bowl the first delivery to the incoming batsman. He held it in his hand and waited, throwing it up like an apple. I had shown him how to bowl overarm and he obliged by sending down a delivery which could only be described as the slowest, juiciest and easiest I'd ever faced. I took a couple of steps forward, got to the pitch and belted the beauty high over Amir who continued to stand with his arms folded and head tilted. The ball vanished in the ditch and a surge of joy rippled through my body. I stood there with my high follow–through, for at least five seconds, admiring the shot and licking my lips in anticipation for more gifts from the novice bowler. I looked around at the other lackeys and they remained silent and bewildered, as though I had drastically diminished their power with one flash of the blade. I was in charge now: no more blindfolds, bombs and hostage–type situations.

Amir finally ran to the ditch to retrieve the ball after being ordered by Abbie. The dear leader sent down another present – the longest of long–hops – and I launched it in to the ditch again. I did the same for another seven deliveries, missing only the fifth because it was a full toss that surprised me. But that was when, through the corner of the eye, I spotted someone in the distance standing by the shed, resting their elbow against the rolled–up rug. It was nice to have a spectator but when I realised that person was Wasim it became a distraction rather than an inspiration. More balls came down from Abbie but now the concentration was gone. I must have missed three of the next five and on the sixth I skied it and, to my amazement, Abbie ran about 15 yards to pouch it with ease. By that time, my chest has tightened up, the cough had returned and my dancing feet had turned to nougat. There was no need for the elements to intervene and stop play.

I handed the bat over to Abbie and shuffled across to the bowler's mark extremely slowly. I could see Wasim walking towards the group and, in a way, I was thankful because it might mean play would have to stop. I knew I couldn't persuade Abbie to stop now – he was ready for a bat and couldn't wait to crack the ball to Basra – so my grandson may have to do something worthwhile for once.

Abbie took guard and I rolled my arm over as best as I could. He missed the ball, flailing wildly at thin air, looking very ugly and ungainly in his foot movement and follow through. But that didn't deter him. He simply ran behind him to retrieve the ball and, instead of lobbing it back to me, threw it up a few inches and smacked it as hard as he could to the legside. He grinned with pleasure and ordered Hashim to retrieve it as fast as he could. Luckily for me, Wasim had got over the ditch and was now just a few yards away. He stopped in the cover point area. Abbie eventually turned around and was surprised to see Wasim standing there with his hands on his hips.

'Jerry's here,' said Wasim.

'Bring him out,' said Abbie.

'But he wants to talk alone.'

'Tell him it's out here or nowhere.'

Who was Jerry? It wasn't my main concern because a short, but relatively mild, coughing spree had begun. Wasim glanced at me but I couldn't shift my face to provide any sort of expression so he turned around and walked back towards the house. Abbie watched Hashim throw the ball back to me and took guard again. I cleared my throat and gathered myself but this time I could only manage an underarm ball. Abbie gave it the proper treatment, of course, by whacking it past Rahul at mid on. I managed a further three, excruciating deliveries when I spotted Wasim over the ditch returning with another man by his side. I felt a massive sense of relief and raised my hand to Abbie to tell him I needed a break. He looked disappointed but I didn't care: I needed to sit down immediately. So I dropped the ball and sat down cross legged behind the stumps. Eventually, Wasim and the mysterious man reached the playing strip and it was obvious that the man with Wasim was not an Iraqi. Even more startling was the fact he was wearing a black bandana, beige t–shirt and army bottoms. He got closer and I wondered whether my eyes were deceiving me. He had to be an American soldier – but what the hell was he doing here?

I sat behind the stumps for half an hour but couldn't concentrate. Jerry joined in the game as much as he could and actually hit some monstrous sixes over long off which he put down to his love of the Cleveland Indians. He didn't say much else but my brain was swirling with paranoid fantasies and outright fear. Was Jerry in league with these jihadis? Who were we fighting at Shami's house yesterday? The answer was so obvious that I hadn't asked the question: surely they were American soldiers. If not, who?

Wasim had joined in too, after some initial reluctance. He was in a surly, uncommunicative mood so I let him be. He spent most of the time chasing after the ball anyway which didn't improve matters: the snail–like manner of his pursuits in the field illustrated what he thought about the process.

It took a long time to get Jerry out – and even then he wanted to carry on. Abbie finally knocked over his stumps but the newly–converted cricket–lover simply looked over his shoulder, picked up the fallen set of blue stumps and stood them upright again. He merrily took guard again so I was forced to raise my finger to give him out. He didn't understand that part of the game but after a sketchy explanation from me, he handed his bat over to Shami who couldn't wait to have a hit despite his arm being in a sling. After that, Abbie and Jerry strolled off for a chat – Abbie kept fiddling with the back of Jerry's bandana and there was an intimacy between the two men that I hadn't expected. The game carried on but I wasn't paying attention: I was watching the two men in the long leg area chatting and smiling. What were they talking about? Weapons? Sectarianism? Occupation? Or was Jerry another man after the affections of Ayesha? After a short discussion of about ten minutes or so, they both headed back towards the house. Abbie waved at me as he walked off the pitch and encouraged me to continue playing. But the thrill was gone and it had been replaced by a deep feeling of unease and uncertainty. Wasim stopped playing too and followed the men back to the house. This infuriated me on two levels because, firstly, I wanted his help in getting back to the house and, secondly, he'd turned his back while a bowler – Hashim – was in the middle of his run–up. Granted, he wasn't much of a bowler, in fact, he threw it, but that wasn't the point: a field change couldn't be made in the middle of a delivery stride. So I politely asked Hashim to collect the cricketing equipment while I, as fast as my stodgy lungs would allow, awkwardly jogged after my grandson to ask him what he was playing at. I finally caught up with him over the other side of the ditch and decided the time was right to give him some home truths – or find some out anyway.

'Who's Jerry?' I asked.

Wasim ignored me and carried on walking to the house. He reached the shed and punched the rolled–up rug with his left hand. This made him walk even faster and I found it difficult to keep up. He went into the house and sneaked into a room I'd never been in before. It was only a few feet away from a back entrance and had a pale yellow door which opened so easily that it could slam you in the face if you didn't hold it. Luckily, I saw how Wasim attacked it and acted accordingly. I walked into the tight, narrow kitchen and suddenly realised why I'd seen so little of my grandson during my stay at Khalifa HQ. There he was sat on a small red stool by the ancient fridge watching Ayesha sprinkling coriander into a simmering pot. Ayesha had taken her hijab off, perhaps because of the heat, and she kept pushing her straggly, zig–zag hair back over her shoulders so it didn't interfere with the overflowing pieces of lamb in the pot. She offered a glance of acknowledgement as I waited by the door but that was it; my snarling grandson didn't even manage that. He folded his arms and gawped at Ayesha like a good little servant boy awaiting instructions for his next errand.

'Final time, lad,' I said. 'Who's Jerry?'

'Jerry is not my business,' said Ayesha, unexpectedly. 'Abdullah does many things…and I do mine.'

The assurance of her response threw me off course. I watched her closely as she stirred the pot and rubbed her eye, blinking furiously as she tried to get rid of the tiny splashes of water escaping from the pot. I knew I would have to wait for the exact moment to pop my next question: she had already intimidated me with her first answer. But then something struck me. As I watched her putting one hand on her hip and stirring with the other, a thrilling fantasy popped into my head. Wouldn't it be great to bring this woman back to England to cook for me and look after me while Nadia and Salim were out earning a living? Nadia simply couldn't do those things anymore because her career was more important so surely a sick old man – who had his given his life for town and community – had a right to explore these possibilities? It was an intoxicating and captivating thought and would have to be asked with all the delicacy of an umpire probing a bowler about picking the seam. As it happened, the thought was obliterated as a cold and brutal revelation sent my head into another tailspin.

'I hope you're better now,' said Ayesha. 'I know they look after you better in England. Everything is free. Wasim is taking me and I will see it.'

I looked at Wasim with disdain. So this is what Mister Martyr had been planning? Not content with taking on the Americans, the British and the Shias, he now wanted to take an Iraqi bride back with him to England and show her the wonders of rain–swept Rochdale where both grandfather and newly–wed granddaughter could do the Asbo dance in front of the derelict Turner Brothers site. Was he mad? How would he pull this off? There was not a cat in hell's chance of it happening.

'We're getting married on the first the day of Ramzaan,' said Wasim, without looking at me. 'Nobody can stop us. Her mother's met me and she's happy about it.'

Ayesha looked over her shoulder at Wasim. It was a sharp glance and I detected a hint of disapproval. She sighed and covered the pot with a lid. She then picked up a grater and a small coconut and started grating it into a small bowl. There were already some grated carrots in the bowl and she eventually mixed the two together. To my surprise, she then started to scoop the raw coconuts and carrots with her fingers and eat them. She offered me some but they didn't look too appetising.

'You understand these things so I tell you,' she said. 'My mother needs an operation to clear a blood vessel in her heart. Our main hospital doesn't have the equipment...private hospital does but we don't have the money.'

'We're going to send money back to them,' said Wasim, interrupting unnecessarily. 'We'll visit and stuff.'

'My two young sisters are students,' said Ayesha. 'Abdullah gives me some money but not enough. I have to help my mother...'

'And your father...where is he?'

Ayesha gave me a piercing look as though I had insulted her. I could also tell Wasim was getting irritated because he was tapping his foot against the stool. His patience obviously snapped because he got up and walked towards me. He rushed past me and opened the door. His drastic action affected my balance for a moment but I managed to hang onto the towel rail by the door. I was doing fine until my hand moved across and touched the wet crimson towel on the rail. Suddenly, the damp sensation swarmed through my body like an electric shock and made me feel sick and dizzy. The strong, sizzling fumes from the pot were also emboldened and got up my nose, causing me to sneeze repeatedly. I could feel myself falling backwards and knew I had to leave instantly. I turned around and walked through the door without looking at Wasim.

'Wait,' said Ayesha.

I couldn't wait. I had to lie down because I was shivering.

'My father met a woman in Kuwait City and we never saw him again,' she said.

I didn't digest what she'd said because it was too loud. I thought about asking Wasim help me get back into the bedroom but there was too much pride at stake. I didn't look back and stepped into the corridor. I wasn't sure which way to walk but I could see the bristly corner of the rug in the main room and headed towards that. I kept my head down and looked at my toes. There were a couple of lackeys sat in the main room with their backs against the walls and legs outstretched but I ignored them. I got to the bedroom quicker than expected and, thankfully, there was no–one in there. I sat down on the bed and tried to take my shoes off but the rapid nature of my breathing didn't allow it. So I lay down with my clothes and shoes on. I tried to relax but my lower part of my right lung felt as though it was being singed. I realised the strain of the cricket may have caused the flare–up but sometimes you had to sacrifice yourself for the greater good. I turned to my other side but my hip was extremely stiff and painful. I knew it wasn't comfortable on either side so the fallback position of lying on the back, hands and feet crossed was the only solution. I adopted that position for about five minutes and was beginning to relax when the loud sound of an engine revving up could be heard outside the house. I ignored it for a while but when my ears began to pop, there was no escape. I sat up and glanced up at the window over my shoulder about three feet above my head. After a few more seconds of indecision, I awkwardly stood up on the bed, with my legs shaking and my vision blurred. I took a deep breath and looked through the grimy, wire–netted window. I cocked my neck forward and could see Jerry sitting on a standard Yamaha motorbike slipping a luminous green earphone underneath his bandana and into his ear. He then waved to someone at the door, who I couldn't see but presumed was Abbie. He revved his engine and tightly gripped the handlebars. Suddenly, he glanced up at the bedroom window and looked straight at me. His sparky, energetic eyes met mine and threw me off balance. I moved away from the window and slumped down on the bed. I leaned back and heard the motorbike move off a few minutes later. I could only draw one conclusion from looking into Jerry's eyes: he was the only one who knew what he was doing.

I woke up with a stiff neck and saw Wasim reading namaz in the corner of the room. He crossed his hands in front of his chest and then raised them up to his ears. Christ was it Maghrib already? I must have slept for hours. My empty bag was lying next to my grandson's feet which sent me into a cold sweat. Where was my cricket equipment? Did I bring it back or had I asked someone else to take care of it? I stumbled out of bed as fast as I could and ignored my whispering grandson. I walked out of the room and down the corridor. I got into the main room and Abbie was the only person there, also reading Maghrib prayers. He was sitting near the wall on his velvet blue and red prayer mat with his hands on his thighs. I walked in behind him and stopped a few feet away. I waited for him to look left and right but he took longer than expected, relishing the slow movement of his head and the melodic, drawn–out verse. He finally moved his head westwards and I moved forward.

'What happened to my cricket gear?' I asked.

'I still haven't finished,' he said, cupping his hands and reading his final prayer. 'But as you're a guest I'll tell you. Hashim fell in love with it and took it home for his son.'

I felt a sharp pain on the right side of my head as if it had been punctured by a set of needles. I wanted him to turn and face me but his rude gesture of keeping his back to me incensed me further.

'He nicked it? Wasn't it your job to stop him?'

'You should be happy; you've found someone who loves your silly game.' He raised his cupped hands closer to his face and closed his eyes. 'Now don't speak to me until I've finished.'

'Where is he?'

Abbie didn't answer and simply read louder, raising his voice even more when it came to 'Ameen'. I wanted to kick his back but I had pins and needles in my favourite foot so that was a non–starter. I swore silently and walked back to the bedroom in turmoil. I walked down the corridor and opened the bedroom door. Wasim was bending down picking up the folded grey blanket he'd used for a prayer mat. I walked towards him and grabbed him by the arm.

'See that?'

'What?'

'My bag is empty.'

'So…'

I pulled him across towards the bed and tried to sit him down but he was too strong: he remained standing. He folded his arms and looked down at the floor.

'Don't start, nana jee, I feel right close to Allah–thallah right now…'

'Come on we're leaving right now, get your things…'

'Don't you want your cricket gear back?'

'I'm too tired for that. If you want to stab people with the wickets and attack people with the bat, then go ahead I couldn't care less. I'm here to take you home – and I'm doing that right now.'

Wasim sat down on the bed and took off his tightly–worn keffiyah. He rubbed his head and looked up at me. 'You've lost your mojo and you're a bit mad, I get it. But I still ain't going.' He took his sandals off and lay down on the bed. 'Cricket just doesn't work here, nana jee, it's the killing fields.'

I opened my mouth but a pathetic whisper came out. Was my voice now affected too? I strained to try and answer but there was little I could do if my decaying organs were not responding. I rubbed my throat and wondered how much longer I could go on fighting with someone who was clearly not listening to me and, further, may have been causing my health to deteriorate.

'Are you okay, nana jee?' asked Wasim.

I heard him but couldn't react. He got up off the bed and came towards me. He put his arm round me and ushered me towards the bed. He laid me down awkwardly and took off his keffiyah. He folded it up and laid it across my forehead.

'Do you want some water?'

I shook my aching, shrinking head. Wasim was inches from my face and provided a scrap of comfort. It was as though the issues of war, martyrdom, cricket, disease and family had been sidelined for a few seconds and it was just about him and me: a grandson showing compassion for his sick grandfather. It was the first time I'd seen that glint in his eye since I'd arrived in Iraq.

But it didn't last long. A few minutes later, Abbie walked into the bedroom. He looked annoyed but stood there for a few seconds assessing what he saw in front of him.

'A man called Gulzar is here.'

Gulzar? There was an instant surge of adrenaline. No medicine was needed. For now.

# 10.

The coughing, scarring and whispery breathing remained undisturbed but there was a glimmer of hope that my secondary ordeal – which I'd named Sadr and Sadr in Abbiestan – was in remission. As I soon as I brushed away the green blanket and set eyes on Gulzar, I could see the whole picture emerging again: a flight (or three) back to Britain; breakfast, lunch and dinner at Edmund Street; Elisha's tears of joy; a long, treasured walk across Lenny Barn and a nice afternoon tea with Len. It was an intoxicating feeling – and all because of his face. He was standing by the clapped–out portable fan with his arms folded and his sparkling green eyes fixed on Abbie. I wanted to hug him but knew it would exert too much energy so I waited by the green blanket desperately trying to keep my excitement under control. He eventually sat down on a flimsy brown cushion by the wall and looked up at me. For a few seconds, he straightened his leather belt and then used a tiny notebook as a fan to keep cool. He rubbed the stitches on his chin and trained his eyes on Abbie again.

'You've made him lose weight and look 50 times worse,' said Gulzar. 'Do you have no shame?'

'Weak old men have no place in this country,' said Abbie, spitting out a seed from a date into his hand. 'You can't stay here tonight.'

'Like Faris? Was he free to choose?'

Abbie looked angry and didn't answer. He threw the seed onto a white saucer on a small table but it missed and fell onto the floor. He didn't pick it up and started walking towards the back entrance. He got to the door and opened it. He glanced at me and then left the room. Gulzar watched the door close and then briskly got up. He walked towards me and gave me a warm, lingering embrace that was surprising as well as invigorating.

'Where's that stupid grandson of yours?' he asked, gently letting go of me. 'If I'd known he'd bring you here, I wouldn't have let you come. I thought you'd stay at Bilu's.'

'He's in the bedroom,' I said. 'Who's Faris anyway?'

Gulzar sighed and turned away from me. He then faced me again and pointed at the green blanket. He didn't say anything as he brushed the blanket away. He put his arm round my shoulder and we both walked into the corridor. He eventually got to the bedroom door and stopped outside it. He waved the notebook in my face to relieve my sweating. He took a deep breath and prepared to open the door.

'Pack your bags; we must drive back to Baghdad tonight,' he said.

The words were important because they provided confirmation. An extraordinary weight was lifted off my shoulders. Baghdad was like paradise compared to where we were. I walked through the bedroom and had a spring in my step. But as Gulzar walked in ahead of me, I scoured the room and was embarrassed to find it empty. Wasim wasn't there and I was furious that he'd escaped my clutches once more. I walked in and fidgeted around for a while, checking my bag fraudulently to see if my cricket gear had miraculously returned. Gulzar looked out of window and then sat down on the bed. He leaned forward and crossed his hands.

'...An elusive boy, your grandson,' he said. 'A bit like Faris.'

I stopped messing around with my bag and zipped it up. I turned around and faced him. He was hunched over with his head almost touching his chest. Some of the sparkle and vitality from his eyes had diminished.

'I wasn't totally honest with you about my family,' he said. 'It's true all three of my children are dead. There was a big accident and most of my family were in that car. But my son wasn't in that car...he was here...'

'With Abbie?'

He sighed and got up off the bed. He walked towards me and put both hands on my shoulders. 'Yes, Faris was part of the Khalifa Brigades,' he said, looking beyond me. He then grabbed my hand tightly with both hands, closing his eyes in the process. He eventually let go and walked back to the bed. He sat down and leaned forward again.

'He was 17 when he met Abdullah in Baghdad. He was killed just after the invasion. Abdullah says American soldiers shot him at a farmhouse a few kilometres from here but I'm not so sure...'

'Can't you do anything? Won't the police investigate?'

He looked up and offered a knowing smile. 'There was no body. The Americans say one thing, Abdullah says another and the witnesses say a third.' He pressed his index finger into the stitches on his chin. 'Once you and Wasim are safe and out of the country, I will continue to seek the truth. But for now, you are the priority.'

'I'm so sorry,' I said, shaking my head. 'And I thought I had it bad chasing Wasim around the country...'

'Where do you think he is?'

'Probably in the kitchen with that woman.'

'Who? Ayesha?'

I nearly choked on my considerable saliva.

'You know her?'

We walked down to the kitchen and Gulzar told me how he came to know Ayesha. He said he had known her for two years because she had been cooking for the Brigades when Faris was part of the group. He had first met her after Faris had been killed because she'd come forward to offer information about his son's relationships in the group and how he might have died. None of this led to any further clues about Faris's death but they did strike up a friendship and, eventually, Ayesha opened up to him about her sick mother. Gulzar said he was happy to help out and took her mother to a hospital in Erbil where she could have the operation she needed. Then, only a few weeks ago, she told him about Wasim and Abbie and how they were competing for her affections. She said Abbie had given her an ultimatum: she had to marry him in order to keep her job. She couldn't agree to that so Abbie had told her never to come back again.

The revelations came thick and fast and the sheer amount of startling information made me dizzy. It didn't surprise me Gulzar was a lawyer. He had impressively condensed a plethora of explosive details and put a fresh spin on a situation that wasn't as clear cut as I'd first thought. But I could only fully absorb the last detail; namely that Ayesha had left. I was now totally confused about how I should approach my grandson. Was he here? Perhaps he had left too?

Gulzar stopped at the pale yellow kitchen door and I walked in a few feet behind him. He glanced over his shoulder and then yanked the door open. We walked in and waited by the door. I looked down and saw Wasim sitting on the grimy white tiles with his back awkwardly against the stool. He was looking blankly down at the floor with his mobile phone by his side.

'I'm going to fuckin' kill Abdullah,' he said, without looking up. 'I'M GOING TO FUCKIN' KILL HIM.'

'There's no need for that,' I said, walking towards him. 'Gulzar's here to help us now. Come on, we've got no time to waste.'

Wasim shook his head in disbelief. 'She phoned me on the mobile I bought her. Fuckin' charming. I should have charged her.'

I bent down as best as I could and put my hand on his shoulder. He pushed my hand off and looked up at Gulzar.

'Who the fuck are you?' he asked.

Gulzar walked forward and, to my surprise, grabbed Wasim's shoulder a little more aggressively than I expected.

'Do you have no respect for your grandfather? Now get up.'

Wasim still wouldn't budge and, provocatively, folded his arms. 'I'm not leaving until I sort Abdullah. He's gone to Shami's; he'll be back in a few minutes.'

Gulzar now tried to get both his arms underneath Wasim's shoulders but my grandson continued to clench his teeth and resist. I felt uneasy about the amount of force Gulzar was using but what was there left to try?

'I'M NOT FUCKIN' GOING ANYWHERE,' he shouted.

Wasim drew his head back and headbutted Gulzar on the chin. It was a glancing blow but it still pushed Gulzar back onto the floor. I got in front of Wasim and held his face with both hands.

'What are you doing? Have you gone mad?'

There was a moment of silence as I looked into the expanding whites of his eyes. Suddenly, we all flinched at the noise of an almighty explosion at the back of the house. The sound of bullets pinging against the back walls could also be heard. Two came through the wire–netted window and whistled against the pale yellow door. Wasim quickly got up and raced towards the door.

'SHIT, MY KLASHIE'S UNDER THE BED,' he said.

Gulzar frantically followed Wasim out of the kitchen as a rocket–propelled grenade smashed through the window and blew up half of the kitchen. But I was in a state of paralysis. The force of the blast left me shaking horribly and I was sure my chest had a giant hole in it. There was a salty smell in my nose and my eyes were burning. A red stool flew towards me and missed my head by inches.

'COME ON, LET'S GET OUT OF HERE,' said Gulzar, holding me by the arm.

Gulzar tried to drag me along with him but my twisted back and wooden knees left me rooted to the spot. The kitchen wall had been sliced off and lay on its side like a slab of polystyrene. A golden fireball illuminated the lush field in the distance. Suddenly, the sense of panic diminished because of what I saw in front of me. It was captivating and exhilarating. The bright blue wickets glowed in the night sky underneath the glittering stars. They were like beacons of hope in amongst the garden of carnage. They remained upright and shone like never before. It was a glorious sight: a crackling sense of menace in the air but a sturdy, reassuring presence in the middle. I felt a sense of pride that I'd made a mark on this land. I started to breathe easier and managed to turn around, happy in the knowledge that my legacy was safe. Gulzar grabbed me and dragged me away as a bullet smacked against the upper rim of the yellow door.

'COME ON, NANA JEE,' shouted Wasim, standing in the corridor. 'FUCK THE CRICKET.'

The good breathing lasted only a few seconds as the searing heat roasted my nose and the toxic fumes sped up my nostrils. I clutched my right ear because the sound was unbearable. Or was I going deaf? I shuffled as fast I could down the corridor and didn't look back. I desperately wanted to look over my shoulder for one last look at the golden centre but felt my neck would snap if I attempted it. I imagined running back and grabbing the wickets before they were levelled by the bomb merchants – it made me feel better if nothing else. My eyes went into spasm but I could still see Wasim making giant strides down the corridor like a pumped–up Olympic sprinter. He was right down the other side. Gulzar was thankfully, only a few feet ahead of me and waited until I reached him. I had a fast, shallow breathing now and was grateful as he grabbed me and pulled me away with him. We rushed down the corridor but my legs were weakening with each flimsy stride. Walking or running fast was impossible. It was also harder to keep my balance but I kept thinking about forward defensives and straight drives. The number of bullet rounds didn't diminish but the sound was fading slightly. Gulzar had to work harder to drag me through with him. His sturdy fingers were digging painfully into my shoulder and I longed for us to see the main room, the green blanket and then the bedroom. I closed my flickering eyes and hoped for the best. I felt like a hard red cherry being flailed for six, flying through the sky, not knowing where I was going to end up; not knowing if I was going to land safely in someone's warm lap or smash a window or break a limb. So I kept flying and stopped counting. After a few knocks and stumbles, I tentatively peeped out and saw the outline of the toilet and the bedroom. The relief was instant but temporary; the sound of gunfire could now be heard at the front of the house. We got into the bedroom and Wasim was already there on his hands and knees pulling out his Kalashnikov from underneath the bed. He also had a duffel bag unzipped, loaded with ammunition.

'Get up, we're leaving,' said Gulzar, walking towards him.

I could tell Gulzar was in no mood for compromise. He kicked away the duffel bag and grabbed Wasim's neck. Wasim stood up and tried to shrug him off but Gulzar was too strong.

'GET OFF ME, YOU TOSSER! I'M GONNA FIGHT.'

'That's what my son said...'

'YEAH, AND HE WAS A WIMP JUST LIKE YOU!'

I realised Gulzar was ready to tonk my grandson so I rushed quickly towards them. I wasn't fast enough, however, because Gulzar elbowed Wasim in the head – while still holding his neck – and then threw him onto the bed. He then picked up the duffle bag and the Kalashnikov and flung them at Wasim who managed to avoid them.

'WELL, WHO ARE YOU FIGHTING AGAINST? TELL ME?'

Wasim was about to answer but a bullet smacked against the grey–brick wall right next to the window. I lowered my head and stumbled across to my bag. I kneeled down as best as I could and tried to put the bag over my shoulder but it was so weak that the strap kept falling off. And then something occurred to me.

'That is the Americans, isn't it?' I asked, turning around and looking at Gulzar.

Gulzar looked doubtful and walked towards me. He took the bag off me and slung it over his shoulder. 'Come on, let's go. Leave him if he doesn't want to come.'

Wasim was in a zone of deep concentration as he started to load his Kalashnikov again. I watched him and realised my exasperation and frustration was its optimum level. The black forest of my right lung was on fire and couldn't handle another snub. So I walked up to him and sat down on the bed. Gulzar shouted something but I didn't hear it. My head was like a furnace and my speech was strangled and distant. I opened my mouth and mumbled something. It didn't come out right. So I cleared my throat and tried again. Nothing but a squawk. I pursed my lips and took a deep breath but my heart began to race so I abandoned that. I looked at Wasim but he was ignoring me. What a pathetic little boy, almost dribbling over his weapon like he did with his Super Mario Brothers Nintendo on his sixth birthday. I put my hand on his weapon and gripped as tight as I could. Finally, there was a glance. He scowled and gave me a blank look but his eyes activated my own speech muscles.

'Do it for your grandad, Wasim. You may not see me again.'

He sighed and turned away. He gave Gulzar a frightful, filthy look. He turned to me again and his expression softened. He managed a slight nod which was worth its weight in gold.

'Okay, but I take my rifle with me.'

I looked at Gulzar who nodded. 'But only if you leave it in the front seat, where I can see it,' he said.

Wasim grabbed me by the shoulder and helped me up off the bed. 'I still hate this world, though,' he said.

I shook my head but decided not to challenge his latest line of wisdom; Gulzar was already walking towards the door. I felt uncomfortable with Wasim's arm on my shoulder – he was overdoing the nursey stuff – so I politely told him I didn't need it. I scoured the room one last time to make sure there was nothing I'd left behind and it evoked an unexpected rush of sentimentality, probably because it was still in one piece. I stumbled towards the door but as it swung open it caught my left knee creating a vicious, agonising pain. I clutched my kneecap and knew I couldn't move, never mind walk or run. Bullets rasped against the wire–netted window but they became a secondary concern. Gulzar turned around and looked down at me. He put one arm round my shoulder and one round my legs and swept me up off the floor. It was so swift and effortless that Gulzar was already scampering through the main room before I had any time to object. My eyes were inches away from his chin as I bobbed up and down with every thumping stride. I noticed the stitches on his chin ran much further than I thought – right down to his throat – although his light stubble did a good job of camouflaging them. We were close to the front door now and it was already ajar. Sparks flew across the rumbling black sky and a vicious draught came through the door to seep into my tender, aching bones. Wasim was a few yards ahead again and had his Kalashnikov at the ready, the stupid boy. Gulzar stepped out of the door and it was almost pitch black, save for the distressing, thunderous noises of random fire. I closed my eyes and couldn't control my drooling – a zooming ball of saliva trickled down my neck and onto my chest. Where the hell was the shooting coming from? And at who? With each passing shot, my bladder's defences were taking a pounding. I counted to six and back again, to relieve the pressure. Gulzar nearly tripped over as he searched for the path and his grip on my body loosened. One of my legs was dangling dangerously close to the ground but he managed to regain his balance and somehow kept me on board. I opened my eyes and was stunned to discover we were rushing headlong for a vehicle that was partially on fire. I felt sick and needles danced in my throat. Ibrahim's white and orange cab was parked haphazardly on the edge of the dirt–track road and its front left wing was in flames. Gulzar let go of me and rested me down a few feet away from the car. It may have been battered and bruised but it was my shield for now.

'WASIM, OPEN THE BOOT!' shouted Gulzar. 'THERE'S A BLANKET AND SOME WATER IN THERE.'

Wasim frantically picked out the partially–torn black blanket and the small container of water from the boot. He rushed to the front of the car and threw the blanket over the front wing. It had minimal impact. He tried to open the container of water but dropped the bottle as a volley of gunfire pelted the front of the house. I couldn't watch. I looked down at the ground and prayed outside for the first time in 33 years.

'SHAH, GET INTO THE CAR,' shouted Gulzar, as he got in the driver's seat and started the engine.

The prayer didn't get very far. I stumbled across the back door on my hands and knees and got in. My knee was so sore that I was sure I had done permanent damage. I slumped on the piping hot seat and looked out as Wasim emptied the whole bottle onto the wing. The flames diminished slightly but they were still raging. Gulzar ushered Wasim to get in the car and Wasim ended his fire–fighting attempts by spitting at the flames in frustration.

Wasim got into the back seat because the front passenger seat was too close to the fire. As soon as he closed the door, Gulzar drove off with intent across the bumpy dirt–track road. I looked out to the right to see who was firing at us but the black woods were calm and silent. There was someone, somewhere in amongst that dark wool harbouring the kind of grudge that sent me into a deep depression. If only I could have helped them like I helped Hashim, many more could have embraced the beautiful game.

As we drove away, Gulzar raised his finger and touched the cube underneath the mirror, changing it from the American flag to the green Islamic one. Somehow, it did the trick because the fire slowly began to die down. I breathed a lengthy sigh of relief and turned to look at Wasim. He was sitting right up against the door, looking out of the window. I raised my hand and touched his shoulder.

'Did you not see Hashim?' said Wasim.

'No...'

'He was lying dead in the middle of the pitch with his son.'

I slept for most of the journey and had never been so grateful to see that Lidl bag again. Amazingly, the bag was still floating around near Gulzar's house although the barefooted beggar, who'd initially taken it off my hands, was nowhere to be seen. I wanted to pick up the bag and take it home because it provided solace and comfort after the traumatic experiences I had suffered but it ended up perched on the end of a broken telegraph pole and, hence, could not be shifted. But it did help clarify my thinking. A few hours earlier, I had been questioning the whole exercise and whether it had been right to enter the country and repair a private matter, no matter how noble. Now, perhaps because I was still in one piece, I came to the conclusion I had been right to take the plunge because I had carried out my mission of finding my grandson while dampening down his militant tendencies. I assessed it had been the right thing to do. It had been an adventure – and my life had been short of those.

I took a final glance at the carrier bag before I walked into Gulzar's house. The front door was wide open, which surprised me because of the security situation, but the reason was clear as I went in: sitting in the living room were Azaad, Ibrahim and, to my great surprise and pleasure, Bilu. Azaad and Ibrahim sprung up from the sofa and hugged me with warmth and vigour. Their faces lit up and their pats on my back gave me an immense source of pride and vindication. Bilu remained sitting in the corner of the room, not looking our way, but his mere presence was enough to give me an incredible boost. Ibrahim ushered me over to the sofa and I sat down next to Bilu. I put my hand on his thigh and he nodded in acknowledgement. He then grabbed my hand and started cracking my fingers. I smiled and politely asked him to wait until later to get to work, pointing to my knee. He obviously didn't understand and pushed his index finger into the back of my neck.

Wasim remained standing by the door and was still, perhaps, unhappy with Gulzar because he had thrown his Kalashnikov out of the moving car during the journey. He told Gulzar that he wanted a 'feast to remember' because he was starving. He may have got his wish because from, what I could tell, Ibrahim and Azaad's wives were here preparing a bumper meal for us, although I never saw them. Strangely, I wasn't that hungry, even though I hadn't eaten for properly for six hours. A small snack and long sleep would have sufficed. But I knew I couldn't be so ungracious after all that Gulzar had done for me. I had to stick it out.

So we took our shoes and sandals off – and in Wasim's case, trainers – and sat down on a big white sheet on the floor which was nicely embroidered with four tiny red ships in each corner. I found it difficult to cross my legs so I leaned against the sofa and stretched them out. Azaad and Ibrahim brought through all the food from the kitchen and placed it down, making a point of pushing most the dishes in my direction. I was very tired and sleepy but the sight of a steamy dish of tangy bitter melon filled with mince meat provided a much–needed jolt of energy. I hadn't recalled telling Gulzar it was my favourite dish but I didn't care – the lizardy green skins of the melon gave my drooling a purpose. Wasim hated bitter melons – he said they were like poison – but he laid into the other dishes with relish, particularly the chicken and aubergine concoction which he eventually devoured with his hands once the crispbread had run out. During the course of the meal, I asked Gulzar about Abbie and if he knew what had happened to him.

'It was probably him shooting at us,' he said.

On any other day or night, I would have probed further but Gulzar's answer was curiously satisfying. It made a strange kind of sense. I didn't really want to know anymore about what went on in this country, who was fighting who and whose fault it was. I came here to find my grandson and spread the game. I wasn't satisfied with the cricket aspect but at least I found Wasim. I couldn't control anything else that happened so there was no point in exploring further; I figured there were too many layers to unpick, too many grudges and too many conflicts. There were enough of those going on in Edmund Street.

It was nearly 12.30am when we finished our meal. Gulzar got up and put his hand on my shoulder. He whispered in my ear that I should get compensation for my industrial disease when I go back to England. Before I could offer my stock answer, he walked off into another room. I was about to follow him because I was desperate for the toilet but he came back quickly and handed me a brown, oblong–shaped biscuit tin. I took it from him and placed it on the floor, near the empty dishes. I looked up and realised everyone was looking at me. I slowly opened it and immediately saw two Austrian Airline tickets, clear and unmistakable. What a relief it was to be reunited with them. I picked them out and felt them but, wait, what was that underneath? I slipped my fingers across the bottom of the tin and felt some beautiful little pebbles. They were delicate, smooth and shiny; grey, black and faded, corky–ball red. But how many were there? I started counting and my hand trembled like never before. One, two, three, four, five...SIX.

'They're from all parts of Iraq,' said Gulzar. 'The River Tigris, Basra, Erbil, Kerbala, the Euphrates and Mosul. I got my friends to send them.'

'But how did you know?'

Gulzar pointed at Wasim, who was still raiding the fruit bowl. I realised what I'd always known: that no grandson of mine could be so wild, zealous and ignorant. There had to be some of my genes swimming around in his muscular body.

'He's a good lad really,' I said.

# PART TWO

*The little war on our doorstep*

# 11.

Wasim flicked through my 1979 World of Sport annual as we took a breather before checking in at Erbil International Airport. The journey from Baghdad had exhausted me so much I had to sit down and recharge for a few minutes before the next stage of luggage handling and passport checking. I was sat next to Wasim but had Fareeda on my mind. She would have been so proud of my actions in bringing Wasim back home and she would have taken a certain joy in feeling the six Iraqi pebbles in her fingers. Those six jewels were for her. Wasim snapped me out of my nice thoughts, however, and handed me back the treasured annual. I let it rest on my lap for a few minutes to show my disapproval but it didn't matter, he was already checking his mobile in that classic manner people did when they claimed to be occupied. I wondered if this was the right time to tell him the exact nature of my illness. Wouldn't that shake him out of his superiority complex? I decided against it because the clean, sparse environment of an airport didn't feel right for a grubby tale. It was too pristine. He put the mobile in his pocket and then reached down into his bag. He smiled at me and then pulled out what looked like a small kitchen knife wrapped in a blue embroidered handkerchief. What the hell was he doing? Amazingly, he displayed a puppyish pride as he raised the knife up towards me to show me its gleaming blade.

'She were a good cook,' he said. 'If I can't take it, I'm not going.'

'Are you insane? Give me that.'

I snatched if off him and met less resistance than expected. He was angry but said nothing. The soft smile had turned into something sinister but I couldn't care less: I wasn't going to have my successful run chase destroyed at the last minute. I wrapped up the knife in the handkerchief and knew precisely what to do. I spotted an airport official a few yards away tending to a little boy who had something in his eye while his fashionably dressed mother, in sunglasses and a hijab, held the toddler's hand. I got up and walked towards them. I stopped inches away and put my hand over my mouth as I cleared my throat. The official finally looked at me although he was more intrigued by my stubby, swollen index finger. I handed him the knife and handkerchief and told him I'd found them near my seat. He didn't even look at them and put them in his inside pocket. He gave me a pleasant smile and then continued to tend to the boy. I walked back towards Wasim and sat down. He ignored me and got up.

'I'm going to the bog,' he said.

'Be quick. We're going to check–in now…'

He didn't answer and walked away to the toilets. I watched him stride off in that easy swagger of his and imagined the reception he would get back home. It didn't make me feel any better. I envisaged wall–to–wall feasts, intimate hugs and even heroic pats on the back from some people. A few would be disapproving, of course, but they would keep their thoughts to themselves. Did I get this type of reception in 1967 when I entered England for the first time? Course not. A revolutionary thought then popped into my head. I had an old friend called Maajid Mir, who shared a damp kitchen floor with me all those years ago in Peel Street just a few weeks after I'd arrived in Rochdale. There were at least 22 other people in the house because, even in those days, I liked to be up with the numbers. But now Maajid, who had a big, bushy moustache, golf ball cheeks and hairy forearms, owned properties where asylum seekers and immigrants could live while getting themselves attuned to the environment and populace. I knew he had one such property in Clement Royds Street. I hadn't seen Maajid for at least five years, when he somehow found out about Fareeda's funeral and came along, but now his house would be the perfect place for Wasim to learn some harsh lessons about the world and how his grandfather had struggled when he first set foot in Rochdale. Wouldn't it be great to see Wasim slumming it with 20 or 30 asylum seekers from Somalia and Afghanistan? I wanted to take it even further. I wanted to call Nadia straight away and tell her to empty Edmund Street for one night so that Wasim would think his family were so sickened by his disappearance that they had left the town. He had to learn. These exciting thoughts were gathering momentum when Wasim returned. He sat down by my side again and continually rubbed his hands.

'I can't face Mum,' he said. 'Can I stay at your house for the first few nights?'

The Maajid idea was extinguished almost as soon as I'd thought of it.

'I've sold it. I live in Edmund Street now. I sleep in your bed.'

He stopped rubbing his hands and looked up at me.

'No worries. We've got a couple air beds in the attic. The front room's warm enough.'

We reached Manchester Airport and, apart from some tight, compact breathing after take–off in Vienna, I was in better shape than expected. The curious sensation of the right side of my body being a bit heavier than my left had been with me since I first boarded a plane but I shrugged it off as something to do with my right lung not being able to cope with being up in the clouds. The vocal tics also died down but there was one big problem: the cold. As soon as we stepped out for a taxi, a blistering wave of mouth–numbing air seeped down into my body and refused to budge even when I got into the black cab. It was particularly bad on my neck and no amount of rubbing was going to change that. I hoped it wasn't a taste of things to come as it was only a mild, drizzly evening and the freezing winter nights were still some months away.

I fell asleep in the cab as soon we pulled out onto the M56 and I only woke up when my head ricocheted off Wasim's broad shoulder and onto the back seat. By that time, we had pulled up at the traffic lights on Spotland Road, with the Falinge flats to my right. We were home. I rubbed my eyes and instantly perked up when I saw a pregnant woman kissing a tattoo–heavy, ear–studded man outside the boarded up Albert Hotel. The woman's arched body was in such an extraordinary position that I was impressed by her dexterity rather than appalled by her conduct. I wished I could be so flexible.

Despite this intriguing sight, the town felt cramped and claustrophobic compared to the wide open spaces of Iraq. I had never seen it in this light before. The tight streets and shop were clumped together while the few people milling around were shoehorned into a space that wasn't big enough. I also started sneezing almost straight away. My sinuses had improved dramatically in Iraq, perhaps because of the environment or because of Bilu, but here I was back to that old Shah again, spluttering, coughing and clearing my throat.

As we entered Edmund Street, Wasim reached into his bag and pulled out an immaculately–folded red and white checked keffiyah. He carefully rolled it round his head and tied it near his ear. I sighed wearily but didn't have the strength for another dispute. I asked the cab driver to pull up right outside our home but he went a bit further. Wasim got out of the car first while I paid the driver. I gave him a generous two–pound tip but he was more interested in looking at Wasim; I could tell he didn't approve. I walked slowly across the pavement and stopped at the end of garden path, standing behind the low brick wall. Wasim looked over his shoulder and rattled the letterbox impatiently.

'Fuckin' lost my keys in Quetta, didn't I?' he said.

How embarrassing. The whole street could hear the clatter of that letterbox and, unsurprisingly, I saw Mrs Gleeson's head pop round her curtains to see what the fuss was about. The front door opened and Nadia stepped out with her arms folded and her hair untied. I looked at her puffed–up face and instantly felt guilty. For the first time in decades, I was scared of my daughter. Her eyes darted around Wasim's face but then she ran forward and put her arms round me. She hugged me tighter than I could remember and it was a rough, awkward embrace rather than a delicate one.

'Jesus, you fuckin' scared the life out of us,' she said. 'Please don't do that ever again, Daddy, you're everything to me.' She let me go and but then rested her forehead against mine. Her harsh, piercing glare was intimidating but provided a curious sense of safety. 'Do you understand? Everything.'

I nodded and glanced at Wasim who was stood there sheepishly, fiddling with his keffiyah.

'Don't you think you're hugging the wrong man?' I asked.

She completely ignored me and spoke frantically. 'I was about to contact our MP and the foreign office but thought better of it and what about your medication? How did you manage in those Kashmiri villages? It's a miracle you're still around.'

I had totally forgotten that no–one in the town knew that Wasim and I had been in Iraq. It came as a shock but it also gave me breathing space in terms of not having to go into detail about a country that fascinated everyone right now. The conversations would be feisty and endless: all in good time.

'I managed,' I said. 'I taught children how to play cricket.'

Nadia shook her head and slowly let go of me. She looked over at Wasim and there was an unbearable silence between mother and son. I had to step in and say something but my mind went blank. It didn't matter because Wasim stepped forward into the house without saying a thing to his mother.

'Take that off before you go in,' said Nadia.

Wasim didn't listen and walked into the house, stroking his keffiyah like some sheikh who had a bob or two to spare. Nadia sighed and was about to say something but I had heard enough. I put my tired hand on her shoulder and prepared to walk into the house. A few minutes ago, I had been full of hope that our return to Edmund Street would be met with joy or, at the very least, relief that a wayward boy had been brought back from the brink but the frostiness between Nadia and Wasim had been unwelcome as well as unexpected. Did I know them as well as I thought? I stepped into the house and sensed the atmosphere wasn't the one I'd left behind.

* * *

One of Nadia's pet hates was making dinner for guests without warning and that's what she had to do on this occasion, although of course, we weren't guests. She thrashed out a couple of shapeless chapattis but, luckily for us, she already had a hefty pot of aubergines and potatoes prepared for the evening meal. It was one of her favourite dishes. She had taken a fancy to it despite hating it the first time she ate it under duress by Fareeda. She was about 11 or 12 at the time and I only remember it vividly because she was still wearing her Redbrook School uniform on a very hot summer's evening. It felt strange to me that someone dressed immaculately in a navy blue sweater, light blue shirt and red tie could be so utterly engrossed in a meticulous VHS recording of *Falcon Crest*. Why not *Grange Hill*? She never watched that. Nadia, however, told Fareeda she wasn't hungry but Fareeda was adamant her daughter would consume a portion of the evening meal because she had spent hours in the kitchen preparing it. Eventually, Fareeda got her way but Nadia vowed she would never touch 'the animal–like' aubergines again because they made her throw up. How times change. Nadia now made her dish in a different way as the aubergines and potatoes were cut smaller and mashed together but it still had a tangy, satisfying impact and I ate more than my stomach could handle. Wasim ate almost nothing – only half a chapatti and a couple of water melons – and disappeared upstairs. Nadia joined him and I didn't see mother and daughter again for a couple of hours. I spent most of the evening with Elisha in the living room. Salim wasn't at home and I didn't bother to ask why. There was more than enough time to talk about that later. Elisha mostly talked about her brother and how much he had changed in the couple of years she hadn't seen him. She didn't mention the actual trip at all. It was clear from Elisha's demeanour – the folded arms and the slightly sarcastic tone – that she wasn't exactly elated her brother had returned. But she was more than happy with me, I suspected. She even took one of her wristbands – the blue one – and put it on my wrist. I didn't know what it meant but it was a nice touch. It was the first genuine heartwarming moment since I'd returned.

Wasim finally appeared again and had changed into a shalwar kameez and slippers. He had even taken his keffiyah off. He walked towards me and sat down on the sofa. He looked at Elisha and she got the hint, getting up and leaving the room. Wasim slipped his feet out of his slippers and put them on the sofa, holding them close to his chest. He looked up at the ceiling and sighed.

'It was Turner Brothers, wasn't it?' he asked. 'They made you sick. Why didn't you tell me?'

'Your welfare was more important...'

'We'll go down there and fuck them up.'

'Good luck because they don't exist.'

I realised I had underestimated the extent of Wasim's naivety. He genuinely did not know that the factory had shut down in 1989 and was now a derelict site. I tried to pass it off as a teenage thing and give him the benefit of the doubt but it wasn't convincing. A more plausible explanation was that Wasim was totally unaware of the community on his doorstep:

what they did and how they managed. Instead, he was connected to another community, more disparate and more widespread and the two rarely overlapped.

He got up suddenly and walked barefoot towards the oval mirror above the mantelpiece. He glanced in the mirror and then walked back towards me.

'I'll hire a solicitor tomorrow,' he said. 'Amjad's a good man, he's done some work for a sister who wasn't allowed to cover herself in a job interview.'

'Is this what you and your mum were talking about?' I asked.

Wasim sighed and shook his head. He sat down again, but much closer to me. He put his hand on my thigh and moved his head much closer.

'Nana jee, you don't understand. We have to get these people back. They've poisoned people. We can't let them get away with it.'

His darting eyes couldn't stay still. They flitted across my face at lightning speed. His giant eyeballs triggered a fresh theory in my head. It was about the nature of jihad and what my grandson had just experienced in Iraq. In most people's eyes, that is what he was: a jihadi. But what inspired him to go all that way to fight for a cause most people didn't understand or agree with? What had motivated him? I deduced that religious scholars, imams and persuasive groups of friends had all worked their black magic to get him thinking a different way but there was another component that couldn't be ignored: injustice. This was the clincher, the game–breaker and the matchwinner for him. In his mind, there was an injustice or a perceived injustice to be fixed or put right. If that component didn't exist, the selling of armed jihad would be more difficult. Now, as I looked into Wasim's eyes, he was showing that exact zeal for something completely different: a disease caused by a former industrial giant. He was engaged and enthused. He wanted to get them back. Here was another injustice to get worked up about. Here was another jihad.

But could I get him onside? Suddenly, I was ambivalent about not getting some sort of recompense from Turner Brothers or their representatives for what they had done to me. I still felt hugely sceptical that writing letters, hiring a solicitor or joining a campaign was worth the hassle but I also realised the opportunity to get into Wasim's head might not come again. I may have a chance of getting my grandson concentrating on the things that really matter: local and community struggles that have a real impact on people in their day–to–day lives. It was clear he was genuinely aggrieved about how my condition had come to pass but now I had to use his fiery idealism for my own benefit and for the sake of the wider community. I hoped I could turn his attentions away from a global fantasy into something more achievable, tangible and long–lasting.

'What about getting a job first?' I asked.

'I'll just sign on for a while,' he replied. 'This is more important. I feel sick just thinking about it.'

* * *

I knew a lot of Kashmiri parents who could not deal with the community burden. By this, I meant they were never brave enough to travel for holidays anywhere other than Kashmir, wouldn't let their sons or daughters marry whoever they wished and could not be seen listening to English music or reading English books. Even if they had the urge, they wouldn't dare take the plunge because it might mean the community would frown upon them and their respect within that circle would be compromised. Fortunately, I had kept my distance from that unspoken code of honour and the trigger for this way of thinking probably came after my marriage to Fareeda because a vicious rumour had spread in the village that Fareeda liked women and that was the reason her marriage was delayed until the age of 33. It wasn't true but it did hurt Fareeda and her subsequent journey to England was one she was desperate to make. That was one of the reasons why the community burden was never really indoctrinated into Maple Street – we only had two Kashmiri families from Briar Street, the Kamals and the Qazis, who visited us on a regular basis and even then they were superficial, cake–rusk dipping afternoons rather than substantial, chapatti–clapping evenings. So this doctrine of friendly isolation carried on when I moved to Edmund Street. Many people in the street knew of me but didn't know the real Shah. There was a further loosening of ties when I became an umpire. That was definitely seen as an indigenous pastime with its stereotype of village greens, cramped pubs and gentlemens' agreements.

But I could not escape the drawbacks of the

community burden as I was forced to sit opposite at least four families (I lost count at about 11pm) the morning after Wasim and I had returned. News had spread like wildfire that Wasim was back and there was nothing any of us could do to halt the well–meaning, but overbearing, tide. Wasim was happier than me because he hadn't seen his friends for more than two years so he escaped in Zaki's BMW and headed off to the town centre. I wasn't so lucky and had to share jalebi and milk tea with Mr Shafiq who continually spoke about the four–floored villa he was building in Mirpur with the income from his Hajj travel business. He did, however, notice my throat–clearing and coughing and wondered if I'd picked it up from Kashmir. It was easier to say I had. I wasn't quite ready to start my campaign for justice in Mr Shafiq's presence.

The visitors thankfully drifted away before noon. Nadia, who hadn't been herself since that conversation with Wasim, had been dropping hints all morning that she had a busy afternoon at university (to get rid of the so–called guests) and it worked a treat because they left earlier than I expected. I went back to bed straight away because I was exhausted. Nadia had bought me a new inhaler and watched me carefully to ensure I took my medication. She was adamant a couple of steroid tablets had to go down the hatch too. I could tell she wasn't happy – but also that she worked things out.

'So you were in Iraq,' she said, putting the glass of water down on my bedside table. 'How could you not tell me about the letter? I'm his mother.'

'And I'm his grandfather. I had to do something. You and Salim have got your own problems.'

'Oh fuck Salim,' she said, rushing towards the door. 'Tell me about Iraq tonight. I only promise to forgive you if you tell me absolutely everything.' She left the room and I looked out of the bedroom window as a blackbird perched on a chimney above Mr Whitworth's house. It flew away almost instantly but Nadia came back within seconds. She came in through the door again. 'Oh, I nearly forgot, you've got an appointment with Howarth in three weeks. I'll come down with you this time.' She shook her head. 'You sold the Proton too. Unbelievable.' She closed the door and left the room.

It would have been better to have stayed in Baghdad rather than see Howarth again. What would he say anyway? That I had a few more scars on my lung? That I had progressed slower or faster than he expected? I really didn't hold out much hope for a positive outcome; I was simply another patient on his overloaded conveyor belt. He could offer me words and toxic remedies but little else. But no matter how much I dismissed the appointment's validity, the thought of making the journey to the infirmary didn't help me sleep. Eventually, I had to get up and make an extremely uncomfortable trip to the bathroom to release some of the wedged mucus from my throat. There was more: a sharp pain in my chest, particularly when I bent down, something I hadn't experienced with such ferocity before. I must have been adjusting to the cold weather again, I thought. I walked back to the bedroom knowing I wouldn't get any sleep but was desperate to get back under the duvet. After a few minutes, the doorbell rang and I didn't want to answer it so I walked up to the window and pressed my nose right up against it to see who it was. I expected another 'community gossip' but I got a pleasant surprise. It was Len and I suddenly felt the day wasn't that bad after all. He had a batch of leaflets in his hand and offered me one as soon as I went down and opened the door.

'Where the hell have you been?' he asked. 'I called round a couple of times. Your daughter said you'd gone to visit relatives. You shouldn't be travelling in your state, anyhow.'

'I had to sort something out. Come in, I might have a new recruit for your daughter...'

'No, I can't stop. Here you go. It's all sorted. Charity match, next month. Workers 11 against Bosses 11...'

I took the leaflet with little enthusiasm.

'I don't know about this.'

'I do. And besides as luck would have it, Sylvia saw my little ad in the *Observer* and got back in touch with us. She wants to help out and do the catering. I was gobsmacked, really, it was totally out of the blue but I'm meeting her now so we'll see...'

I felt a strange euphoria which propelled me forward to grab Len's hand. 'What are you wasting time here for then?'

'Because I was worried about your health. Anyhow, it seems to have brought me some good luck, so I'll be eternally grateful on that front. You look better though, I have to say. There was a rumour you'd gone abroad…'

'Yes, I went to Iraq to rescue my grandson and spread cricket in the country.'

Len laughed and patted me on the shoulder. 'Course, and I'm Dickie Bird.' He looked at his watch and walked off.

'What about the police thing? I may have found someone who wants to join up.'

'I'll tell my daughter, she might pop round.'

Len always doffed his cap when he was leaving, even to me, but not this time. He tied an elastic band around the batch of leaflets and strode down Edmund Street. His left arm swung for the first time in decades. But as he turned the corner down into Silver Street, I caught sight of Salim's beige Toyota Carina pulling in. Should I close the door or leave it open? It didn't matter because by the time I'd made my decision, Salim had already parked up. He got out of the car and fixed his eyes on me with a force I couldn't recall.

'Where the fuck were you?' he shouted, from at least 20 yards away. 'You could have been killed.'

# 12.

I felt embarrassed that Salim had chosen to humiliate me in the street but he had that look of incredulity in his eyes and that meant there was no room for reason: better to let him swing wildly. He looked a bit dishevelled with his overgrown goatee beard, shirt hanging out and the laces on his right Puma trainer dirty and undone. I wondered where he'd been but, as expected, he turned the tables on me and ushered me inside with an uncomfortable arm on my shoulder. A few minutes later, in the corner of the living room, I was forced to come clean on my small, but memorable, adventure. I had expended a lot of energy in my conversations with Len so I reached into my pocket for my wallet and handed Salim the letter Wasim had written to the family. He took it but didn't move his eyes from my face. He unfolded it and, finally, looked down at its contents. It took him a matter of seconds to absorb the main fact that his son wasn't where he thought he was. He smacked the letter on his thigh as though he was swatting a fly. He looked up at the ceiling and let out an almighty sigh.

'I called literally hundreds of contacts in Kashmir,' he said, finally lowering his head to look at me. 'But all this time, superhero grandad here were running around in Iraq with my son trying not to get shot.

Are you sick or what? Have you still got your head screwed on right?'

I had to swallow before I replied because their simply wasn't enough saliva to lubricate the vocal cords. The events of the day had caught up with me. I could not afford a long, drawn–out dispute with my son–in–law. It had to be short and, not particularly, sweet.

'Why didn't you call the police or the local MP?' I asked. 'Were you scared they would ask questions of your troubled son and what he was up to?'

Salim's lip twitched, a rare sign that he was getting annoyed. He threw the letter back in my direction and walked off towards the kitchen. In a way, I could understand his concern. I was officially sick and had travelled thousands of miles to a foreign country and, yes, could have been killed. It could have been deemed a highly irresponsible act but, on the other hand, who else was going to stand up and be counted in terms of getting to the heart of Wasim's teenage fantasies? Who else was prepared to put themselves on the line to keep the family unit together? I didn't see it from anyone in this house. A few seconds later, I could hear the tap running. I got up and headed out of the living room, desperate to get upstairs for a nap. He quickly returned and, curiously, stood in front of me to stop me leaving. He then folded his arms but used one of his hands to rap his knuckles on his forehead. He had an occasional habit of rapping slow, lumbering tunes on it like a confused drummer.

'I shouldn't have brought the illness into it. Sorry on that score.' He moved his hand away from his forehead. 'But you went to Iraq, for fuck's sake. Even Blair's shit scared of going there.' He stepped away from the door so I could get out. 'I can tell you need a rest, that's okay. I'll get your medication if you need it. But you need to tell us everything. Wasim's my son and if I'm going to knock some sense into the cocky sneak then I need to know the details.'

'Knocking sense into him hasn't worked so far, has it?'

He shook his head and opened the door for me. He ushered me through but didn't say anything. I hadn't noticed it before but his eyes looked a little bloodshot. Had he been taking drugs? There were so many gangs prowling every street corner that I wouldn't have been surprised. But I had given up trying to work out Salim and what made him tick. His value system was completely different to mine and he had proved it by being away for so long since Wasim and I had arrived. Granted, he didn't know we would appear out of the blue but it was obvious there was a pattern of behaviour developing and he wasn't too enamoured with us for returning and disrupting his lifestyle. There were other factors too: he had never suffered a day's illness in his life, not even a cold, so it wasn't surprising he couldn't relate to my condition. He also sold flimsy mobile phones while I had made real things of use to everyday people: motorway signs and brake pads. There was too much between us for reconciliation now. I had bigger things on my mind.

It was early evening when Wasim rushed into the bedroom with a bulging, wallet–type folder under one arm and a yellow plastic bin in the other. I hadn't slept at all and was sat up reading Len's leaflet, bewildered by how quickly my old friend had organised the charity match. I put the leaflet down and watched Wasim place the bin by the side of my bed. It was thoughtful of him because it would save me a trip to the bathroom. Most of the time there was nothing to release from my throat, even if there was an immediate urge from my volcanic stomach, so now I could simply lower my head and spit whatever stuff came out without having to move. Wasim sat down on the other side of the bed and pulled out a thick pile of white paper from the folder. He laid the sheets out neatly on the bed like a pack of cards. His eyes flitted across the pages and he was deep in concentration. He paused and rubbed his chin. He picked out one of the pages and handed it over to me.

'These are mostly from the *Observer*,' he said. 'They've shafted a lot of people...'

He handed me one of the loose pages and it was a story titled 'Asbestos took my wife away me'. It was pretty self–explanatory and I only decided to read the first couple of paragraphs which told the story of a woman who worked at Turner Brothers for 33 years and had been diagnosed with Mesothelioma. The disease lay dormant for over 30 years and she died in 2002. I did not want to read any more because it was too painful and made me think of Fareeda. She knew of a man in Heath Street in the late 70s who had died of asbestos–related disease, or so his wife claimed, and Fareeda subsequently wanted me to find another job in the town. But I didn't listen because I was settled and had a decent wage. I figured that so many people worked there, about 3,000 in my time, that I was certain a giant company like that would protect us as much as they could. I handed the page back to Wasim and, although he took it, he wasn't even looking at me. He was scouring the other pages and handed me another one. His enthusiasm for the cause was admirable. I raised my hand and asked him to stop.

'Nana jee, this is important,' he said. 'I won't ask you to read another one. You can rest after this.'

'No you read it, my eyes hurt...'

He took the page back off me and read me the whole article which claimed families, of asbestos workers, were also at risk. The article highlighted a case where a woman in her 40s got Mesothelioma from sitting on her father's knee: he had worked at Turner Brothers and regularly came home for lunch in his asbestos–covered overalls. I looked up at Wasim after he had finished and it was the same kind of expression I had seen many times in Iraq: a blank, stony certainty; a semi–blackmail posture that required immediate acquiescence. He was sure he was doing the right thing and I needed to go along with it. Now, that my 'disease' could hurt the family too I had to join the campaign for justice, anything else would be wrong or, even downright, dangerous. There was an uncomfortable silence between us. It couldn't wait. I had to change direction completely.

'Do you intend to see your jihadi friends again?'

Wasim huffed and turned away from me. He got up and walked towards the window. He picked up the Kwik Cricket bat and did a quick slog to long on. He then put it down and walked over to the dumbbells near my bag. He picked one up over his shoulder and slowly raised it head, all the while not taking his eyes off me.

'This is still my bedroom,' he said.

'…And it's my disease, why do you want to fight it?'

He put the dumbbell down and slowly walked towards me. He sat down on my side of the bed, and to my surprise, gently picked up my hand. He examined my index finger and then held my hand tightly.

'There are no brothers like that in this town,' he said. 'Amir was from Bolton, Shiraz from Middleton and Liaqat from Cheetham Hill. We used to meet at a house in Glodwick. Some nights we drove down to an imam's house in Birmingham. I might see them again I might not. I'm not sure. Amir got married and had a kid, Liaqat got a job in Leicester and Shiraz ended up in Kandahar so I just don't know. All I do know is that Mum cried her eyes out for almost an hour when she spoke to me. I didn't expect that. It hurt me. I thought she wasn't affected by what I did. She blamed me for nearly taking you down with me…'

'Was she right to blame you?'

'…Suppose so, I'm not sure. All I know right now

is that I want to help you. If I'd known how ill you were I wouldn't have been so horrible in Iraq. I'm sorry about that...' He glanced up at the Islamic map on the wall and then moved closer to me. 'I want you to tell me everything about Turners and what it was like in those days. I know it was difficult for people when they first came here so I'd like to know all about it.'

I nodded and cleared my throat. A substantial ball of phlegm rocketed up into my mouth. I gestured for him to move aside. I shifted across the bed and lowered my head down into the bin. The release was almost perfect: my throat felt light and clear. I didn't know where to begin but a freezing January night in 1967 when Cyril Smith was the guest at a reception at the Golden Mosque would be a good place to start. It was the end of Ramzaan and he was welcoming all the new immigrants to Rochdale. He was wearing his Alderman's necklace and towered above most of the five–foot nothings.

'I was scared of Cyril Smith because I wasn't sure if he looked like a beast or the King of England...'

They listened attentively at the dinner table as I retold the Iraq journey from beginning to end. I was on decent form, probably because Wasim had dredged up some long–buried nostalgia from me earlier in the evening and it had made me feel a hundred times better: a wonderful meal of bitter melon, tangy pancakes and sweet orange rice also helped; the only downside was a greenish–looking banana which felt more like biting into a tree than a fruit. Throughout the evening, Nadia shook her head and rolled her eyes a lot but it was more in good humour than outright disapproval. Elisha interrupted with questions like: 'Did you go to Abu Ghraib' but she meant well. Wasim stayed silent for the duration. His father was sat next to him most of the time so it wasn't surprising. Salim did leave the table once to make a call on his mobile but returned within a few minutes to listen to my experiences in the safe house with Abbie and his crew. He obviously didn't like what he heard. He playfully shoulder–barged Wasim and, when his son didn't respond, he followed it up with a stronger, harsher push. There was silence in the room but then Salim asked me to continue and merely said he was 'testing his son to see how hard he was'. After I'd finished (and I was immensely proud of myself for getting to the end without coughing and pausing for breath) a strange thing happened. Salim watched Elisha follow her mother into the kitchen to help her with the dishes and then moved closer, sitting on the chair next to me. He fiddled about with his mobile for a few seconds, pretending to look busy, and then put it down and looked up at me.

'Kudos to you for having the courage to go to Iraq,' he said. 'I respect that. You had an adventure down there and brought Wasim back in one piece.' He offered a handshake and I was so surprised that I took a long time to raise my hand. 'Sometimes, blokes need to do their own thing…'

'Would you have gone?'

He picked up a sliced orange and tentatively put it in his mouth. 'Booking time off work would have been difficult but, yeah, course, although you nicked the letter so that saved me a job.'

A job? Is that what all this amounted to? He'd been going so well before that point. He wrapped his mouth around the orange slice and slowly tore off the peel with his teeth. Some of the juice dribbled down his chin but he wiped it away with his finger while putting the peel back on the empty plate. He then touched his silver wrist chain and got up from the table. He touched Wasim's shoulder and then smiled at me.

'I heard you two slept together in Baghdad,' he said. 'No room for that kind of behaviour here...'

He winked and left the room. Wasim glanced at me and but didn't smile. I was surprised by his expression because the standard set of affairs, when his father had disappeared, was to see his swagger and certainty return after a feeble, head–down, arms– folded period when the two men were together. Not today.

'They wanted to build some new houses at the old Turners site,' said Wasim, with a firmness that caught me off guard.

'Who?'

'I don't know: twats. But they wanted to have a children's nursery too.'

I was shocked to hear him swear like that. He had never been so crude in his own home before. Perhaps, he was simply fed up with his father.

'Has it been granted?' I asked.

'I'm not sure but there was a big protest against it.'

Most of this was news to me. I had been ignorant of what had been going on in the town although there was some mitigation because I had been quite reclusive for months after Fareeda's death. It didn't surprise me that developers were looking to build new homes on the site because nowhere was safe. It was a source of deep irritation to me that whole swathes of land, playing fields and old mill sites were being flogged for identikit housing. Nadia was still seething about her former middle school, Redbrook, being demolished. I shared her frustration but, on the other hand, the playing fields were used for the new home for our cricket club. Sadness and loss for one person, an opportunity for another; it was always divisive. Wasn't there a better way?

Wasim got up and said he was going to set up his airbed in the front room because he was extremely tired and wanted to have an early night. He asked me to come in with him and, because I felt slightly guilty about sleeping in his bed, I agreed. I hadn't been in the front room since I'd returned but I could see it was a bit awkward fitting any sort of bed in there because of the computer, the three piece suite, the Sanyo stereo system and the sturdy wooden coffee table. But he had made the best of it. The table was resting on one of the armchairs which had been pushed right back towards the window to provide more room. The stereo system was also perched awkwardly on another armchair and looked as though it could fall onto the carpet at any minute. Admittedly, it was a bit of a squeeze. It was hardly a hovel but I wondered how long Wasim would have to sleep there. He unrolled the silver blue Aerobed, which was lying haphazardly near the Sanyo stereo, and then plugged it in. He pressed a button on it and the flimsy piece of kit began to puff up nicely into a solid mattress. He covered it with a nice blue bedsheet and then threw down a pillow and a thin–looking brown duvet. The bed was ready. He sat down on it, cross–legged and folded his arms. He looked straight ahead as I sat down on the empty armchair.

'Ayesha's dead,' he said, in a low voice. 'I tried to call her yesterday, again and again, but couldn't get a line. In the end, her sister picked up and said she was killed in that attack on the safe house.' He drew back his knees and pushed them up to chest. He ran his palms down his face and then put his arms round his knees. 'It's over now. I won't talk about it again. It was stupid…'

'You can still get a line?'

'Sometimes…it's expensive but we've got our ways.'

'I don't get it. She was killed in the same attack? I thought she wasn't there.'

'Her sister said she was. I don't care anymore. She was messing me around anyway.' He looked to his left and grabbed his Puma holdall. He unzipped it and picked out a leaflet and a couple of books. 'The books are really for me but I got this leaflet off the web.'

He had shrugged off a woman's death – one that he supposedly loved – as though it was a minor detail in a now–forgotten frenzy of romance, self–discovery and fundamentalism. It was hard for me to take in. I wanted to ask a few more questions about Ayesha but realised that side of Wasim's life was now drawing to a close so it was pointless. Moreover, I was afraid of his reaction because he did genuinely seem to love her. Best not to rock the boat; he had been extremely well–behaved since his return.

He moved across the airbed on his knees and handed me the leaflet. It was about International Memorial Workers Day at the Town Hall and I looked down at the date which read April 28 2006. I realised it was another thing I'd missed. Was there any point in pursuing claims or joining a campaign? I'd obviously missed it all. I read some of the information on the leaflet and it made me feel extremely unpleasant and breathless. A hundred thousand asbestos– related deaths worldwide and 5,000,000 may die from exposure, it claimed. Who cared if it was true? I wanted to hand it back instantly and head upstairs but some of the pictures on the leaflet caught my attention. They were quite small, not much bigger than a postage stamp, but they included images of asbestos–related victims and I couldn't help but have instant solidarity with them. The workers may have been from a different era but they were looking straight at me as though they knew what I was going through. There was an intimacy that only we would share. I thought I had blurred vision for a moment but I realised it was my eyes moistening. I looked at the other images: workers on the factory floor, street protests, shipyards, dumping sites and, finally and most chillingly, Turner Brothers itself. It resembled a giant ice cube tray on its side because of its multiple dark windows and oblong shape but still had an indestructible and imperious look about it. The red–brick chimney shot up into the sky like an erect elephant trunk; powerful and ominous. It had a faded grandeur; a holy, haunted relic that made it feel like part of another century, located thousands of miles away somewhere far away. But it wasn't: it was on our doorstep less than half a mile away up Rooley Moor Road. I could visit the derelict site at any time but why would I want to? Part of my flickering soul was hiding somewhere behind the factory gates but many bodies had already been thrown over the gate and dumped around the town in the name of profit and progress. I could not face the ghostly presence again: the factory may have been long gone but its poisonous legacy wasn't. I looked at the images of the sick workers again and found it hard to take my eyes off them. I shuddered at the prospect of more victims – and families – continuing to suffer in the town. Yes, the factory had given me the chance to build a future for me and my family but was it worth it to be poisoned by its so–called magic mineral? I thought about the likes of Paul and Wasim who were scrambling around trying to find jobs and wondered if I was being too harsh on my former employer. But no, the leaflet had hardened my stance. The images of sick, dying workers had made a powerful, searing impact on me that no amount of words could ever manage. I usually wasn't taken in by that kind of propaganda but the ultimate message was raw, painful and truthful. There was a killer in our midst – and I had a duty to warn others.

# 13.

Nadia drove me to the infirmary for the follow–up appointment with Dr Howarth. I had a chest x–ray first which I felt was unnecessary but Nadia came in with me to provide comfort. She held my shirt and jumper while the radiographer eased my chest up against the plate and my hands onto the rubber handles. A waft of icy air seeped into my ribs as the radiographer got the image she wanted. It was uncomfortable but quick. After that, there was a long wait for Dr Howarth's consultation which took us past noon, by which time Nadia was extremely hungry. She was ready to head off to the canteen when Dr Howarth eventually appeared, looking even younger and leaner than the last time I'd seen him. We sat down and waited for him to get going but he took an extremely long time to get his papers, files and other correspondence in order. He glanced at Nadia but didn't look at me.

'Er Mr Rafeeq,' he said, still fiddling around with his notes. 'How are you?'

'Decent, I suppose.' I looked over at Nadia and she rested her hand on mine. 'I mean, I can get from A to B and, obviously, I've still got Nadia. While she's with me, I've got nothing to fear.'

Dr Howarth nodded and cleared his throat. He took off his jacket and finally looked me straight in the eye. His sleeves were already rolled up but he pushed them further up.

'Has your lifestyle changed dramatically recently?' he asked.

'Don't know what you mean…'

'Smoking…travelling to a polluted environment… that kind of thing?'

I shook my head as Nadia squeezed my hand. 'Why? What's the problem?'

There was a pause as Dr Howarth had another roll–the–sleeves–up moment.

'Well…' he said. 'Your x–ray shows the level of fibrosis has progressed dramatically from when we last saw you. The scarring has spread and now covers a substantial area. I'm surprised how quickly it has developed. Have you noticed any difference in your symptoms?'

'Well, the climate makes a difference. Hot weather seems to soothe my throat and helps my breathing. I now feel colder generally and there's a bit more mucus but winter's just round the corner so it's nothing special.'

'Hmm…did you go on holiday?'

'No, I was just speaking generally. The sun softens my lungs. It's like my Siamese twin. I'm lost without it.'

'But you mentioned the hot weather. It hasn't been too warm around here recently.'

'Don't you listen?' interrupted Nadia. 'He hasn't been anywhere. Just tell us what the prognosis is and what medication we need…'

'Okay…I can't really speculate on how the disease will develop,' he said. 'What I can recommend is oxygen therapy at home, if and when Mr Rafeeq requires it, and an increase in the medication he already takes. Perhaps, a dose of antibiotics will also help to reduce the chance of infections. Have you had your flu jab yet?'

'Er no, I haven't got round to it…'

'Call your GP and get it done immediately.'

He had said the same thing to me last time but I had simply forgotten. Nadia would ensure I wouldn't forget this time, although I still felt it wasn't wholly necessary. It wasn't that I was against vaccines; it was more that it would create an extra trip to the doctors and I didn't have the Proton anymore. I simply didn't want to be a burden. I wanted Nadia to wrap up but she continued to ask detailed questions of Dr Howarth, particularly about the how the oxygen therapy would work. She was slightly brisk and forceful, I thought, and felt she had the measure of Dr Howarth, perhaps because he was about the same age as her. As she continued to press on minor points (how big are oxygen cylinders?) I had to absorb the harsh reality that the Iraq venture was probably the reason for the dramatic escalation in my symptoms. It was baffling because, in general, the warm weather I encountered over there had actually made me feel better. Was it the placebo effect? Was I simply feeling perkier because I had succeeded in my mission to bring Wasim back home? Perhaps, but if that was the case how did the scarring on my lungs become so bad?

Chemical pollution? The rot and sewage of Sadr City? Depleted uranium? Did it matter? Not now because the evidence of deterioration had been laid in front of me. I had paid the price for my trip – some would say, folly – but it was a price worth paying. I had kept the family intact and gone to a part of the world that most people would only see in their news bulletins. I had also taken a great game to a great land. I could take strength from those achievements in the dark, breathless nights that lay ahead.

Wasim now had the bit between his teeth. He had provided me with information about the two main supports groups in the area – the GMAVSG (The Greater Manchester Asbestos Victim Support Group) and Save Spodden Valley – while also filling me in about an annual Action Mesothelioma Day and a special asbestos memorial in the Town Hall. I read most of the smudgy internet printouts in my bed while he called GMAVSG and asked them detailed questions about compensation and other legal matters. I wondered why he had phoned because he had already arranged a visit from his solicitor friend Amjad later that day. But he was on a roll and it was difficult to stop him. There was a manic energy and stop–start focus about him that was mildly infectious – in a good way. Yes, he was overdoing it – he hadn't shaved since his return, insisted on keeping the keffiyah round his shoulders and ate trashy chicken kebabs while sitting on the bedroom carpet – but he had introduced me to some moving accounts of victims and workers who had suffered similar diseases and I wouldn't have read them if it wasn't for his encouragement and idealism. Yet I did wonder where all this was heading: were we going all the way the courts? To number 10 Downing Street? To campaign globally? What was his endgame? Little things didn't inspire him anymore. He usually wore me out by noon.

Amjad arrived in the afternoon with a mobile at his ear and an open file in his hands. He was a tall man with an awkward gait and a serious–looking gaze. He was smartly dressed in a crimson v–neck sweater, beige scarf, suit jacket and jeans. He surprised me by being extremely liberal in his views, the exact opposite of Wasim, and the two men exchanged feisty banter about the perils or otherwise of a secular society. I had never met Amjad before but he did a lot of work for the community on visa applications for young spouses who wanted to join their husbands and wives in the UK. His speciality, however, was personal injury claims – and that's how Wasim had originally met him. Wasim had suffered a slight accident in his father's car just days after passing his test but Amjad wisely told him not to put in a claim. Instead, he helped him find an extremely low–cost garage which fixed the car so no–one at home would notice. To my knowledge, no–one ever has, apart from me, of course.

Nadia made tea for him and then joined us in the more formal setting of the front room, which had been cleared of Wasim's messy bedtime arrangements.

Amjad explained the ins and outs of trying to get compensation for my disease and I listened attentively for no more than five minutes. Mrs Gleeson had been walking her dog Ena past the window and I couldn't help but notice her peering in while Ena was distracted by a family getting out of a car. Mrs Gleeson moved on quickly but it was enough for me to miss a big chunk of Amjad's monologue: the only detail I absorbed was that if I wanted to put in a claim for personal injury I had to do it within three years of diagnosis. The rest was as clear as mud. Finally, after a lot of detail about certain Acts and Government legislation, he began to ask detailed questions about my condition and my former employer. The first one was the exact date I started and left Turner Brothers. As an opening question, it was reasonable but it hurt my head and increased the phlegm at the back of my throat. If this was a taste of things to come then I wanted to bail out now. It was such a long time ago, that I only knew which month I started, not the exact date. Amjad had these searching eyes as he waited patiently but my answers were always too vague to be inducted into the fresh legal file he was compiling for me. Inevitably, the question of a face mask arose again. Was I wearing one? No, for the umpteenth time, because I worked in the rubber department and asbestos fibres did not fizz up into the atmosphere; therefore no mask was needed. Nadia kindly interjected on my behalf on occasions when I found the going a little rough and regularly asked Amjad to slow down. It was an endless, repetitive and exhausting interrogation. But he saved his most niggly question when I thought it had all been wrapped up. He asked if I'd been anywhere recently because that could affect a definitive diagnosis. Unsurprisingly, he knew of my trip abroad (although not where) and felt it could affect my case. How that was possible, I wasn't sure, because I had been diagnosed officially before my trip to Iraq but, on the other hand, I did understand that the waters could be muddied. I didn't answer the question and thanked Amjad for taking the time to come round to my house. I had been naïve. I had expected some sort of facility to already be in place to compensate victims in the town. That wasn't the case. Most of them had to battle hard to get what they deserved and some of them had been treated with indifference, or even contempt, simply to get acknowledgement of their condition. I knew some of these people or, at least their families, would be at the forthcoming charity match. I had no intention of going.

The oxygen cylinders arrived early next morning. Nadia asked me if I wanted to get 'hooked up' straight away but I couldn't stand the sight of the ugly things and told her I wanted to get rid immediately. She had a deep conversation with the engineer who demonstrated how to use them while I lay in my bed comparing the Islamic map on the wall to the cylinders. It was like being a victim of chemical warfare.

Nadia didn't leave at the time I expected. She was still in the house by noon. I asked her if anything was up or if she just had a free morning. She said she was fine and went downstairs to make lunch – a warm, tender concoction of potato pancakes, yoghurt and zesty aubergines. She came back upstairs and we talked about Fareeda's love of fat cushions among other things. I desperately wanted to stay awake but the heavy lunch rolled me over before 2pm. When I woke up, she was gone but Wasim was a few feet away taking pictures of the oxygen cylinders with his mobile phone. There was a laptop on the floor and pieces of paper strewn all over the carpet.

'I'm driving down to the old Turners site in a few minutes, nana jee,' he said. 'Wanna come? I've started up a new website. It's going to raise money for a dedicated care facility for asbestos sufferers. Raise money the same way we do for a mosque. That's why it'll work. Door to door fundraising. It's going to be massive.'

'How long have you been here?'

'Ages. Even Mum thinks it's a good idea.'

He finished taking the pictures and smiled as he scrolled through the images on his phone. His offer was enticing because I wanted to get out of this pokey bedroom and get some air – but the kind of contaminated air that may be swirling around the old Turners site wasn't quite what I had in mind. Was he thinking straight? Why take me up there now?

'It has been demolished, you do know that?'

'Course, but I just want to see what kind of shithole it really is now. If they want to build houses on it, then they'll have to take on the whole community.'

He hadn't looked at me once. He finished looking at his photos and bent down to fiddle with his laptop. He eventually glanced up at me after a longer–than–usual silence.

'Oh I get you,' he said. 'Look, nana jee you don't have to come. I'll take you down town, instead, if you like. I've got dad's car for the day. I want to get full use.'

I couldn't refuse. I wanted to buy a thicker hat for my head which was becoming colder by the day. I slowly got out of bed and could see Wasim rummaging through his pile of clothes bunched up in the corner. He pulled out his keffiyah and looked over his shoulder.

'Do you want to wear this on your head?' he said, with a devilish smile. 'I have no use for it now.'

'Just get the car started, lad. Don't push your luck.'

Wasim drove down Spotland Road but could not control his father's squeaky windscreen wipers. He had them either too fast or too slow and they were practically useless as the sheets of rain swirled across from the west, as though the Falinge flats were ejecting all their mess in our direction. I was told by Len recently that Falinge was the 'sicknote capital of the country'. Len was better read than me so I tended to believe most of what he said, although in this case I recall he'd read it in some national newspaper. Not the straightest of bats, at the best of times. But what if it were true?

I mulled this over as I looked out of the window to absorb the toffee and grey low–rise blocks. Why were so many people on benefits? Had Turners polluted the whole area? How did the Highland Laddie pub end up next to Coral's the bookmakers? I remembered being invited for a warm, evening drink one snowy night in the late Sixties by Mrs Lorna Vozniak. She lived in the Featherstone block but had just made her daily check on her elderly mother in Mitchell Street who was suffering from arthritis. She walked past me to return home but noticed I was almost at a standstill, shivering and struggling to get my flask open so I could desperately sup my milk tea. I had just returned from a punishing shift and had no power in my hands. She asked me if I needed any help but I mumbled that I was fine; my English was not great at this stage but it was passable. Amazingly, she then grabbed my frozen hand and examined it.

'You'll be a mannequin if you stay here any longer,' she said. 'Come on, my flat's a couple of minutes away. Get a brew inside you and you'll be rolling again.'

I have to admit it did cross my mind about what people would say if they saw a foreign–looking man going into a flat with a middle–aged lady but the irrational fear of pneumonia and hospital wards won the day – and besides Fareeda wasn't even in the country yet. So the two of us went back to her low–rise flat and spent a cosy couple of hours talking mostly about her mother's claim that she was a neighbour of Albert Tatlock, who I had never heard of. I did not have a TV so I only found out he was a character in Coronation Street about 12 years later. I still don't know his real name. She also made me a lavishly–buttered crumpet to go with my blisteringly strong cup of tea. She apologised because, as a dinnerlady at Oakenrod School, she was used to toning down the food she prepared for children and, at home, she could let her hair down as it were. She told me she would never marry again because her first husband – a soldier from Castleton – had left her during the war for a nurse who was treating him. It was the only time her exuberance and effervescence was checked. She went to make a pot of cauliflower soup and sweet pastry flan and insisted I take it with me. I couldn't refuse and, as she slipped the food neatly into my tartan drawstring bag, she casually mentioned the subject of a multi–million pound development in Ashfield Valley – a scheme that would see more than a thousand modern flats built with central heating, garages and a play area. Some of her friends were ready to move out of Falinge and into the new, dynamic enterprise which was based on a Swedish model. She would not be moving. Never. She loved her home – and job – so much, no amount of glittering inducements would be enough to shift her out of her 'pride and joy'. We said our farewells and I never saw her again. I later read that the Ashfield Valley project, after a promising beginning, had turned sour with problems of crime, vandalism and anti–social behaviour. Most of the 26 blocks had been demolished by 1992 and the rest were refurbished for a new retail and business development: Sandbrook

Park. Nadia told me she quite liked the Odeon cinema and had watched Billy Elliot there. She wasn't too keen on the fast food places, however. I wondered if Lorna was still alive and, if so, whether she still lived in the Featherstone block. She showed good judgment in not moving to Ashfield Valley but what would she think of the deprivation in Falinge today? It wasn't long before I was jolted away from my misty–eyed nostalgia.

'FUCKING GET A MOVE ON, YOU TWAT!' shouted Wasim.

My head swung away from the Falinge flats and up ahead at a learner driver, in a Fiesta, who was crawling along ahead of Wasim. There had been a minor accident on the corner of Holland Street but the traffic was now moving at a decent pace, except for the ultra–cautious Fiesta. Two policemen were at the scene taking some details – one of them was smiling and joking with the driver perceived to be at fault.

'You'll have to tidy up your language if you want to join the police, Wasim,' I said. 'Len's daughter's in the force, she'll help you out.'

'Not that again.'

'Don't tell me, it's about trust.'

Wasim shook his head and moved up a gear. He looked at me and smiled.

'Will it make you happy if I fill in an application form?'

'Proud.'

He simply gave me a thumbs–up and then stuck a ghastly CD in the stereo. No matter, I felt the rehabilitation was almost complete. I had taken him from a position of great peril to one of stability and calm. I was extremely proud of my achievements. I looked in the wing mirror as the Falinge flats faded in the distance.

Nadia brought up a tray of coriander naans and bitter melon for supper. She rested the tray on the small table beside my bed and rushed back downstairs. I wanted her to stay with me (it had been such a wonderful day) but it became apparent she had more pressing matters. I could hear her having a row with Salim downstairs and it put me off my food. The day had largely been symptom–free but, as the voices down below became more strained, I could feel a shortness of breath developing and the gathering storm of needles in my throat. I had to abandon my meal and head to the bathroom to clear my throat – but I was adamant no amount of stress would be allowed to affect my balanced mood. I came back to bed after a flimsy bout of coughing and finished my meal. The food went down exactly how I wanted it to go and then I lay down, putting my head under the duvet. After a few minutes, I heard footsteps thudding up the stairs. Nadia came in and sat on the bed. She looked preoccupied and distant. She got up and picked up the tray. She said nothing and headed for the door again.

'What's he said now?' I asked, sitting up in bed.

She waited at the door and looked down at the greasy plate. Her hands were shaking and the tray looked as though it was about to slip from her hands.

'I got a job offer in London,' she said, without looking up. 'I sent some designs down there. They liked them. I really want to go…'

I could not deny it: there was surge of joy, elation almost, that my daughter had gained some recognition after years of toil. She had taken inspiration from her mother who passed on her eye for quirky clothes and unusual design. If she was looking down on us now, tears of pride would be running down her cheeks.

'I want Elisha, you and Wasim to come with me,' she said, finally looking into my eyes. 'Salim doesn't like it but I don't care about what he likes or doesn't like anymore. He couldn't even have a mature conversation about it. He's gone to see his mates, anyway.'

I tried to respond but excess saliva flooded my mouth, allowing only a pathetic mumble. I swallowed the saliva and licked my lips.

'But what about Elisha? Her school and all that?'

Nadia didn't answer but tightened her grip on the tray. I may have been wrong but I was sure she was about to throw it across the room. She took a deep breath and left the room without replying. I tried to get out of bed and follow her but when I reached the door a searing pain raged across my collarbone. A wave of cold entered my body and my right arm felt completely numb. I started to shiver and got back into bed straight away. The trembling continued even as I wrapped the duvet – and an extra blanket – tightly over my body. A few minutes went by but there was no noticeable difference. Now, I couldn't even tell if

I was hot or cold. A bout of coughing started; it was so deep and involuntary that my eyes were watering. I eased to the left and flailed around trying to pick up my jumper from the chair but it was no use; I knocked the chair over and the jumper ended up on the floor. I made fists of my hands and curled up as tight as possible. Thankfully, I heard the thudding footsteps again. The sound of the door jolted my left shoulder. My jaw trembled and I had bitten my lip. Nadia walked in and kneeled down by my bed. I glanced up and touched her warm hand. Nadia took off her shoes and snuggled in beside me in bed. She moved closer to me and held me in a deep embrace. The warmth of her body sent a tingle around my icy bones. No matter what, we would stay together. She had the right to choose.

The morning came quicker than ever. Nadia screamed as the door crashed open. The door came off it hinges like a flimsy slab of polystyrene, thudding onto the carpet. A vicious draught was coming in through the frosty landing. The light came on as if by magic. Uniformed men swarmed in like an army of giant ants. They must have come down from the sky. They wore big boots, dark glasses and helmets. Some had guns and waved them around wildly. Was I in Iraq again? Nadia jumped out of the bed but one of the men pushed her back onto the bed, nearly making her fall over. She retreated and grabbed hold of me.

'IS THIS HIS BEDROOM?' said one.

'WHAT?' said Nadia.

'IS THIS HIS FUCKIN' BEDROOM?'

'YES, BUT MY FATHER IS ILL. SHOW SOME RESPECT.'

The shouting, screaming and pointing of weaponry battered my ears and left my temples on the verge of eruption. I tried to keep my stomach in check but last's night wonderful meal became an ugly, ferocious fluid which partially missed the bucket and ended up on the carpet. A scorching pain ripped into my abdomen and remained until I released some more dreadful, smelly sick – this time onto the side of the bed and my hand. From the corner of my blurry eye, I could see one of the men – who looked about 8ft tall – use his weapon to tear down the Islamic map from the wall. Somebody shouted at him about 'evidence' but I could hear little else. The piercing, ringing sound in my ears was all too dominant. My mouth became saggy and I started to drool. Nadia helped me get my stone–heavy head right over the bucket. Another man walked round the bed towards us. He stopped a few inches away. All I could see were his trousers tucked inside his big black boots. He whipped out a small bottle of water from his equipment belt and handed it to Nadia. She unscrewed the cap and delicately eased the bottle towards my lips. I took a drink but found it hard to swallow. She helped me lay back on the bed. As I settled down, I could see most of the other men searching Wasim's drawers, cupboards and files. His laptop, dumbbells and bags were being taken away. The invasive noise was still too much for me – a pounding migraine had started on the right side of the head.

'Suppose you're gonna tell me those oxygen cylinders are for the old fella here,' said the water carrier.

Nadia didn't answer.

'Is that your son downstairs?'

'Where is he?' screamed Nadia.

'In a nice little van.'

I gestured to Nadia that I didn't want any more water. She handed the bottle back to the water carrier.

'Keep it. Looks like he needs it.'

Nadia stood up and moved closer to him. She looked into his dark glasses and placed the bottle carefully back in his equipment belt. I couldn't tell if he was angry; I couldn't see his face. She sat back down on the bed and slipped her ankle–length boots on. She stood up and moved across to me. She placed her hand on my shoulder and softly asked me if I needed anything. Peace and quiet was all I needed. She picked up the bucket of vomit and calmly walked towards the invisible door.

'Where are you going, love?' asked the water carrier. 'The lad's already gone.'

She held the bucket up and walked out. A few feet away, one of the men was ruffling through my bag which made me feel sick again. He pulled out the blue Kwik Cricket bat and threw it onto the bonfire of evidence already gathered. The water carrier smiled and moved away from the stuffy window, leaving the sun to pierce my eyes. It drained the last ounce of energy from me. I lay my head on the pillow and could feel my eyes closing. There was only one thought swirling around in my head: how many days detention without charge was it? Fourteen, 28, 90? I really should have kept up with these things.

# 14.

Salim came rushing into the bedroom as I ate from a carton of sticky dates and watched the sun go down. I glanced at him but he only had astonished eyes for Nadia who was sat on the carpet texting a man about making the necessary repairs to the front, living room and bedroom doors. She had the *Manchester Evening News* open on her lap with a saucer of croissants and a mug of coffee resting on top of the newspaper. She didn't look up at her husband. Salim put his palms on his head and walked over the bed. He sat down and folded his arms.

'We were fuckin' raided?' he said. 'DON'T TELL ME WE WERE FUCKIN' RAIDED!'

Salim got up and walked over to the window. He looked outside and ran his hand across the back of his head. He smacked his fist against the window.

'Have you been down there, yet?' he asked, looking at Nadia.

Nadia didn't reply.

'Nadia went to the station this morning,' I said. 'They took all the details. She couldn't do anymore today.'

'Who asked you? It was your fuckin' fault anyway. If you hadn't gone out there, he'd still be a free man. It's you they should be interviewing, not him.'

I spat out a huge seed into a saucer and picked up another date. 'I've just given a statement.'

Salim nodded his head sarcastically. 'Yeah, about counting pebbles, was it?' He walked briskly to the door. 'I'm bombing down there, now. We've still got time to sort this out. He hasn't been charged with anything so we have a right to some answers.'

'Not a wise move.'

Salim put his hand on the unhinged door which had been resting upright against the wall. He got his fingers round it and slammed it down onto the floor.

'WAS GOING TO IRAQ A FUCKIN' WISE MOVE? EVERYTHING FUCKED UP AFTER YOU MOVED INTO THIS HOUSE.'

Nadia sprung up from the floor and rushed towards Salim. She stopped inches away and looked into his eyes. She took a deep breath and calmly raised her hands up and down.

'Can't you see we're trying to get things repaired,' she said. 'We don't want to break anything else.'

'Fuck that. I'm gonna sue the bastards.'

Nadia moved away and sat down again.

'He'll be released soon anyway,' said Salim, picking up the door and resting it against the wall again. 'Just like that bullshit Old Trafford plot a few year ago. Most of them were Iraqis. Funny that. Fuckin' war has been bad for each and every Muslim.'

Nadia took a bite of her croissant and then used both hands to compile a text message on her phone.

'So you're not going to London, then?' asked Salim.

Nadia paused and rubbed her forehead. She shook her head and carried on texting.

'Right, I'm off to see my son, then.'

Salim waited for a response but none came. He straightened his silver wrist chain and left the room. I picked up the last date from the saucer but chose not to eat it.

I had never met Len's daughter, Alice, but she appeared with her father on the doorstep of Edmund Street on the fifth day after Wasim's arrest. To say it was a shock was an understatement. She was off–duty, or so she said, but that wasn't going to stop me taking guard like the most cautious of opening batsmen. She was wearing a camel–coloured jacket, faded light blue jeans and Reebok trainers. She also had a black beanie hat pushed down almost over her eyebrows. I thought she could have been the girl working at the local Lidl store rather than a copper; perhaps that was her intention. I invited them both in and Alice went immediately to the kitchen and prepared tea and butter Crinkle biscuits for the old men. I nudged Len, who had a copy of the *Observer* tucked under his arm, and asked why she was here. He shrugged and started reading his paper. We sat at the dining table and finished our tea – I had decided to stop eating biscuits all together because they caused me indigestion – and Alice wasted no time in getting to the heart of the matter. She turned her chair away from the dining table so she could stretch out her legs and fold her arms.

'I heard Nadia on local radio yesterday,' she said. 'She didn't sound too good. Dad knew her so I just thought I'd come down and show my support.'

I placed my ice–cold hands on the steaming cup which fired a warm, soothing sensation throughout my body. 'Do the police usually have tea at suspected terrorists' homes?'

She smiled and looked at Len. She finally took off her beanie hat and straightened her short, spiky hair. I noticed a small scar on her forehead, just above her eyebrow. It became bigger when she smiled.

'I wouldn't know a terrorist from a taxi driver,' she said. 'The only Asian lads I know are cabbies, restaurant workers and call centre guys. I went to school with a lot of them. The sexy, glamorous work of stopping bombs is done by bigger beasts than me. I'm not allowed to get involved; they're very precious.'

I looked at Len. 'Did you put her up to this?'

'Yes, he did,' said Alice, with a smile. 'He couldn't wait to get over here and tell you about my mother. He might be getting back with her.'

'Bit premature to say the least,' said Len, rolling his eyes.

Alice playfully slapped Len on the thigh. 'Well, it's better than immature which is what you two have been for the past 18 years.'

Len looked uncomfortable and got up from the dining table. He lit up a Woodbine and paced casually to the door. Alice watched her father and then moved forward in her chair. She touched me on the knee which made me notice how stiff it was.

'How are you feeling?' she asked.

'My bones feel brittle after that so–called raid but, generally, I'm not too bad.'

'Fucking raids,' she said, resting back in the chair. 'Macho posturing.' She stuck her hand into her beanie hat and stretched it out as wide as possible. She laid her hat on the table and moved forward again. 'Anyhow, when I had cancer, I ran a half marathon. I didn't want to do it, at first, but when I saw the community rally round and create an unbreakable spirit it made me proud. We can do the same again.'

It had taken me a long time to work out. I simply could not swallow the fact that Alice, who Len had spoken about for years, had chosen this precise moment to visit the house. There had to be more, apart from the obvious reason of a neighbourly copper fishing for useful information. When Alice's intention became apparent, it partially lifted the soiled cloud of the raid. I was heartened that a young woman put such a premium on family values.

'So it's all about the charity match, then?' I said. 'You're desperate for Sylvia and Len to get back together again.'

'Kind of,' said Alice. 'Mum's uncle Geoff worked at Turners in the Fifties and was sick for a long time…'

'She didn't tell me about Geoff,' said Len, interrupting his daughter.

'She didn't tell you a lot of things. Anyway, her firm's organised all the catering. It'll be a shame to cancel it now.'

'We won't get another slot till next season,' said Len.

I expected to feel pressurised but that wasn't the case. Alice's compassion felt genuine. She had given me an unexpected boost and, crucially, allayed any scepticism I initially had about her. I couldn't imagine her in uniform. Had she arrested anyone lately? I couldn't see how that was possible.

I sighed and looked at Len. 'When's the match again?'

'Two weeks on Friday…'

'Have you got another umpire lined up?'

'No, it's just me and you, like old times.'

Alice had swung it for the workers. She knew I was mobile enough to attend; I knew it too. Further, I probably could hit a few balls and do a bit of fielding at long leg too if I wanted. Whereas I had been meek and hesitant, she had taken the initiative and pulled the main players into line. Weren't daughters the greatest gift to the world? What would happen if Nadia did happen to move to London and left me to cough and splutter my way down Edmund Street? She was unlikely to do that now but could anyone blame her? Perhaps, she was gone already.

Alice reached into her pocket and pulled out a card. She handed it to me and was quick to speak first.

'Just so you know, I have suggested these solicitors to Nadia already. He helped me and might do the same for you.'

The card said 'Lawrence Fitton and Co' but I didn't read the rest; the print was too small. I nodded and slipped the card into my trouser pocket. My hand stayed in my pocket to count pebbles. Somehow, this flimsy piece of card provided hope. I wanted to get Wasim down to the game, in his whites to prove he wasn't a bad kind of lad. I reckoned he'd be released by then anyway. If not, surely there was a chance of bail while his case was ongoing? They'd let him out for that because he now cared for asbestos sufferers. I had no doubt about that.

'It's a Friday, you say?' I asked, suddenly feeling five pebbles between my fingers rather than six.

'Is that prayers day?' asked Len. 'You don't go to the mosque anymore.'

'We're in need of all the help we can get.'

Nadia came in through the back door flicking her shawl over her shoulder while taking her earphones out. I could see her through the living room window as I sat at the dining table hurriedly trying to finish the plate of brown rice and chick peas she had left me for lunch. She came into living room and hesitated, perhaps not expecting me to be there. She walked over and handed me one of the earphones, urging me to put it in my ear. It wasn't something I usually did but today, I would make an exception. I awkwardly smuggled the earphone in and waited. It sounded pleasant enough, if a little thumpy. At least, it wasn't a racket which is what I expected. I listened for a couple of minutes until I was irritated.

'De La Soul,' said Nadia, taking the earphone from me. 'Wasim was 12 when he danced to that.' She looked out of the window and said nothing for at least a minute. 'He's been charged with inciting an act of terrorism overseas and a couple of other things too…I didn't pay attention. They said he was part of a group but the rest aren't in the country now so they're off the radar. Typical fuckin' sheep, he's the one that got caught.'

'How is he?'

'I haven't been allowed to see him today. Only thought that place existed in the papers and the TV…'

'Where?'

'Strangeways. At least he hasn't got a control order, I suppose.' She moved away from the window and walked across to the mantelpiece where I had neatly piled up a sizeable stack of mail. She picked up one of the envelopes, checked the address but put it back again. She walked back to the dining table and sat down. She picked up a solitary chick pea from my plate and put it in her mouth. She reached across and held my hand. 'Sorry, but it's all going to come out now. You might have to take the stand.'

'But he's changed. He's been taking care of me. He's started a campaign.'

'Lawrence said they've got evidence on that, as well…'

'Sorry?'

She picked up my glass of water and took a sip. 'During the raid, they picked up a list from his laptop of people suffering from asbestosis, cancer and other lung diseases; they'd all worked at Turners. They were all Muslims…'

'…I don't understand.'

'Lawrence says the prosecution will use that as a sign of separatism; that he hadn't changed at all, that he was racially and religious intolerant, that he wasn't fully integrated. I honestly couldn't believe what I was hearing…'

'But he was using that list as a starting point, as a means of inspiration. He wanted to raise money door to door, mosque–style, that's all. There would have been a new building for sufferers. I can't believe it, the authorities have gone mad.'

My voice was breaking and my jaw was like a rock. I felt dizzy and confused.

'Where's that Amjad solicitor, anyway? Can't he do a better job for us?'

'Can't get hold of him. Seems to have disappeared.'

Nadia's mobile rang. She spoke for a few minutes. After ending the call, she got up and stood in front of the mirror. She threw her shawl onto the sofa and tilted her head, running her fingers across her eyebrows. 'Mrs Lorenzo is so disappointed you couldn't take up the post. She wants to thank you for your interest and wish you the best of luck for the future.' She turned and looked at me. 'Best of fucking luck. We've really had some of that, haven't we?' She walked to the sofa and sat down. 'Mama would have dealt with all this better, don't you think?'

I got up and headed towards the door. 'I need to lie down.'

'Have you had your medication?'

I shook my head. Nadia followed me into the hallway. She put her arm round me as we walked up the stairs.

'Sorry about the job,' I said.

She smiled and squeezed my shoulder. 'London scared me a little anyway. We've got a bigger fight on our hands now.'

We walked into Wasim's sparse, cold bedroom. Nadia looked around and shook her head. 'You can't sleep in here, anymore.'

'I've got attached to it.' I walked over and sat on the bed. 'At least, they've taken the oxygen cylinders away…'

'Oh I forgot, I need to order some more…'

'Don't bother. They're not needed.'

She walked over to the bed and straightened my pillow. 'I don't need another crisis. The doctors must have some idea…'

I looked doubtful and lay down on the bed. Nadia drew the curtains.

'So when's he in court, then?'

'In a couple of weeks. Might be a marathon…'

'What about bail?'

Nadia shook her head.

I turned over in bed and put the cold duvet over my battered body. 'I haven't stepped inside a court in 73 years, and I don't intend to start doing it now.'

Nadia sat on the bed and pulled out her phone. She handed me one of the earphones but I refused.

'We're all De La Soul, now,' she said.

* * *

I had expected Salim and Nadia to pull together in the hour of need but, obviously, it was too much to ask. Their relationship had broken down completely but I hadn't realised how much until a couple of days before the charity match. I was having an uncomfortable morning, having to get rid of vast quantities of phlegm while trying to deal with the new sensation of being hunched over more than usual: no matter how much I tried to straighten my spine, it simply curved round again making my shoulders sag and my neck stiff. I felt a touch better when everyone had left for school or work but the pain and discomfort was its height when, at about 11am, Salim popped into the kitchen with another woman, who he introduced as Nikki. Wasn't he supposed to be at work? He grabbed a tube of Pringles and filled up a huge plastic bottle with water. He headed back outside. He acknowledged me but said nothing. About half an hour later, he came into the living room – where I was taking my lunchtime nap – and sat down beside me.

'Soz about that,' he said. 'You know it's finished between me and Nadia. That's Nikki; known her since sixth form. I'm moving in with her in a few weeks. It's difficult round here now, people are looking at us because of Wasim and all that shit. I know it might be hard for you but, believe me, it's rough for me too.' He got up and walked to the door. 'Oh, and please don't tell Nadia I brought Nikki here…'

'She's knows about your…arrangement?'

'She's known for ages.'

'Why do you need so much water?'

'Thirsty engine. I'm driving down to see the folks. They want to know about the raid and stuff.'

Salim's parents lived in Northampton. They had moved there after getting annoyed by the amount of community intrusion in Rochdale. The last time I saw them was at Fareeda's funeral. I wondered what they thought of their son now and his dalliances with his sixth–form sweetheart?

Salim walked off but turned around as though he'd remembered something. He walked towards me and stopped inches away.

'Got pregnant, didn't she,' he whispered in my ear. 'Fuck could I do?'

He offered a resigned shrug and walked out of the house. I wondered how long Nadia had known about these disgraceful antics. Months? Years? It didn't matter now because he was going. The sooner the better. We could take care of the Wasim issue ourselves. But something he said intrigued me. 'People were looking at us,' he said. I'd hardly been out so I wouldn't know. Were Edmund Street's beady eyes fixed on us? As far as I could tell, only Mr Shafiq had visited after the raid to ask how we were getting on and offer his sympathies. The rest had stayed away. In fact, many more had come when we had returned from Iraq. Were they scared or ashamed? With this in mind, I got changed and prepared to go out for a walk. The plan was to amble down to the Variety Food Store on Spotland Road and browse around for nothing in particular. That way I could gauge the mood of the locals and see how they responded to me. As usual, things didn't work out that way because my gorgeous–smelling socks (Nadia had bought a batch of ten online) led me to make fists of my toes and carry out soothing exercises with my feet. By the time I'd finished, Elisha came home from school and the momentum was gone. She was at least 15 minutes early and looked extremely glum. I was at the bottom of the stairs and she breezed past me without making eye contact.

'Have you been bullied?' I asked. 'Are they taunting you about your brother?'

'Don't be silly, nana jee,' she replied. 'I got a lift off Debbie's dad. That's why I'm early.' She got up to the top of the stairs and peered over from the landing. She hesitated and then spoke breathlessly. 'Rachel threatened me. She's been dumped by Ali but blames me for it. Ali asks me for advice and I give it. She just can't take it.'

Elisha waited on the landing for a moment and then disappeared into her bedroom. I walked up the stairs and stood outside her bedroom for a few minutes. Ali and Rachel's love affair wasn't exactly top of my to–do list but I felt Elisha needed my support so I knocked on the door and waited. She came to the door and had just unfastened her hair. The red lamp on her dressing table made her face glow. She had the same nose as Fareeda, I thought.

'If it's about my brother, I don't want to know,' she said.

In the days leading up the charity match, an image of Fareeda dominated my thoughts. She was captivated by a Play for Today drama in 1975 which involved a barrister called Rumpole. I had heard of the TV series *Rumpole of the Bailey* (although I had never watched it) but the story of that particular episode fired Fareeda's interest because a black man had been accused of a stabbing. I remembered having to get up early for my shift at Turners and went to sleep halfway through but Fareeda remained on her wicker chair, her eyes fixed on the flickering, black and white Ferguson TV. It was as though Fareeda was fantasising about what could happen to the son she never had in a hostile land far from home. That man on the stand could have been her son. Ours. Now, I felt Wasim was that boy. Nadia kindly dug out the drama for me on DVD. I learnt it was called *Rumpole and The Confession of Guilt*. I didn't enjoy it at all.

There was little benefit in all this Rumpole business but it did prepare me for a number of calls from Lawrence the lawyer. He wanted to glean some information from me but I had I absolutely no intention of encouraging him. He did get me thinking about the nature of the judicial process, however, and it didn't seem too appealing. I always imagined Crown Court as a Test match arena: the respectful hush of the public, a calming dash of cerebral white, barrister matchwinners putting shine on the ball and a jury in the pavilion absorbing every detail. The reality was probably more brutal, particularly in a terrorism case, but I had no desire to experience it. I could see myself coughing and slurring my speech when taking the stand. It was out of the question.

I put it all out of my mind on the Friday of the

match. Nadia made me a wonderful breakfast of pancakes, yoghurt and soft–boiled eggs which set me up perfectly for what I knew was going to be an extremely long day. Len had agreed to pick me up outside the Golden Mosque when afternoon prayers were finished. I hadn't been to a mosque for Friday prayers for 17 years. The two Eid's? Without fail: but once I left Turners, the small mosque–going community I had been part of was broken up and I simply made no effort to revive it. Once I started umpiring, this state of affairs became even more acute. So I walked into the Lower Sheriff Street mosque, where I'd been welcomed with open arms almost 40 years ago, and took off my shoes. I realised I hadn't done my wuzu and figured it would be too late now anyway so I soldiered on and carried out my prayers. If this impurity disqualified me from an official prayer then so be it: the charge sheet was long enough as it was. However, I noticed something else even more disturbing: my body was stiff and dangerously rigid. In fact, I found it so difficult to sit with my hands on my knees that I thought my ankles were going to break. It was an agonising experience – and I was thankful when the imam put me out of my misery and asked the packed hall to look east and west. It had been a mistake to come; I was ill–prepared.

I rushed out as soon as our cupped hands brushed over our faces. Thankfully, no–one recognised me, although I noticed the brothers Ghulam and Liaqat Deen from Pilling Street staring at me as I walked out. I didn't know them very well at all but that never stopped them from passing judgement on the apocalyptic state of the country – and why we should all go back to our real home. One day, I would put them straight. I walked out and enjoyed the cool breeze on my warm cheeks. I spotted Len in his daughter's Vauxhall Astra on the corner of Lower Sheriff Street and walked briskly towards him. The engine was running and he didn't notice me until I got in.

'You're early,' he said. 'Faith difficult to find, was it?'

'No, my body was…'

Len smiled and put a CD into the stereo. 'Look, I'm only driving this horrible thing as a favour to you. If it was up to me, I'd burn the lot of them.'

'You sound like my grandson.'

We both laughed and Len drove off. Dusty Springfield's *All Cried Out* played on the stereo. I knew this because Len told me it was Sylvia's favourite song. He couldn't stop talking about her on the way to the match. I felt hopeful again.

# 15.

Only in this town. Before the match began, two brothers called Wayne and Dan Turner entertained us royally by letting everyone at the club throw fruit at them, make fun of them, humiliate them and chase them round the pitch with cricket bats and balls. I didn't get it at first but, eventually, Len put me in the picture and it all became clear: Turner Brothers. Everyone wanted to have a go at them; that's what we were here for. I joined in and tried to hit Wayne with a pebble but missed by a long way.

But once the serious business of the match began, I soon realised I'd made a mistake by staying away so long. The pitch was like a green electric current fizzing through my body. Len and I smiled as we strode out into the serene strip of gold in the middle. I checked my pockets to ensure I had all the little treasures: bails, hanky, scorecard, coins, packet of Polos and, of course, pebbles. The bails came out and everything felt right again. A gust of wind blew them off the wickets the first time but once I replaced them, I felt a strange calm descend over me, as though I'd finally returned to a sacred and holy place. Play began about 10 minutes later. There was light applause as The Bosses' opening batsmen came out into the middle. They were booed and jeered mercilessly. The field was brought in by The Workers' captain Stuart Parrington so they were almost on top of the batsman. As the first gentle delivery came down, I was stood at square leg and the sound of willow onto leather provided the kind of comfort and longing I thought had gone forever. I felt alive again. As I strode forward after six balls, I stood behind the wicket and started counting those pebbles. The bowler ran past and delivered. It took an eternity to reach the other end but when it did The Bosses' opener smacked it away past point for four runs. The Bosses were in charge.

The match itself went very fast, particularly the second innings. A steady drizzle fell during the latter half of the innings but it didn't disrupt the game: we were used to inclement weather. At the interval, we enjoyed Sylvia's buttered scones, hefty tuna rolls and tangy lemon cake with custard. I was amazed how easily most of it went down. The Bosses eventually won the game by 62 runs after posting 132 in their 20 overs; the Workers' batting was woeful. Once it was over, Len disappeared with Sylvia even though the bugger said he'd stay with us for the entirety. It was the first time I regretted not bringing Nadia with me. Everyone was eating, chatting or drinking in the Pavilion suite while I looked and felt sheepish sitting at a table on my own. There was a buffet, specially prepared by Sylvia, but I had no room for any more food. I had made the decision to use the payphone at the club and call Nadia to pick me up when Stuart Parrington walked towards me, with a paper plate stacked full of pizza slices, onion–heavy salad and cheesy garlic bread. He also had a bottle of Holsten Pills dangling between his index and middle finger and smiled as he sat down next to me. He tried to start eating with his plastic fork but threw it across the table and picked up a pizza slice with his hands.

'Len's giving us a lift home,' he said, wiping the crumbs from his mouth. 'Did you come down with him?'

'Wished I hadn't...'

'He's in the kitchen with Sylv. Got his mojo back.'

There was an uncomfortable silence as Stuart finished his meal. I sensed he wanted to know how ill I was but was too afraid to ask. He took a lengthy swig of his bottle and grimaced.

'My dad collapsed a few yards from the mill but they still didn't give him a penny. Only 42–year–old and they made up fairy stories about a phantom lung condition.' He looked up at me and felt reassured enough to continue. 'Turnout was so shit today. I expected a few more to come down.'

'What was your father's name? I might have known him.'

'Robert...'

I shook my head.

'No–one really knew him,' said Stuart. 'He kept himself to himself.' Stuart's mobile phone beeped. He reached into his trouser pocket and checked his messages. 'Mam's asked me to pop into the offie on the way back. She wanted to come but didn't want to dredge it all up again.'

I pictured Stuart's mother sitting there in her flat, house or bungalow and wondered how many more people there were like her in and around the town. Lives shattered but no—one listening: an army of muted voices in the wilderness.

'We just take it in this country,' said Stuart. 'We go abroad and start wars but we sell our folk down the river.'

I took a deep breath and cleared my throat.

'So you didn't agree with Iraq, then?'

Stuart looked at me as if I'd propositioned his mother.

'Afghanistan was right, fuck the Tallie Scallies but Iraq's gonna make us bleed.'

Something within me shifted. I reached into my trouser pocket and laid the six pebbles across the table.

'Do you know where they're from?' I asked.

Stuart picked a couple of them up and rubbed them with his fingers.

'Probably, Hollingworth Lake, somewhere like that...'

I carefully picked one of them up.

'They're from Iraq.'

Stuart nearly choked as he took another swig of his beer.

'You're gypping us. Did some fucker fire them as bullets from a magic gun?'

I smiled and shook my head.

'Well, how the fuck did you get them, then? Did you go down there?'

I continued to look proud like a veteran soldier finally getting the praise he deserved.

'I went out there to spread the game.'

'Bull. They don't play cricket out there. Why would you go all that way for something like that?'

'It's true. They were quite enthusiastic. There was one boy – Madrid Boy I called him – who had a lot of potential.'

Stuart grinned and took another swig of beer. He took one of the pebbles and dropped it into the bottle. He looked through the bottle and watched it floating on the small amount of beer that was left.

'Nah, you must have gone for another reason.'

'That pebble's quite precious. Can I have it back?'

'It's being westernised…'

He continued to peer through the bottle.

'Don't lie like the government. Tell us why you went or I'll drop all six in the bottle…'

I had underestimated Stuart but, as Workers' captain, I shouldn't have. I remember Len telling me he was a member of UNISON and worked as a voluntary care worker in and around the town.

'It was for the cricket,' I said. 'I don't get involved in politics…'

Stuart picked up another pebble and plopped it into the bottle.

Before I could respond, I felt a hand on my shoulder. I turned around and saw Len wiping his hands on an apron. He sported the widest smile I could remember. It was the stroke of luck I needed, although it only lasted a few seconds.

'Am I still on for a lift then, Len?' asked Stuart.

'Aye, no problem. Primrose Street, yeah?'

Stuart held his bottle up to thank Len and then took a swig. One of the pebbles ended up in his mouth and he bounced it around for a while before spitting it out onto his hand. He smiled and offered it back to me.

'Used to being wet, aren't they?'

Len approached Spotland Bridge and slowed down. He had a Fisherman's Friend in his mouth and kept looking down at the screen of his mobile phone. I didn't know he actually had one. He told me it was a present from Sylvia. His constant flitting from mobile to windscreen made me nervous because the rain was teeming down and his windscreen wipers were failing to cope. I was in the back seat, keeping my eye on Stuart who was in the passenger seat without his seat belt on. He hadn't said anything since leaving the cricket club.

'Turn left here,' said Stuart.

'But Primrose Street is up the other way.'

'I know where I live. Just turn up here. I want to visit my gran.'

Len indicated left and then raised his hand impatiently to ask whether he should go up Edenfield Road or Rooley Moor Road. Somehow, I knew he'd point towards Rooley Moor Road. I felt a surge in my chest because I hadn't been up the 'Rock and Rooley' for nearly 20 years. As we drove up, I thought about the sons, daughters, mothers and fathers rushing away after marathon shifts, eager to get home for some warmth and comfort. They all headed away from a monstrous pit of reward and despair, unaware that, one day, it would become an irremovable stain on the face of the town. Yes, the giant factory had been demolished but, as we drove further up the road and the rain lashed down in a southerly direction, it was though the dirty fucking mill was having one last release at our expense.

'Turn right up here,' said Stuart.

'There's no way through there, lad,' said Len.

Woodland Road was inaccessible, or at least it looked that way, with the overgrown bushes on one side and green railings on the other. Len put his indicator on and pulled in, mounting the kerb. Stuart reached down into his bag, pulling out a Size 7 Duncan Fearnley bat and a munched–up cricket ball. What the hell was he doing? He opened the door and a violent waft of wind and rain swept over me making me shiver. He started running down Woodland Road and then, amazingly, slung the bat as far as it could go like a powerful hammer thrower. Len got out too but I was staying put whatever happened. I felt a jolt of icy air ravish my body and a mild sickness was also gathering. Stuart stopped and turned around.

'Where were the fuckin' mill? Here?'

Len shook his head: he'd never been up here before. I had, but I swear I couldn't remember this exact spot. Wasn't the mill behind us or further down the road? Everything looked different now.

'Come on lad, let's get you home,' said Len, walking back to the car.

Stuart raised his index finger to Len and then turned around. He dropped his trousers and started urinating on the long grass. 'FUCK YOU, MURDERERS,' he shouted. 'THIS IS WHAT YOU DESERVE.' He zipped his trousers up and smiled at us. He then ran ahead and picked up the cricket bat. He tossed the ball a few inches in the air and smacked it into the distance. He ran forward and disappeared into the woods. 'AZBASTARDS, AZBASTARDS… AZ–FUCKIN–BASTARDS…'

Len shook his head and got back into the car. He looked at me but I couldn't respond. My ears were ringing and my breathing was becoming extremely shallow. There was a sharp pain in my right shoulder making my body veer towards the left. I was beginning to drool and my mouth was drying up rapidly. I put my hand on the window in the hope of a fresh sensation but it just felt numb, cold and lifeless. My whole body felt as though it had just come out of an underheated swimming pool: shivery, sweaty and ever–so fatigued. Then I coughed – so painfully and acutely that I thought all my insides would come out – and tilted my head forward against the back of the passenger seat. I tried to reach over to Len and tap him on the shoulder but the power in my arms was diminishing by the second. I coughed again and the pain was unbearable. Black spots were appearing in front of my eyes. The weakness in my body was almost total. Oh how I'd love to see that chimney again. Love it.

\* \* \*

Bleeping sounds, heavily–equipped beds and plastic chairs. A nurse to the left washed her hands in the sink. A frail old woman lay in the bed by the window, oxygen mask on but eyes rolled up to the heavens; a young man, in overalls, sat by her side holding her hand. I tried to take a deep breath but my rock–like chest was buried under the spaghetti junction of wires and tubes. I felt as if a medicine cabinet had been dropped on my head with the flying wreckage of the pills and syringes wreaking havoc across my body. My snooker–ball eyes would surely pop out at any minute, the sickly–sweet mouth as dry as a desert. It was a relief to be lying down: it felt oddly blissful and safe.

The nurse looked over her shoulder and smiled. She quickly finished cleaning her hands and then disappeared. She returned a few minutes later with Nadia and Elisha. As I watched my daughter and granddaughter walk in, I longed again for Fareeda. Her soft hand on my ice–cold claw would have made everything all right again. Elisha walked ahead of her mother and approached me. She reached over and kissed me on the cheek. Her supple, delectable features shouldn't have to see this; it felt all wrong. Nadia sat down on the chair and put her hand on my leg.

'You're going to be fine,' she said. 'Why did you go up there?'

I mumbled a reply but it didn't come out too well. After licking my lips, the next one fared better.

'…Stu's idea.'

Nadia looked away from me. She gestured for Elisha to leave but Elisha shook her head. Nadia then shifted her chair forward and moved closer to me.

'You'll be moved to a ward tonight,' she said. 'You've been in for two days already. Pneumonia. If we keep the antibiotics going, you'll be fine.'

'…Don't fucking feel fine.'

The swearing felt good. No wonder, I felt so terrible: I'd been here for a couple of days, pumped relentlessly with wild drugs. My back was like an ironing board. Where the hell were we anyway? Instead of questions of mortality, I was thinking more about an article I'd read in the *Observer* that said emergency services might move to another town. Had we gone? Was I in some other Lancashire town or further afield? How about moving the whole fucking NHS service to India or something?

'We're in the infirmary,' said Nadia, in reply to my question. 'They won't be moving for years yet…'

'Mum's put in a request for Wasim to be allowed out for a few hours,' said Elisha. 'You know, just to see you and that…'

'It's unlikely,' said Nadia. 'Look, forget about him. I've tried to track down Dr Howarth to come and see you. I don't trust these other doctors.'

'I brought Fareeda here that morning…and now I'm here.'

Nadia tutted and grabbed my arm. 'Stop talking like that. That guy, Stuart, he's in the waiting room now. He wanted to see you and apologise but I said I'd ask you first.'

'…Later, not now.'

'Mum, tell him about the letter,' said Elisha. 'It'll make him happy.'

'Not now, Leesh.'

'If it's from Wasim, I don't want to know.'

Nadia shook her head. 'It's not from him. Anyway, you're not in any state for it now. Let's wait till we get you back in the ward.'

'I may not get in the ward. Who's it from?'

'NO! you'll find out later.'

'…Fareeda would tell me.'

Nadia took a deep breath and gave Elisha a cold look. She reached into her handbag and pulled out a tatty envelope, which had already been opened. I recognised the stamp on it immediately. A rush of adrenaline was unexpected and welcome.

'It came a couple of weeks ago,' said Nadia. 'It was addressed to you. I wanted to protect you from any more stress and trouble. But I was curious, so I read it. I felt I had a right after what I've been through.'

'Not a good habit; reading other people's mail.'

'You should know.'

Nadia put the envelope back in the handbag.

'Oi, what are you doing?'

'It's not the right time,' she said. 'It was from a man called Gulzar.'


The murmurs of improved breathing were felt after Len and Stuart visited me on the ward. It may have been a placebo effect but the small triumph of letting my chest expand while feeling about 30 per cent less pain was real. A small team of doctors came to do their rounds and confirmed my tentative analysis: they were happy with my progress, the antibiotics were working. I wasn't sure about that: I'd get a better understanding from Dr Howarth. But where was the lazy bastard? Didn't he care about his patients? At least, the asbestosis hadn't progressed, however, or at least that's what the tall, ever–so slim specialist said to me after a surprising late afternoon visit. He also asked me about Fareeda. It was a nice touch. I didn't need Dr Howarth after all.

In the evening, with the help of the nurse and Nadia, I sat up in bed for the first time. I was as stiff as a wicket and the breathing improvements I'd noticed earlier in the day had diminished. But I did manage to eat a light roll and some soup. Most of it got stuck in my throat and was thrown up but the rest brought some much needed strength. Nadia was on her mobile for most of the evening: she was in and out of the ward and didn't have many words left for me. I felt guilty about the amount of strain on her but was desperate to ask her about the Iraqi letter. She said she would read it to me later in the day but hadn't mentioned it all.

'What did Gulzar say?'

Nadia was eating an apple, texting on her mobile in deep concentration.

'Who?'

'The man from Iraq?'

Nadia continued to text and reached into her handbag with her other hand. She handed me the envelope. I took it tentatively and my shivering hands pulled out the letter. I opened it and then looked up at Nadia but she continued to tap the keys on her mobile. I was on my own.

*Dear Shah,*

*I hope you are well. When you left us, you seemed in better health and I hope this is the case. Playing on those beautiful green fields will surely help. Stay away from work at all costs!*

*I remember our time together in Iraq as though it was yesterday. You were a true friend and you brought so much wisdom and wonder to our blighted country. The situation has improved slightly since you left but not much.*

*As for my own situation, it has improved a great deal. Ibrahim's sister–in–law, Misha, and I have been engaged for three months and have decided not to wait too much longer to get married; people disappear very quickly over here so we don't want to have any regrets! It would have been great if you could have been here to give your blessing but I suppose we can't have everything.*

*But there are some people who are not happy with this union – not Ibrahim or his family, they have been very supportive – but others who feel I should have waited longer before banishing the memory of my first wife, my children and my parents. They have not been through the fire like some of us. They are the lucky ones: their families are well and their homes remain untouched. There are thousands of these green zones in the country. But I am no green zone. I need comfort and support like everyone else. Can I not start again?*

*My friend, I have rattled on like a UN session. I just wanted to share with you a little piece of joy I feel and desperately wished you could be over here to, how do you say, straight bat a few people. Obviously, that isn't going to happen but I hope you can be here in spirit.*

*One more thing, although it is a trivial one. A British man came to my house – God knows how he got the address – and asked a few questions about Wasim. He seemed to know a lot about him but wouldn't tell me the nature of his business. So I told him nothing and he sloped off. Looked like a legal man to me. Takes one to know one!*

*Is Wasim okay back at home? I hope all is well. He was a confused boy and I pray for him. I'm sure he won't think of going against the family again.*

*And finally, I hope you kept those pebbles. Spread them around in that little town of yours to show solidarity with the ever–suffering people of our country.*

*Your eternal friend, Gulzar.*

I folded the letter and looked up at Nadia. She was already looking right into my eyes. She had a tear in her eye. She got up and carefully took the letter out of my hands.

'Wasim's not worth getting upset about,' I said.

'Who says it's about him?'

Nadia put the letter in her handbag.

'Elisha's cooked an omelette for the first time,' she said, smiling as the tears rolled down her face. 'She's bringing it over this evening.'

I was discharged after five days. I could barely walk and the cold was tearing into my bones but I understood the need for beds for sicker people than me. I couldn't avoid the sight of my bed being manically stripped and prepared for the next poor bugger unfortunate enough to be wheeled in; hundreds of Turner victims must have passed through these wards, I thought. Len, who hadn't said much throughout my stay, helped me get into the back of the Nadia's car. He then walked off and said he'd catch the bus despite Nadia urging him to get into the car. I could understand Len's concern about my health but his gait and manner were less assured than I remembered them. But it didn't take long for me to understand why. Nadia told me he had broken up with Sylvia again which wasn't really a surprise – but the reason given by Sylvia could have plunged me back into A&E immediately. Sylvia blamed Len for being two and a half times over the limit – and nearly getting me killed in the process. I felt that was harsh: the weather – and perhaps the stress levels – were the main factors in my sudden deterioration but was it really true that Len – careful, precise, safe Len – had downed a few before taking the wheel that night? He would have never contemplated such a thing. Love may have been in the air but Len always saw the bigger picture. Nadia then handed me a recent copy of the *Observer*, opened at the relevant page.

### DRINK DRIVING UMPIRE SUSPENDED

This was Len we were talking about? He had been breathalysed at the infirmary after bringing me in. He had been arrested and spent the night in a cell. He was to appear at Magistrates Court in a few days. He had been suspended by the cricket club until the case was settled. I didn't read the whole story: I felt sick. The charity match felt like a distant memory now. Did it really happen? How much was raised? I didn't know; I didn't care. I simply wanted to get home and plant my head underneath the sheets for a long time – and read Gulzar's letter again for some hope.

After visiting Wasim in Strangeways one rainy afternoon, Nadia tentatively suggested we should move out of Edmund Street when I got better. She said it wasn't because anyone had sent hate mail or been abusive – on the contrary, most people had been supportive – but because she felt 'soiled' due to the raid. After a short discussion, however, she withdrew the suggestion saying it was a 'demented' idea in the first place. For the first time, I sensed I was becoming a burden on my daughter.

During those early days back in that misty bedroom, I wondered how Wasim was getting on in that horrible cult prison, although I did read a story in the *Manchester Evening News* that it had improved in recent times. No matter, I would never set foot in there. This was not because of any fear of criminals, I had been to a war zone after all, but more the strength and toxicity of antibiotics, pills and other medication which were leading to more disturbing symptoms of anxiety and mood fluctuation. Yes, my body was the main reason I couldn't go very far – the stony chest, the spine curving by the day and the matchstick legs – but I was afraid the man Wasim would see in front of him would act less appropriately than some of the inmates he shared the prison with. So I chose to do the next best thing: ask Nadia to hastily dictate a couple of letters on my behalf and send them to the young lad. That would keep his spirits up. I still believed he'd be found innocent, without my input.

Len, however, wasn't so lucky – or maybe he was. He was fined £1,500 and banned from driving for 12 months. He walked a lot anyway so I hoped it wouldn't bother him much. He rang Nadia to pass on the message to me. He apologised for not telling me about it at the hospital. Thankfully, the cricket club lifted his suspension. I sensed he was embarrassed because Alice was so desperate for her mother and father to get back together. Alice being a copper probably didn't help either. But I felt he should have come round so we could have talked things over like we always did. I missed him, particularly at about 4.30pm on weekdays.

But I did have Gulzar's letter to keep me going. Nadia had 'loaned' it to me and I kept it under my pillow for comfort. On cold, dark nights I reread it and thought about the sweltering days we spent together in Baghdad: his house a little corner of calm in amongst the carnage and destruction. I dreamed that, one day, Gulzar and Misha would turn up on my doorstep and have dinner in the house. After lunch one afternoon – which consisted of a soft jacket potato and runny lentils – I even envisaged them sat at the dinner table offering tales of romantic scrapes, wild gunfire and epic family gatherings. But they were not there and Nadia snapped me out of it. She was sitting at the dinner table, hands on her chin, looking out of the window having not eaten her stodgy jacket potato. She had been very irritable all afternoon, since coming home for lunch from university.

'Amjad, our nice solicitor, told the police about Wasim's activities,' she said. 'Wasim told him in complete confidence about the Iraq stuff.'

There was a long silence during which I tried to absorb what Nadia was telling me. After dabbing the potato skin leftovers on my empty plate with a spoon, I finally realised the seriousness of her revelation.

'But we invited him into our home,' I said. 'To deal with Turners…'

'Doesn't matter now. He's moved to Birmingham, to join a better firm.' She got up and started clearing the dishes. 'We can't even send him any hate mail.'

'But I thought they were friends. How could he give him up like that?'

She held the plates in her hand and looked straight at me.

'Because Wasim's a terrorist in everyone's eyes but ours.'

# 16.

Nadia decided to set a routine for me every Sunday morning. I didn't enjoy being taken out of my comfort zone but once Elisha had cooked breakfast for me – usually an overlarge and wonky–shaped omelette – I was nicely fuelled–up and gave her mother the benefit of the doubt. So at 10am for the next few months, we got into her car and drove to Hollingworth Lake. It may have been less than four miles away but it felt like forty. Generally, the pattern was the same: take a walk on the ragged beach, watch the geese gather and then find a secluded spot to sit down and eat the sandwiches Nadia had made for lunch. Occasionally, Nadia would get chips and mushy peas from Mr Thomas's chip shop – while I continued to watch the boats sail by – but this only happened when she was chirpier than usual which wasn't often. One time, on a busy Sunday, we were sat on a wooden bench watching the smooth contours of the waves when Nadia pulled out a folded, orange sun hat and rested it on her lap.

'Mama used to pull this right over my head,' she said. 'She hated seeing my head bare.'

'You must have been ten when you first wore it?'

'Seven. You're three years out.'

She pushed opened the hat with her palms. She tried to put it on her head but it was much too small for her and slipped from her clutches, landing underneath the bench. She picked it up and handed it to me.

'When I read Gulzar's letter, all our troubles didn't seem that bad,' she said. 'Your illness, Wasim's arrest, Salim's shagging, Amjad's sneakiness…It put it all in perspective.'

'Salim and Amjad are history. I'd kick them into the sea if they were here.'

She offered her first smile of the day and got up off the bench. But she didn't move forward, she simply stood with her arms folded. The silences from her were becoming more frequent. On average, this was a short one, followed by a mild cough.

'I saw this woman on the news a couple of years ago,' she said. 'Probably Pakistani or Kashmiri…she was outside her house looking bewildered as TV crews asked her about her terrorist suspect son. She had a very bright shalwar kameez and looked odd in front of these suited men pushing mikes and tape recorders under her nose. I didn't feel sorry for her; I pitied her because she was so powerless and vulnerable. I thought to myself: 'Why doesn't she say something? I'll never be like that'. Well, fuck me do, here we are…'

She reached down and picked up a pebble. She threw it as far as she could and then sat down on the bench again. I wanted to say something but I couldn't get the image of that woman being hounded by news crews out of my mind. She was the kind of woman I knew well. Hundreds of them came over as brides every year. Fareeda was like that woman; the only difference was she would have responded to those media hordes. Of course, she would.

'Who's to blame for Wasim?' said Nadia, turning immediately to me after a long pause. 'Me or you?'

She lowered her gaze so I knew she was being serious.

'No–one is…come on, Nadia…'

She looked away. 'Well, someone is because he's one fucked–up boy…' After a minute or so, her mobile beeped and she reached into her handbag. She scrolled down the messages. She shook her head and laughed. 'How about the father? Salim still texts me about a pair of jeans he left here, a tube of toothpaste left there, a fucking towel and so on…some people. He might even remember his son one day.'

'Did he visit?'

'He's been a few times but Wasim generally blanks him…'

She put her mobile away and looked towards the lake again. 'Wasim never knew what he wanted,' she said. 'He changed his interests almost every week: one week it was boxing, then cars, then martial arts, then bodybuilding and then…well, we know the rest. I remember him coming in one day, just before his 17th birthday, doing a Black Panther salute and then punching his sister quite hard on the shoulder. It was quite scary. He seemed to like too many things but nothing very deep. I know people say these lads aren't integrated but they're wrong. They're integrated all right, they're just not immersed. Elisha's totally immersed culturally, that's the difference.'

She walked forward a little and smiled at an elderly couple walking past. 'But the funny thing is while all that's been going on, I had this stupid idea for a fashion business…' She came back and sat on the bench. '…Elisha wore a hijab round the house for a while. At the time, I thought it was a plain, colourless garment and then the other day, I saw a woman wearing one with a small US flag on it and it just hit me – hijandchips.com – I could create stylish hijabs with British icons or landmarks. Some would have fish and chips on them, some would have famous buildings, some would have images of famous films. It would give these young Muslim girls another choice and a sense of belonging. The idea didn't seem that stupid after all.'

I started to cough and laugh at the same time. 'Hitch and chips, what kind of stupid name is that?'

'HIJ…short for hijab!'

She was serious too, which was slightly worrying. But something else was happening while we were having this mildly flippant conversation. My eye became fixed on the beautiful red boat in the distance that was sailing away quicker than all the other boats. The more I looked at it, the more my chest and throat tingled. The air I was breathing in became crisper and fresher. I could take deeper breaths as I became almost hypnotised by the moving red boat. It then slowed down as another boat caught up and eased by its side. I turned to look at my daughter and she was watching me. I smiled and took her hand.

'Are those chips from Mr Thomas any good?'

I could not deny it: the Hollingworth Lake Sundays, as I called them, were improving my condition – albeit slightly and with little reduction in pain. I still had to wear three layers of clothing in bed – sometimes a hat too to cover my head – and there was still the hot and cold flushes tingling across my body, particularly, on bitterly cold mornings. But the biggest difference was in mobility and breathing. I could bend down and get my shoes from under the settee, talk on the phone without getting a thumping migraine and do windmills of my arms without getting extreme pain in my chest. Elisha also helped with light stretching exercises which helped unstiffen my arms and shoulders. During this time, Dr Howarth turned up at our front door to surprise us all. He was happy with my progress but felt I should do more physiotherapy. How much could an old man do? Was it an official visit? Did specialists usually turn up on doorsteps or was it a rogue trip? He stayed for rather a long time and told me he couldn't see me in the infirmary because he had been on a short break in Wales with his wife. It was his first holiday for eight years. They were extremely overstretched at the infirmary and he was worried about the changes his local health Trust were bringing in which included the moving of wards and possible closure of A&E. I was surprised he was so candid. It was always nice to hear fresh gossip but the less I heard about hospitals and infirmaries the better.

A few days letter I received a letter from Wasim. He said he felt guilty that he couldn't conjure up 'a magic potion' to cure my health. He also gave me a detailed account of his journey to 'Bad Mington Court' as he called it. He was escorted by a guard who was also an Oldham Athletic fan: they got on well and spoke of the so–called 'racial segregation' in the town which they felt had been 'blown up out of proportion'. He also told me about his 'school dinner' food, the 'shitty' mags he was reading and the 'ever–shrinking' walls he had to look for 'endless' hours a day. He signed off with 'all the best' and not 'Allah Hafiz' which got me thinking about his state of mind and whether faith was still playing a big part in his life; there wasn't a single reference to 'Allah' at all. I felt better after reading his letter but it didn't last long when Nadia came in and told me he'd been in a fight with an inmate a few hours ago. When the hell was his trial anyway? Couldn't they get the kangaroo hearing over with? The boy was obviously suffering. Wasim's state of mind would provide more ammunition for the salivating national scribes and the *Manchester Evening News*. If I had the strength, I would spend every day in Hollingworth Lake while the trial was on.

Gradually, a six–day routine was now set for me and I was working within my limitations. The period between 8.30am, when the house went quiet because Elisha and Nadia had left for school and work, was the most difficult and restless. I tried reading the *Observer*, watching TV shows like *Homes Under the Hammer* or taking a walk in the tiny garden but none of them gave me any comfort as I waited for the clock to run down until Nadia rushed home to cook me lunch. She was often late but it was worth the wait to see her face come through that door. Some days, she didn't have any lectures in the afternoons at all, so I felt I wasn't being too hard on her. After lunch, I took my medication and then a peaceful nap which helped propel me to the time when Elisha came home. We did a few stretches together and got into lengthy conversations (which she always won) about discipline in schools, poor teachers and religious figures. I admired Elisha's enthusiasm and thirst for knowledge. She claimed she had only caught this bug because she had become close friends with Hannah Reece in the past six months. Hannah wanted to be a relief worker because the 'world was going to shit' and she didn't want to do the same job as her mother who was an adviser at Rochdale Job Centre. She said she would leave school at 16 and travel the world: I hoped Elisha would not do the same. These hours with my granddaughter flew by and dinner always came so soon. The only downside was Elisha provoked me into talking so much that I was ready to go to bed immediately after the meal, generally before 9pm.

But then on one frosty Autumn morning, when I could hear the hailstone smacking against the bedroom window, it all changed. I went downstairs and saw Elisha in the kitchen preparing breakfast for me. She was on half–term holidays and looked extremely relaxed. She had the radio on: a ghastly, ferocious racket fit for an invading army. I mumbled

271

a few words but she couldn't hear me. So I switched the radio off.

'Oh nana jee, I was enjoying that!' said Elisha.

'Is your mother here?'

Elisha gestured to the back garden and turned the radio back on. I tentatively stepped forward and opened the back door. I stepped out and a swirling blend of wind and hail blew into my face causing me to stumble. Nadia was sitting on the steep steps in front of me with her back to me and hailstones nestling evenly in her shoulder–length hair. She heard the door open and turned around. She swiped her hand through her hair to shake off the flaky hail.

'It was as cold as this on the morning Mama died,' she said, blinking as the drops of hail fell into her eyes. 'Even though the sun was out.' She turned away and looked out of the garden into the tight terracing of Pilling Street with its imposing row of chimneys. 'She was right about Salim, wasn't she? Maybe, I should have listened to her.' She looked up at me and smiled. 'Should have taken my chances on Zain; first cousin marriage, genetic deformity and all that…'

I walked forward and put my hand on her shoulder. 'Come inside. It's too cold.'

'It's early, I've got the day off. Mags and Sheena are coming round later to talk about our new business. They can warm me up.'

I sighed and was unsure of what to do next. There was room for me to sit down on the cold, harsh step but I didn't fancy it. I looked over my shoulder and noticed Elisha gesturing to me that breakfast was nearly ready.

'Two girls have stopped talking to me at uni,' said Nadia, wrapping her arms round her knees and resting her head on her forearms. 'A lecturer's also been a bit funny; abrupt and to the point. Even Ali's staff at the kebab shop have been staring more than usual. I've joined the dots. My boy's a wrong un...'

'Don't be stupid,' I said, sitting down awkwardly by Nadia's side, grimacing as my knee cracked painfully. My buttocks felt as hard as the stony step.

'People respect you a bit more, Daddy. They won't give you gyp. They think I can take it.'

'You've taken enough now. Do you want me to visit Wasim – and meet Lawrence too?'

Nadia sprung up from her relaxed, semi–lying posture. She looked at me for a few moments and then shook her head. She put her hand on mine. 'But you're not well enough. That's why I've protected you from all of this stuff so far. I can manage. Looks like Wasim's got an uphill battle anyway.' She released her hand and looked down Pilling Street again. 'Mention the 't' word these days – and you're a goner, no ifs or buts.'

'Don't talk like that,' I said, grabbing her hand again. 'He's a changed boy. He wants to do good things for people.'

'Daddy, you're so naïve.'

I coughed and felt a gush of wind cutting into my neck. I let go of her hand and got up. 'Naivety is what got you into this country in the first place.'

Nadia smiled and playfully tapped me on the leg as I departed. 'Anyway, the trial date's being put back all the time. Complex investigation and all that. Yeah right.'

I opened the back door and prepared to walk in.

'I don't think you should get involved,' said Nadia. 'I'll never forgive myself if anything happens to you.'

'I'll be fine. I'm doing this for you, not for him.'

The nights leading up to the prison visit, in terms of sleep, were niggly, scratchy affairs. I kept thinking about my failure to assess the strain and burden on my daughter. She had been going through a much tougher time than I expected. On one particular morning – in the early hours – I was so occupied by Nadia's slight drop in standards in terms of her cooking that I staggered to the bathroom and threw up a pathetic amount of liquid while trying to deal with a searing pain just above my stomach. When I got back into bed, there was already a small pile of vomit near my pillow which I hadn't noticed. I felt angry for punishing my body more than required.

But as so often happens, on the very same morning, Len turned up at the front door to relegate my problems so far down the chain that I questioned whether I had been sick at all. He was extremely apologetic and, in chronological detail, told me how he had come to take the wheel of his car after having a tipple at the charity cricket match. He had an unlit Woodbine and a glass of Ribena in his hand and spoke of being 'high on a romantic cloud' and 'wanting to prolong the night'. He shouldn't have bothered: I needed him so much I even let him light up the fag indoors – while I retreated as far away as possible to the corner of the sofa.

'Come to Strangeways,' I said, making a calculated judgement that the moral balance of power was in my favour.

Len looked surprised and rested his forearm on the mantelpiece. He took a drag of his Woodbine and looked in the mirror, pushing his cap back a little. 'There's something you need to know.' He turned and looked directly at me. 'A fella called Bernie Kershaw was in the stands at the charity cricket match. He runs a successful business called Kershaw Kip Ltd: it sells beds, sofas and furniture. Anyhow, he contacted me after the match and told me his father has died of Mesothelioma – another Turners victim. So he wanted to make a big donation and start a campaigning charity that helps local victims. He's got a name in mind too: Pride of Our Town.'

'Good name…'

'Well, he does that sort of stuff for a living. But that's not all. He's also got a long–term plan to buy up the old Turners site and bring his company to town. You know, create some jobs and all that.'

'But it's polluted?'

'Even if it is, he reckons the people in town will trust him to clean it up rather than some outsiders.'

I looked doubtful and used the armrest to get up from the sofa. I walked to the dinner table and picked up my paracetamol tablet and glass of water. 'Great. But why are you telling me?'

'Because I'm packing up my umpiring.'

I dropped the tablet into my mouth but the dryness of my mouth led to the tiny white pill getting stuck in my throat, causing a bitter sensation and a painful bout of choking. Len walked over and ensured I got the water down in safe fashion. 'Come on swallow, hard now.' He helped me sit down at the dinner table and I finally got the tablets down my throat.

'Had a good innings but I want to do something else now,' said Len. 'Something really helpful for the community in this town. I had a chance decades ago to be elected and it didn't happen for us. Now I could make a real difference. This fella knows his onions. He told us there were a law lords ruling lately that said people with pleural plaques, asbestosis in other words, weren't allowed to get compensation. This has made him a bit mad – and that's why he's started this campaign, just for this town.'

I settled down and finished the glass of water, which was nowhere near enough. 'But you said umpiring was in your blood...'

'It was, but worse things get into your blood and you have to fight them.'

The instant headrush from the tablets forced me to get up and walk back to the sofa to lie down. I picked up a cushion and balanced it on my forehead.

'Checked him out proper, this businessman?' I asked.

'It's been going on a couple of months now. His assistant – or what–have–you – has been communicating with me. They've got a man doing the website already and the charity's in the process of being registered so we're already up and running.'

'How many jobs does he think he can create?'

'About 200 at least, he says, but who knows? It's a long process with the planning application, building work and, you never know, there might be protests too.'

I slowly lifted the cushion from my forehead and rolled over onto my left side, with my back to Len. 'So many martyrs in this town…'

'Not the word I'd use but I follow you. There are literally hundreds of people in this town suffering, or at risk, from this disease and it's my duty to help them. And you, of course.'

I sighed and rolled back onto my right side. 'So are you coming to Strangeways or not?'

Len shook his head and took a final drag of his Woodbine before stubbing it out on his own portable ashtray on the mantelpiece. 'Sixty eight years without having stepped in a single jail cell or prison and now you want us to do two in the same year?'

'Just make sure you don't have any Vodka in the car.'

Len smiled and slowly raised his index finger for the last time.

Nadia's mood had changed: the twin appointments of visiting Wasim and meeting Lawrence had been organised. She even agreed, after a feisty exchange, to let Len take me to Strangeways. But as I watched Len drive down the A56 from the back seat, I knew I had made a mistake. Wasim's environment was causing me anxiety. How bad was Category A status? How big was his cell? Did he eat enough? Did he get enough exercise? Was there any Islamophobia? It was a stupid oversight on my part. Due to the exceptional family circumstances, I felt Nadia's presence may have caused a tense, claustrophobic experience but it was actually the opposite: I had much less freedom with Len; I couldn't tell him what was on my mind. Wasim's dreadful plight was engaging me so much that, as we approached the red–brick, Victorian building with its tall, fountain–pen tower and dome, I even envisaged this thuggish institution as a mosque: replace the red bricks with Arabic calligraphy and the minaret and dome are already present, I thought. If Nadia was here, none of this silliness would have come to the surface.

But I needn't have worried. About 25 minutes after we arrived, Nadia suddenly appeared – out–of–breath, slightly red and with her hair straggling down one side of her face – to insist I couldn't go into the jail alone. Len had helped me to the entrance and then, stubbornly, went back to sit in the car because he was adamant 'family business was nowt to do with him'. I had already been searched from top to tail, frightened by a metal detector and frisked so hard I thought the guard's giant hands would be stuck to my body for ever. Of course, I had been prepared for it but it was more invasive and disturbing than I expected. Nadia got through the search much quicker and had some banter with the guards. We eventually got in to see Wasim about 15 minutes later than scheduled; reducing the visit to 45 minutes.

The visiting area was like a giant, disused canteen with endless rows of wooden tables with numbers on them like C2 or D4. There were embedded plastic chairs on each side of the table – one side red, one blue – and a raised wooden parting in the centre to separate prisoners and visitors. The ceiling didn't look level and the orange rails, boulders and bars across the windows completed the suffocating, imposing environment. There were also a few tall, anorexic plants dotted around, the odd vending machine and, of course, a few white–shirted guards. One of the guards was sat cross–legged on a podium, elevated above the prisoners, looking down on the rabble like a king on his throne.

We took our seats and counted three families already in there, talking to their young men, no doubt cursing their hard–luck stories. We waited a couple of minutes and, eventually saw Wasim approach us wearing an odd–looking green vest – like a lifejacket – and an extremely loose pair of grey tracksuit bottoms. As he walked towards us, I was sure it was a completely different person: he was bulkier, smaller and had more white in his eyes than I'd ever seen in Wasim. A few feet away, and the trick of the mind disintegrated as fast as it had arrived: it was my grandson all right; he had either been eating raw meat or spending hours in the gym – or both. He looked quite enthusiastic and sat down opposite us. He reached over the centre partition and touched my hand.

'Big respect for being here, nana jee,' he said. 'Heard about the pneumonia stuff: what does the doctor say?'

'Better now – but I've got Nadia to look after me…'

Wasim laughed in a loud, scattergun manner.

'Course…' he said, trying to get the next word out as he continued to laugh. '…It ain't gonna be my Dad who's gonna tuck you up at night.' He was laughing so much that he drew the attention of the guard at the podium who was watching our table. 'My old man taught me a lot. He was in here the other day and couldn't stop apologising for leaving Mama to deal with all this shit. He's always been there for me but not there, if you know what I mean. What's the reason for him fucking off anyway? He obviously didn't have the balls to tell us.'

There was a moment of silence. I looked at Nadia and a knot of strangulation floated across my throat but thankfully it passed.

'I get it. As usual, I'm the last to know. I'll find out soon enough when he comes running back home.'

'Like you did?' said Nadia.

'Mama, don't start.'

Nadia closed her eyes and ran her forefinger and thumb down the bridge of her nose. 'Your nana jee's here for you.' She opened her eyes but didn't look at

Wasim. 'He's going to talk to Lawrence later in the week. People are more inclined to believe his story than yours.'

Wasim gave his mother a cold look but her gaze was elsewhere.

'How are they treating you in here?' I asked.

'Eh?'

'Are you getting on okay?'

'Er, yeah. I suppose there were one little thing but it weren't much. One of the guards wanted me demonstrate how we pray and, as I went down to place my forehead on the ground, he shouted 'the last prisoner pissed right there, where your lips are' and then walked out of the cell. There's been a couple of other name–calling things but that's about it. I do seem to get wound up much quicker though. I need to get out of here so I can get back to helping you, nana jee. We're gonna fight those mill crimes to the death.'

'Let's get you out first and deal with the rest later.'

'Did you put him up to this?' asked Wasim, looking at Nadia. 'He's fucking ill, don't you understand? He nearly died when he was Iraq – and now you want to him to drop dead in court. Fucking hell, missus!'

I tried to swallow but the shortness of breath was immediate and severe. A big ball of saliva had formed in my mouth, but after licking my lips and dry mouth, my chest expanded and the breathing returned to a manageable rate.

'We're not in Iraq now,' I said. 'We're in jail. If you don't want my help, I can find the door.'

Wasim grimaced and held his head in his hands. He unlocked them and did a slow neck roll. He looked over his shoulder at the guard, giving him a resigned, nonchalant look.

'I used to think big, very big, but this place makes you think small,' he said. 'If I could go back in time and find that man who roped us in, I'd deck him...'

'Who do you mean?' I asked.

Nadia rolled her eyes and looked disinterested.

'Shareef, the lad who worked at the pharmacy, told us a new imam had come in from Muscat and was living in Blackburn,' said Wasim. 'I think I'd just turned 16 at the time and there was a general election campaign going on. I remember that because Shareef said he wanted to vote. Anyhow, Shareef told us this guy was the dog's bollocks, fucking amazing, and we had to listen to what he had to say. He said it would blow our minds. There weren't much to do around Spotland so Liaqat and me agreed to see what the fuss was about...' He took a deep breath. '...I need a fuckin' spliff now.'

'You're in the right place,' said Nadia.

'Anyhow, we got there and it was some kind of community centre and there were only about 15 to 20 people there. They were all watching this weird bloke with a Cossack–type hat and a long robe standing out front with a table by his side. On the table, there were a can of Coke, a wad of dollar bills, a can of Heinz baked beans and a record player...'

'Do we really need all the details?' said Nadia, with a weary sigh.

'No, but nana jee wants them. Anyhow, as the Cossack bloke talked, I laughed at most of what he was saying. He said Coke written backwards said 'No Mohammed, No Mecca'. Then he said the all–seeing eye on every dollar bill was to do with the Freemasons and world domination. Then he played Madonna's *Like a Prayer* backwards and said she was singing 'Oh hear us Satan'. By the time he got to the baked beans, we were giggling so much we didn't pay attention.'

There was a moment of silence as Wasim's relish at telling this story turned to something more reflective.

'...But then he got onto serious stuff. He showed us a map of Arab countries before 1916 and then after. He showed us the oil fields. He showed us the flags of the new lands and the Royals and dictators who controlled them. He then told us how America had become the global superpower. Honest to God, I'd heard nothing like it at school. It made me think about the world in a completely different way. Everything I was seeing on the telly was making sense now. No–one spoke in the hall. We are all eating out of this man's hands. Not the baked beans but you know what I mean. We must have gone to about 30 or 40 speeches in all. They just got more and more interesting.'

Nadia glanced at me. 'He told me he was watching Oldham Athletic at Boundary Park with his mates. I didn't even know what division they were in, never mind when the season ended.'

'Yeah, guilty on that one Mama. I did go to the last home game of the season against Stoke though. Bit of trouble that night too.'

He stopped talking abruptly and looked beyond the both of us. I waited to see if he had really finished because his speed of delivery was wild and unpredictable.

'…The day I heard about the Kashmir quake, I decided to fly out immediately,' he said. 'I couldn't stay here and watch the suffering. Mum told me not to go but she was hardly around anyway. I didn't get the grades for the university I wanted – and I didn't want to go anywhere else – so I thought why not? I tried to look for a job after my A–levels but there was nothing around so I just thought 'I'm off'.' He shook his head and banged the table with his fist. 'People disposed of, man, just like that. Made me sick.' He chuckled nervously. 'Then, of course, we had Iraq. I didn't want to go, at first, but then I saw that chipmunk's face on a TV in Quetta. Wanted to bash it in.'

I moved forward, laying my hand carefully on his. 'I hope you've been completely truthful to the solicitor. It's the only way we'll get out of this.'

'Course I have, like WMD, it's the only way to be. I don't recognise this court but, for you, nana jee, I'll make an exception.'

'I'm being serious Wasim. I'm worried sick about you. That's why I'm doing all this. Nadia is worried sick about you too…'

'Yeah, yeah, I get it. Families are good at worrying.

Honest to God, I'd rather be back in Iraq than this shithole. The Baath Party's got nothing on these screws.'

'Speaking of Iraq, I got a letter from Gulzar...'

Wasim interrupted with a laugh. 'Phew, that's another story. That first Iraqi letter I sent to you was a real mission. There was no postal service in Baghdad, so we had to smuggle that out by other means, through other countries...'

I waited for his laugh to die down. 'Coming back to the point,' I said. 'Gulzar said someone was asking questions about you. They were probably looking for evidence for this case.'

Nadia sighed and folded her arms. 'They've got someone already.'

'What?' I swung round and looked at Nadia.

'I don't remember the name but Lawrence told me the prosecution have a strong Iraqi witness. I didn't tell you because I wanted to protect you...'

I looked at Wasim. 'Did you know about this?'

Wasim laughed. 'Nana jee, of course, I knew about it. Larry Legal has been pummelling the questions my way for yonks. Mama and I felt it was right to keep you away from all of this.'

'So who is it then, this Iraqi witness?'

'...What was his name, Mama? Shakeel something?'

'He's just given a witness statement. Lawrence hasn't met him.' Nadia moved closer to me and put her arm on my shoulder. 'Look Daddy, forget about it. Maybe this was a stupid idea after all. You shouldn't have got roped into it. Whatever happens will happen. I can call off the meeting with Lawrence. He won't mind. We've got an uphill battle anyway.'

I coughed and looked at the guard on the podium. He uncrossed his legs and put his hands behind his head. His security face could have earned a nice little number in Iraq, I thought.

'…I don't remember anyone called Shakeel.'

# 17.

Lawrence put me at ease straight away. His shoulder rose each time he started a sentence but, apart from this oddity, his grasp of our tricky situation was admirable in its calmness and candour. He spoke briefly about my illness and made me promise that I would stop him if things got too detailed or too sensitive. Nadia was also there, in the front room, but not always paying attention. To begin with, Lawrence took an hour or so over lunch savouring the delicate pakoras and chutney she had prepared along with the chicken biryani. Then we spoke about his time in the East Coast of America and how he felt it had toughened him up in terms of the work ethic and dedication needed to become a solicitor. Even then, Lawrence didn't begin the serious stuff: he talked about his father – who was a PE teacher at Green Hill School (later Falinge High) and how he'd wanted him to be a professional Rugby Union player. He did try it, he said, but ended up preferring Rugby League, much to his father's annoyance. So we finally got to the important business, late in the afternoon, by which time I was stiff and tired. Lawrence sensed my unease and rattled on. He listed the things in our favour: my appearance would 'push the emotional buttons' of the jury and, therefore, the chance of an acquittal for Wasim was greater; the ECB (England and Wales Cricket Board) had been contacted and given a glowing reference specifically naming me as spreading cricket in Iraq and being a force for good; my Turner Brothers story would elicit sympathy; a sick grandfather travelling thousands of miles on a rescue mission; and so on. He also said something very interesting about whether Wasim's so–called crimes could be deemed as such because they were committed during what some people would call an illegal occupation. There was much more (something about public interest immunity, whatever that meant) but I couldn't absorb it all and needed a toilet break. When I came back, Lawrence had a laptop on his knees and was bashing away ferociously and then looking at his watch.

'Nadia told me there's an Iraqi witness,' I said, walking back to sit down on the armchair.

'Shakeel Ali Hameed,' he replied, glancing up from his laptop. He sighed and lowered the cover of the laptop so it was nearly closed. 'Don't worry yourself about the prosecution's case: it's pretty strong and that's not going to change. They've got an imam from Blackburn, witnesses from Rochdale, a grocery seller from Quetta, someone from Iraq… quite a few people all saying the same thing: that our Waz was a GI Joe; in this climate it won't be easy to go up against that lot. But now we've got something in our favour: you. I think you can swing it for us.'

I felt quite important as I sat down and picked up my mug of cardamom tea. I took a sip and looked at Nadia, who was fiddling about with her mobile. She glanced up and sensed I was mildly pleased that Lawrence had come to the house. She smiled and carried on poking the mobile keypad with her fingers.

'You know, it's odd, but I believe that Waz made an innocent, stupid mistake,' said Lawrence, warming to his task. 'Yes, it was dangerous, of course, but so was I when I was speeding down the motorway doing 120 while high on weed at the age of 19. Young people do bad things – but the key question is: has he changed? Is he doing those things now? I think the answer is no.'

Lawrence's powerful voice almost made me want to march down to the court now. I imagined myself out in the middle of a packed court, being probed by a sneaky barrister but giving him as good as I got. I would pepper my assured oratory with confident glances at the jury so they'd be in no doubt where the balance of truth lay. The arena would be tailor–made for me and the calm, composed delivery of my story – with the Turners tale at its heart – would see them eating out of my hand.

'I can't wait forever,' I said. 'When's the trial?'

'God knows,' replied Lawrence. 'The average at the moment is about 18 months after being charged.'

'Another year? Bloody shocking…'

'It's a complex case…'

I almost stopped listening. How could I go another year waiting for this pathetic circus to get its house in order? I remember Len getting his case done and dusted in days and then there was Alice who had to give evidence in a more serious case – when she witnessed her partner being assaulted on patrol – but even that was resolved in about seven months so why did these so-called terrorism cases take such a long time? MI5 and MI6 must have something to do with it. It must be about their methods – and about what can and cannot be said in court. They cooked up a nice number before Iraq and now they were cooking up another one about my grandson. Over my dead lung.

'Do you think a jihadi can be cured?' asked Lawrence, abruptly.

'Cure? Not sure about that: changed maybe...'

'So why did Waz go to Muslim sufferers of asbestos-related conditions first?'

I shook my head. Lawrence pulled out a piece of paper from his folder and looked down at it. 'He knocked on more than 60 houses in his door to door campaigning – and 49 of those have been identified as those from the Muslim faith. That's quite a lot, don't you think?'

Nadia looked at me and shifted forward in her seat.

'He might have started knocking in a predominantly Muslim area,' I said.

'Or maybe he just wasn't well integrated...'

'Meaning?' I snapped. 'I thought you were here to help me...'

Nadia raised her hand and Lawrence smiled. It had not been clear to me why Lawrence was being so aggressive but now I knew.

'That was a very mild version of what you'll be facing,' said Lawrence. 'Benjamin Lees will probably be defending for us. He's a good barrister. We tried to form a synth band at Manchester Grammar School. Didn't quite work.'

'What was the name of the Iraqi man again? Shakeel something?'

'Er yes, Shakeel Ali Hameed. They're trying to bring him in. It's why the process is taking so long.'

I got up and walked towards the window. I touched the leaves on the plant pot resting on the window ledge. The scent from the leaves rocketed right up my nose and made me sneeze repeatedly. The cold, runny mucus dribbled from my nose and turned into a woozy light–headedness. I put my hand down on the window ledge but missed, stumbling, but still managing to retain my balance.

'Shakeel, you say? Got more on him?'

Nadia got up and raced over to me.

'Don't worry yourself about that,' said Lawrence. 'Your health is delicate so I don't want you to get in too deep. Just think about your own position and what you're going to say.'

I shrugged off Nadia's help and walked back to the sofa. 'My health is not delicate, okay? I went to Iraq and back in this state. Have you done anything like that?'

'Not really...'

'Well then,' I said, sitting back down on the sofa. 'If it wasn't for a solicitor we wouldn't be in this mess in the first place. Bloody Amjad Nazeer. I'd belt him if I ever saw him again.'

Lawrence closed his laptop and began collecting his papers. He glanced at Nadia and got up. He walked over to me and put his hand on my shoulder. He then reached into his blazer pocket and pulled out a musty–looking C–60 cassette.

'My music is delicate,' he said, handing me the cassette. 'Have a listen some time.'

He walked out of the room and closed the door.

Another year of this and Wasim would probably end up on suicide watch. As for me, who cared if I coughed to death one morning and lay motionless on the bathroom floor? Nadia, of course, was still doing her best but, with winter approaching, I shuddered to think how she'd cope with her studies and the three men – including me – who'd let her down. Even the two things that had kept me going since the bout of pneumonia – the thought of a grandstanding trial and the soothing environment of Hollingworth Lake – were fading in the distance. The trial felt like an eternity away and the lake felt so bone–crushingly cold that I was forced back into the seven-day routine of sleeping, eating, drinking, inhaling medication and reading local newspapers; I did try the internet in the front room a few times but it gave me a crushing headache on each occasion. But then Len came up with a surprise: he called to say Bernie Kershaw wanted to meet me. I was quite flattered, at first, as Bernie's photo (and story) had appeared in the *Observer* outlining his plans for the town and his new campaign. But as I examined the picture on Page

7 of the paper – his piercing eyes, his bulky frame (surely about 15 stone) and woolly turtleneck jumper – I started to become intimidated. He looked a genial sort from his photo but it was his status as the boss of a firm that gave me pause for thought. They had an uncanny knack of getting their way – and I wasn't sure I had the stomach for anymore charity do's or functions.

Bernie arrived in time for afternoon tea and sat by my bed while Len was downstairs in the front room using Nadia's computer to check on the construction of the Pride of Our Town website. Bernie didn't have a biscuit because he had to eat gluten–free products. He spent a good half an hour talking about his trials and tribulations of trying to get a loaf of bread that wouldn't poison him every morning. Since being diagnosed with Coeliac Disease, he said he'd put on a lot of weight because his tummy was finally working properly again. He was also surprised how quickly he'd felt better after diagnosis, like a magic cure, he said. If only a simple piece of toast could cure all the illnesses of the world, I thought.

He reached into his pocket for his wallet and pulled out a small, black and white photo. He handed it to me and asked me if I recognised the man standing on the platform at a train station. I looked down at the picture and immediately recognised the round face and thinning hair.

'Blondie…' I said. 'You know him?'

'It's my father Richard. He started at Turners in 67, a couple of months before you, I believe…'

'Long time ago, now. I must have only spoken to him a few times. Came on his bike and always had a camera with him. Did he work in Textiles?'

'For 12 years. Why did you call him 'Blondie'? He never told us about that. And he had brown hair too.'

'Nobody really called him that. He used to like spaghetti westerns and spouted the odd line of dialogue in the canteen. It's how I remember him.'

'He liked taking pictures too?'

'Hmm, once he was so exact and precise that we were nearly late clocking in. He wanted four of us in a line with the chimney directly behind us. He even liked taking them in rain. They must have been nice pictures: pity I won't see any of them.'

'I know the ones you mean. I've got them all at home.'

I coughed and reached over for another sip of cardamom tea. 'I'd love to see them.'

'It's why I came really. You're in about a dozen of these pictures. When I heard about the charity match it got me thinking about all that Turners stuff and I started going through a few of Dad's things. Then I came down to the match and was amazed when I thought you were the man in the pictures. I knew you were suffering so, really, that was the moment I thought about doing something for people in this town. I was only 15 when he died so I felt a bit helpless. But now I've got the clout to do something and I will.'

After his bout of energy there was a moment of silence as Bernie looked away from me towards the window. He reached over and picked up a handful of cheese and onion crisps (his gluten–free substitute hastily provided for him by Elisha). He looked down at them in his hand and slowly put it into his mouth.

'It took five miserable months for my father to waste away,' he said. 'The weight just fell off him. He looked like he'd been vertically chopped in half. Mesothelioma is cruel but he never complained. He was grateful for what he had. He gave us the values I have now.'

Bernie looked at his watch.

'Shit is that the time? Got a meeting in Bolton in 45 minutes.' He walked to the door and stopped. 'Look, I'd love to come back every fortnight and visit but that's your call. I've got a second place in Manchester – and as we're expanding the business up here, I can pop in at any time, no obligations.' He swallowed his crisps and decided to walk back in for another handful. He waved goodbye and left the house.

The trial was so far away but winter was lurking. Dr Howarth, in a fresh appointment, said my condition had stabilised (a legacy of Hollingworth Lake, no doubt) although it didn't feel like it. The cold was seeping into my lungs and there was no escape: the kitchen was freezing, the living room a little better and my bedroom was the worst of the lot – even with the nice electric heater Nadia had bought for me. She even put long pieces of cloth under the doors, leaving the curtains drawn, but it didn't seem to make a difference: the dirty mucus and phlegm were lodged so deep in my chest that I felt I needed a piping hot defibrillator to suck all the decaying stuff out.

But it was into this draught–a–minute environment that Bernie agreed to return. I was grateful to him because, with Elisha and Nadia generally being gone for most of the daylight hours, he made some of the days go quicker. Len could only visit once because he'd become terribly busy (what was that about bosses and workers?). On some days, Bernie brought his own biscuits and cakes and on other days he had a flask with him – the same one his father had used all those years ago at Turner's. It reminded me that my own flask and tartan drawstring bag were down in the cellar after being dumped there after my move from Maple Street. Most of the time, we shared intimate memories as the steam from the plastic white cups rose above our heads. After a couple of visits, he showed me his father's camera and the photos of me and my fellow workers in and around the factory. For a few seconds as I looked down at the photos and absorbed the camaraderie on display, I almost missed the place – but then as I looked beyond my colleagues at the huge, chugging buildings towering over them the aching evidence in my chest resurfaced. There was no escape: we were connected forever. We were like prisoners in a camp. Bernie sensed my unease and we pledged not to dwell on bad experiences because they weren't helping my recovery. It was the first time I'd heard anyone say the word 'recovery' in relation to my condition. It gave me a strange boost that I couldn't describe.

Bernie came around less frequently in the late winter months but in early spring he rushed in on one occasion offering to get some better care for me and a set of doctors 'who knew what they were talking about'. It came a bit out of the blue but I told him I couldn't deal with the strain of a new doctor or specialist or both: more questions, more investigations and more hassle; I was fine with Dr Howarth. Bernie took it well, and it was on this very same visit that he finally broached the subject I'd expected him to explore many moons before: my errant grandson. It was my only moment of true anxiety in all the time I'd been in Bernie's company: how would he react to a terrorist suspect lurking and living in this house; in this very bed, in fact? I needn't have worried: he had his own story to tell.

'My father's neighbour, Sean Fleming, was an electrician and liked to play five–a–side football at weekends,' said Bernie. 'One morning, out of the blue, he was arrested on terrorism charges. They said he was sabotaging people's houses by dangerous rewiring that may cause explosions or even death. The paranoia spread across the neighbourhood because he'd been in almost every person's house, including ours. While he was locked up, his wife was spat at and his kids were bullied in school. She eventually left. I'm sure you won't be surprised to hear he was released because there was no evidence against him. The charge laid against him was from a man who'd said he'd been electrocuted by a fuse box. Sean never really recovered. He drank a lot –

and he's still alive I believe – but I heard he'd moved down to Hastings.'

'Edward Heath was dead meat…'

'What?'

'Edward Heath was dead meat. A couple of men from Turners used to sing that. From Cork, I think.'

Bernie nodded. 'They'd have been arrested today, nailed on.'

There was a long moment of silence as Bernie remained reluctant to go head–on about our troubles, probably out of respect for me.

'I met one of these Labour MPs down in the Midlands,' said Bernie. 'Round about the time we were being sold the Iraqi story. I took the piss out of him a bit but he actually believed that all the WMD stuff was true. I couldn't believe it; he was dead serious.'

I sat up in bed, picking up my hot–water bottle and placing it under my neck. 'They're all the same…'

'Even Cyril Smith. Did you hear that stuff about him backing Turners?'

'I didn't know about that. I thought he'd look out for our interests a bit more…'

'The big lad only looked after number one…'

I tried to answer but could only mumble an incoherent word. Another long silence. Bernie got up and walked to the other side of the bed and looked out of the window.

'I'm sorry about your grandson. I heard you were getting him back on the right road: he had dossiers about Turners, that kind of thing. You've almost pulled off a miracle there: dragging him from the fire of Iraq and straightening him out.' He edged closer to the window so his nose was nearly touching the glass. 'These raids have got a patchy rate of success. He might get off. Most of the jury probably hate the Iraq war anyway.' He sighed but turned away from the window and looked at me. 'I know two other people down this very street who are suffering the legacy of Turners...'

'Don't know them...'

'Precisely. Because no–one works together anymore. When I see them, I see my father – and it's the same with you. This new group's going to be for all of you.'

There was a knock on the bedroom door. Elisha came in after coming home from school. She glanced at Bernie and then at me.

'Oh how I loved school,' said Bernie, with a smile. 'Time to go.' He briskly walked past Elisha and tapped her on the shoulder. He opened the door and left the room.

Elisha came over and sat on the bed by my side. She felt her tie in her hands, picking out a couple of threads and gently dropping them onto the carpet. She looked quite miserable but that wasn't in any way remarkable.

'Been thinking about it all day, nana jee,' she said.

'What?'

She looked into my eyes and hesitated. She looked away in frustration and took off her tie quicker than usual. She screwed it into a ball, turned and lobbed it against the window.

'Elisha, what's the matter?'

She folded her arms and looked at the bare wall. She scraped the toe of her shoe across the carpet.

'I feel sick about Wasim. I'm having nightmares about him going down.'

My eyes were about to roll but I managed to keep them in check.

'It'll all be fine, don't worry about it.'

She turned directly to me and jumped onto the bed, sitting cross–legged.

'The court case is in two weeks, nana jee, two weeks. Mummy wanted to keep you protected from all this crap so you wouldn't have time to get worried about it...'

My head was spinning and a ball of saliva nearly slipped from my mouth. I shook my head.

'So I haven't been getting all my mail?'

'Everything, but the court stuff.'

I sighed and put my hand on Elisha's shoulder. I lay down and turned onto my side. 'Sorry, I need a rest,' I said.

'Nana jee, don't worry, I've got half–term so I can come with you and get you through it. I'll look the wiggy bastards in the eye.'

'Please, Leesha, got a headache now. Tell your mother I want to see her when she gets home.'

When Nadia did come home she wasn't in the mood for listening. After two minutes of disagreement, she

300

slung her shawl over her shoulder and went into the kitchen to make the evening meal. We didn't talk again until after we'd eaten the courgettes and potato concoction which wasn't one of her best – and the chapattis too, were out of shape and crackly. The trial date was the first thing she cleared up: it had been brought forward because there were lots of so–called terrorism cases in the London area and simply not enough court space to try them so some of them had to be moved up north. This meant they had examined the cases already up here and concluded that, ours – and a couple of others – had the potential for quick results because there was only one defendant and his alleged crimes (in the main) weren't on these shores. So what happened to the complex case theory?

'Always been bullshit,' she said. 'Code for 'we better find some evidence and quick'.'

Nadia was quite snappy, I felt, even though it was me who had been wronged. If I wanted to escalate this, I could but what was the point? I had to grudgingly accept that she was right. She had been shielding me from the twisted thoughts of barrister interaction and that was no bad thing.

'We've ditched the 'Hijandchips' thing,' she said. 'We thought there was a market for it but the designs weren't really coming alive. They looked better on the screen than on the actual headwear.'

'Could have told you that.'

'Should have shouted louder then…'

She got up and cleared the dishes. She walked

into the kitchen and I didn't see her again for about 45 minutes, right on cue for my cardamom tea. When she returned, she had a bowl of pistachio ice cream in her hand and slumped down on the sofa.

'Do you want to do my dissertation?' she asked.

'Come on, Nadia, be serious. We've a court case coming up. We could lose Wasim for a long time.'

'Broke the fucking bank to become a mature student. Good couple of years but now it's a drag. Might pack it in.'

'But you've nearly got the degree in your hands…'

'Feels a lifetime away.' She glanced at me as she turned the spoon upside down in her mouth. 'Salim was on the phone again yesterday. Said he definitely wouldn't talk to the press if Wasim went down. As if I cared…'

There was a period of silence as Nadia finished her ice cream. She then sat cross–legged and rested the empty bowl on her lap.

'Do you want to go for the prosecution case?' she asked.

'When's my turn?'

'A few days after that. I'm going to try and be there for the duration.'

'What about your studies?'

'I was only messing about when I said I wouldn't finish my degree. Really Daddy, sometimes you really do get taken in. Of course, I'm going to finish it. The only reason I want to be in court as much as possible is to support Wasim.'

I nodded and instantly felt better. There was still

hope of a beautiful sun–drenched day later in the year when Nadia would come out in the right sort of black garb and make her father proud.

'I'd like to go for the whole case,' I said. 'But I'm not sure I could see it through…'

'I think you should stay at home until the big day.' Nadia picked up her bowl and headed for the kitchen. 'But that Iraqi bloke, can't remember his name, he's giving evidence first…'

'Who the hell is this Iraqi man? I'm sick of it.'

'Don't get worked up about him. I'll find out for you.'

'If I don't see his face, I won't get a night's sleep for the rest of my life.'

# 18.

The two of us drove up in good time. Nadia insisted I wore the navy blue trousers and beige cardigan she had bought for my last birthday but which had been sitting in my wardrobe, clean as a whistle but terribly unfamiliar and loose–fitting. I had read up on some of the cases that had just gone through at Manchester Crown Court and, naturally, they didn't make pleasant reading: rape, drugs, paedophilia, drunken assaults; it really was depressing. There wasn't a single terrorism case as far as I could tell: except this one. How could we have got it so wrong?

There was immense inner satisfaction that I had reached the court in decent shape – but it wasn't to last. As ever, the corridor of uncertainty can do strange things to people and this was one was no different. I was fine until I saw two barristers – one man, one woman – walking briskly in their flowing gowns, one with a mobile phone to her ear and the other carrying the thickest file I'd ever seen. As they brushed past me, it was as though a waft of toxic air floated across into my body making me violently and physically sick within seconds. The early morning potato pancake had no chance and rose up my body into my throat: some of it landing on the corridor and some of it on the entrance to the men's toilets. I was extremely fortunate that Nadia was on hand to help. The message was clear: I didn't belong here. It was quite intimidating.

Thankfully, I had improved sufficiently to take my seat in the courtroom. There didn't seem to be any other people in the public gallery apart from the two of us: there were at least the same number of reporters sat at the press bench to our left. One of them – a beady, overweight sort – hadn't stopped staring at me since I'd sat down. He only relented when proceedings began and he was forced to finally open his notebook and, perhaps, do some work. Then he came out. Wasim was a few feet away from us, surrounded by etched glass, accompanied by a guard who took off his cuffs and watched him sit down (standing only when the judge sauntered in). He didn't look round and it was a good thing because Nadia would have cuffed him one – the true long arm of justice if there ever was one. But I spotted something on the side of his face: was it a scar? Had he been beaten up? I kept my eyes on him as he made his plea and the jury was sworn in. He cupped his hands as though he was praying. Too late for that, boy. The prosecution started to make its case – and the smooth, stocky bastard was so persuasive that even I began to believe him.

'...Get a good look at the defendant, Wasim Rafeeq, a man who has travelled thousands of miles to actively fight against the Queen's forces. He did not tell his mother, he did not tell his father, he did not tell his grandfather. Would you believe a man who took up arms against the country of his birth while selling his family the ultimate dummy? Of course, it is beyond most people's comprehension. Yet we know what he did believe – global jihad – and we also know that it isn't long before the radical eye is turned in this direction and demolishes those he went to school with, those he played with, those he dined with and those he called best friends before they, too, become infidel fodder…'

And on he went. He delivered his case so well that I wondered why we'd turned up at all. I was desperate for Ben Lees to get up and stop him in his tracks but he calmly went on, even spouting outrageous lies that Wasim had Al-Qaida links. Lees finally got his chance. He got up and looked an impressive sort: tall, lean, glasses with reassuring arm movements; finger on chin and then arms folded and then back again. His voice was lower, however, and didn't have the range and authority of the stocky supremo. But he grew in confidence and did improve after a few minutes.

'…This young man cares more than most. He travelled out of this country to help victims of an earthquake and he came back to these shores and took up one of the most noble causes in the town. So what, may you ask, happened inbetween? A little ditty called Iraq is what happened. Didn't we all fail in that most tragic – and still live – episode. Didn't the state make errors? Didn't the security services make errors? Didn't US and UK forces make errors? Didn't our leaders make errors? Didn't we all, ladies and gentlemen of the jury, make big and small errors? Because if you agree with that, then you must agree that Wasim Rafeeq too, made an error. He was there to help like everyone else. He may have been swayed – but that's all he was: swayed. The evidence before and after suggests he cares deeply about his community and family. After his error, he showed his true character in becoming a carer and campaigner for his sick grandfather. This is the real Wasim Rafeeq, not the lost boy afflicted by the madness of Iraq – for which we all share culpability. His errors were our errors too…'

I felt a surge of hope after Mr Lees had concluded his opening argument but both cases sounded persuasive, detailed and ridiculously plausible (apart from the Al-Qaida links, of course). I looked at the jury – a grey–looking bunch with lots of glasses and woolly jumpers – and made a crude calculation: the Iraq war enthusiasts would return a verdict of guilty and the anti's would do the opposite. The undecided's would veer on the side of caution and probably want to convict. The problem was, apart from the Government attack dogs and newspaper cheerleaders, I didn't know any Iraq War enthusiasts. Yes, there was Eric Davy's dad – who came to support his son at the cricket club – and wanted 'Saddam Out' but even he said 'God, I hate those Americans' so whether he counted in the 'pro's' I wasn't sure. I deduced from this that we were on good ground in terms of Iraq – surely the jury had major doubts about it – and what it would come down to was evidence on these shores, or at least evidence that showed the lad was threatening to harm Westerners. Was there any?

Stocky supremo got up again. He was called Mr Hammond although Mr Hammy felt more appropriate. He called his first witness: Mr Shakeel Ali Hameed. A familiar feeling of strangulation returned to my throat. There was a pause as everyone in the courtroom waited. After an excruciating delay, a man walked in and as soon as I set eyes on the tiny, hunched over frame the jolt in my chest was so severe I thought I was having a heart attack. I grabbed Nadia's hand instantly to stop my fingers throbbing. The sweat gathered on my forehead as I looked again at the old, old man in the shiny shoes ambling into the witness box. I couldn't believe my eyes but it was clear and unmistakable. The man about to give evidence against my grandson was Bilu.

He had an interpreter by his side and it was clear he was going to give his evidence in Arabic. Most of the early questions Mr Hammond put to him went over my head in a fog of confusion, mild panic and bewilderment. How could the man who helped me so much betray me so cruelly and deeply now? I didn't have to wait long. Mr Hammond plunged his scalpel in almost immediately. He asked Bilu if he had found anything while Wasim lived in his shoe–selling slum and Bilu nodded and elaborated. I hadn't heard him speak so much before – and it came as a shock. He was fluent in Arabic and couldn't get the words out fast enough. I looked at the jury and wondered what they were thinking: how much Arabic had they been exposed to apart from the war on terror stories on the nightly news? These alien (and some would say, enemy) sounds in such an esteemed – and triumphantly democratic – institution couldn't have helped Wasim.

The interpreter translated Bilu's evidence in a slightly regal, pompous accent. He said Bilu's shop had been bombed last year and in the clear–up, two more mobile phones belonging to Wasim had been found by Bilu. There were also memory sticks, a compass and a personal diary. Bilu said he had no knowledge of them and they had been stuffed in a hole underneath the sink close to where Wasim had slept. He had no idea why Wasim had left them there: perhaps, he had simply forgotten because he did have a habit of rushing off in emergencies.

Mr Hammond probed the diary first. The jury heard some of Wasim's entries which were hardly surprising to me but sounded quite chilling in a courtroom.

'Together, we'll chop off the invader's hands, throw them on the floor and crush them with our feet. Those who cry in agony will get a megaphone in their ears with sayings from The Prophet (PBUH) to soothe their tortured minds...'

'A black fog is descending on this land and will infiltrate the kufr's heart. He will have nowhere to hide and nowhere to run. If he does not go home, we will create the biggest explosion he has ever seen and he will only go back on the wave of the hell fire...'

I lost count but Mr Hammond was well into double figures in relation to these entries. I stopped listening after the third one. Then it was the mobile phones which showed badly–taken photos of amateurish–looking weapons, a group having a picnic sat on tied keffiyah scarfs, another group smiling while standing over a body in a puddle and plenty more. At this point, Nadia looked at me and rolled her eyes as if to say 'another thing he kept from me' but I could only acknowledge her with a weary nod; a tide of drowinsess descended upon me without warning and I wanted to leave the courtroom immediately for a nap. But Mr Hammond began to wrap up his opening salvo – saying the images and entries spoke for themselves – and handed over to Mr Lees for cross–examination. I hoped I could ride out the fatigue for a bit longer.

'Mr Hameed, I can understand how a hard–working man like you would feel betrayed by what happened in your country,' said Mr Lees. 'You were born into the country of Mesopotamia but it became another country with a new flag and a new leader when you were a mere four years old. You have sweated blood and toiled away for more than 70 years for your new country and what has it given you? Assassinations, coups, wars, sanctions, hardship and finally an invasion in 2003. And yet you were still going strong. Until that is, your shop was bombed last year and your business went up in smoke. After seven decades, that must have been hard to take. Isn't it true you saw an opportunity for compensation and that is the only reason you are here today?'

'Laa…'

Bilu said this a lot and his sidekick followed up immediately with 'no'.

'Wasim Rafeeq was campaigning, at the time of the bombing, on the streets of his home town, so you don't claim he had any involvement?'

'Laa…'

'So why hand over this so–called evidence now? Why didn't you do it when he was living with you?'

There was a long pause and, for the first time, Bilu glanced over in our direction. Had he seen me or was he looking at his old tenant Wasim? He rubbed the back of his neck with his finger and then gave his longest answer. He claimed he was too busy selling shoes. Business had improved because so many people's footwear had been lost, blown–up or left behind when they were running away in fear. He said he had nothing against Wasim: he actually liked him. He had no idea he was involved in serious wrongdoing. But he was sick and tired of his country being a playground for foreigners: they had ruined it. He had been close to attacks and bombings before but this kind of direct experience had led to a lot of soul–searching. He was told it was a sectarian attack but after discovering Wasim's items he wasn't so sure. He felt he had to strike a blow for justice if his country was ever to get rid of 'bad elements'. He did not want to be a bystander any longer.

The repetition of Bilu's words into English left me beaten: it was simply too tiring to hear the same answers twice in different languages. There was also a feeling of suffocation and tightness around the chest.

I realised it would be an extremely difficult morning to get through, never mind the afternoon. I tapped Nadia on the shoulder and explained but she urged me to hold on for a break which she forecasted would come quite soon. So I tried to straighten up once more but my head began to drop to the side towards my shoulder. Nadia looked at me and quietly helped me up and out of the courtroom with as much discretion as possible. She said I was going home. She ordered a taxi and said she'd hang around and fill me in later. I couldn't argue with her because she was right. When I got home I was relieved to get back in one piece but annoyed that I couldn't stay for the duration of Bilu's evidence. I didn't fully grasp how hard it would be to listen and concentrate for a concerted period. It was a draining experience. It was impossible to go back in a few days and be the centre of attention; the pressure would be increased tenfold. Sleep, peace and relaxation was what I needed – and lots of it. A little massage from Bilu wouldn't have gone amiss either but I understood that the Bilu I once knew had gone forever. He was now a grumpy little bastard like the rest of us.

The sleep was good until I heard a knock at the door about 90 minutes in. I rolled over and hoped whoever it was would go away – and they did after about four knocks. But then to my horror, I heard the front door open and someone slowly coming up the stairs. I grabbed my hot water bottle but realised my hands were already burning up.

'Hello,' said a woman's voice. 'Is anyone in?'

At least it was a woman, I thought, less chance of getting a pillow over my head to suffocate me.

The woman came across the landing and stopped outside my bedroom door. There was a knock and then she opened the door. She popped her head around and jangled a set of keys in her hand. It took me a while to recognise her because she kept most of her body behind the door but it was Mrs Gleeson.

'You left your keys in the front door,' she said, placing them carefully on the bedside table. 'Someone could have waltzed into the house and had a field day. You need to be more careful.'

'Er, thank you, Mrs Gleeson...'

'Have to go now; got an appointment with the doctor's.'

She smiled and left the room. Where was the appointment? What condition did she have? I wanted to ask her but didn't have the guts. She went down the stairs and the front door closed. I could only think of Fareeda. I imagined her on freezing afternoons such as this tucked up beside me, advising me and instructing me on what to do next. As I heard Mrs Gleeson's shoes grace the pavement outside, the message was clear from Fareeda: take a principled stand for your family; the rest can wait.

Now the gowns and wigs really were intimidating. There was a deathly hush as all eyes set upon me in the witness box. My bowel was twisted in knots and I was convinced I'd leave a puddle if I got up: best to tense those bony cheeks and hope for the best. Len had joined Nadia in the public gallery to offer support. I was grateful for their presence but they seemed a million miles away. The session took such a long time in getting going that I wondered if they wanted to speak to me at all but once Mr Lees stepped up, he soothed my anxiety almost instantly.

'So Mr Rafeeq, at 73 years of age, having been diagnosed with asbestosis, having lost your wife five years before, having been forced to sell your home after 39 years and having to move in to a new home with all the upheaval that would bring, why did you travel to Iraq to rescue your grandson?'

'It wasn't really to rescue him, just to see if I could find him…'

'Just let me get this clear, you worked at Turner Brothers Asbestos for how many years?'

'21 years and a few months…'

'Hmm, 21 years. And you were diagnosed with asbestosis…let me see…about 19 years after you were made redundant. That must have been difficult for you?'

'It was, but others suffered too…'

'So going back to my original question, how did you, as it were, decide to take the plunge? I understand you received a letter from your grandson.'

'Yes, it was the first we knew that he wasn't in Kashmir, but in Iraq.'

'That must have been a shock to you?'

'It was.'

'Why hadn't the parents – your daughter and

her husband – done more to avert these delicate circumstances?'

'They just didn't know. Thousands of people travel to Kashmir every month. He sent letters, he seemed happy. If they'd known I'm sure they would have done something.'

'So the letter drops on your doormat and you read it. Did you decide immediately that 'I'm going to get him?' I mean, you did know you were travelling into a war zone?'

'I didn't think like that. I read his words and they made me angry. I wanted to do something about it.'

'Didn't you think of your illness?'

'It was better to do something rather than nothing. I didn't want to become housebound.'

'So what did your preparations consist of? I understand you purchased some cricket equipment from Romida Sports shop in Newhey…'

'Yes, there were a few things including the cricket gear. I felt I could help take the sport to a new territory.'

Mr Lees looked down and picked up a letter. 'M'Lady, I have a letter from the ECB – the England and Wales Cricket Board – concerning Mr Rafeeq. I'll read out a short, salient passage. 'We had a programme of spreading the game in Basra where most of our forces were based but we were overjoyed when we started hearing reports of Kwik Cricket emerging in Baghdad. We investigated and discovered that Mr Rafeeq had helped children take up the game and, further, there was a massive surge of sales of cricket bats, balls and wickets. We can only thank Mr Rafeeq for his considerable efforts in taking this wonderful game to a region blighted by war and sectarianism.'

The letter provided an exceptional boost. I suddenly felt like a fluent batsman at the crease; all flowing strokes and smooth, boundary–hitting potential.

'So the journey you undertook,' said Mr Lees. 'It was from Manchester to Vienna and then to Erbil in Kurdistan. Did you take your doctor's advice?'

'I didn't tell him.'

Mr Lees gave me his first strange look, as though he hadn't expected that answer.

'A soldier doesn't consult a doctor if he has an urgent rescue mission to undertake.'

I almost regretted it as soon as I said it but this environment was making me more combative than usual.

Mr Lees then started to probe the Iraqi leg of the 'adventure'. It was quite pleasant talking about this because I had only happy memories of generous people and a rugged but expansive terrain where you could breathe properly. The Iraqi questions were very specific: when did I first set eyes on Wasim? What was my relationship with Bilu like? What kind of exorcism was performed on me as a hostage? I felt I responded to these questions quite well and regularly looked across to Nadia to see if she nodded or gave me the thumbs–up; the fact I couldn't actually tell if she'd done so wasn't really important. Mr Lees was also interested in how I persuaded Wasim to come back home and what transpired once we got here.

'When did you first notice him taking an interest

in your health – and therefore – the whole Turners saga?'

'He first asked me in Iraq but when we came home, he started getting books, going on the internet and looking at campaigns. He really wanted to help. He wanted to start a new group.'

'…And his Islamic radicalism?'

'He hardly mentioned it.'

'Did he pray?'

'Of course, but now he had a cause he really cared about: in his town, with his people. He admitted he had made a huge mistake in the path he had taken and wanted to put that right.'

Mr Lees delved further but concluded his questioning by mentioning the police raid on our home.

'After all you'd done – with your progressive illness and noble intentions – how did you feel when armed police stomped into your home?'

'Sick.'

'Nothing else?'

I shook my head. Mr Lees read out statistics on the success of these raids and pointed out that they had only lead to a tiny number of convictions. Most of the time, they were fishing expeditions, he said. There were no more questions from Mr Lees and Mr Hammond got up and glanced at me. He looked smaller and more muscular close up. His wig tilted slightly to one side and he liked to cross his hands while talking.

'This is as easy as 1–2–3,' he said. 'First, you receive a letter from your grandson, Mr Rafeeq, clearly informing you that he has, let's say, jihadi and radical ideas and that he is fighting allied forces. Did Mr Rafeeq inform the authorities or the police? Of course not. Second, in a pique of madness, Mr Rafeeq boards a plane to Iraq to try and find him. Eventually he finds his grandson but doesn't think it wise to inform the coalition authorities so they can protect the public or at least gain some intelligence. Why on earth not? And third, when the two men returned home, wasn't it Mr Rafeeq's duty to tell the police here that his grandson may have been a threat to himself and others after his Iraqi adventure? Of course it was but Mr Rafeeq didn't do that. Instead, he took a risk that no one would find out and it eventually backfired because a police raid smashed up his house. I put it to you, Mr Rafeeq, that you failed on every level to inform the authorities and failed in your duty to protect your own family and the public at large.'

'That's not true.'

I turned away from Mr Hammond and looked at the judge, in detail, for the first time. She was the same age as Fareeda. She was like the Queen, I thought: looking but not feeling; tanked up in regal attire, a museum piece. I hoped she was on my side. Mr Hammond started talking again so I was forced to look at him again. I thought barristers softened people up and only roasted them at the end of their argument. I had been wrong. He had given me a bouncer straight away and I had no means of dealing with it. I only knew one thing: if I got out of here in one piece I would never step in here again – and it didn't matter if Wasim was taking the stand: good luck to him.

Mr Hammond had the bit between his teeth on Iraq and claimed I'd been naïve in making the trip. It was a relentless, forensic probing of each action I carried out, each scrape I got into and each place I ended up in. I was exhausted when he completed the Iraqi barrage – it must have been at least 25 minutes – but then he ridiculed Wasim's so–called 'awakening' when he came home. The bastard was now really enjoying himself.

'Do you think anyone can be cured of jihad?'

'No, but they can be shown a better path.'

'The defendant took up the asbestos cause – a noble intention, I'm sure – but was it genuine?'

'Of course it was.'

'So why did he knock on so many Muslim–owned houses? Was he getting new recruits to the cause?'

'No.'

'He was still an Islamic radical, wasn't he?'

'No.'

Mr Hammond opened a file and picked out a sheet of paper. 'When he was in prison, the defendant got involved in a fight with a fellow prisoner. One of the guards heard him say and I quote. 'You're all fuckin' white animals. On the day of judgement, Allah will spare none of your pigswill arses.'

'I didn't know about that.'

'Didn't know much did you? I put it to you that, throughout this tawdry tale, you colluded with your grandson to cover up his dangerous, terrorist–related activities.'

319

'No, I simply thought it was a family matter.'

'How, precisely, is blowing up coalition forces a family matter?'

'He didn't do that.'

'But he was prepared, capable and willing to do it.'

I could feel the pressure growing around my lungs. My swallowing was becoming drier by the minute. I found it difficult to listen to any more. Hammond's questions became repetitive and challenging in the extreme. I needed to get out immediately. Why not just feign a collapse right here? I'd be out in no time. I once knew a man at Turner's who had epilepsy and he'd feign a seizure anytime he was in an awkward situation. I remember him winking to a group of us gathered round him after he had a so–called fit while the foreman placed a cushion under his head. I could do the same: I couldn't take this anymore. The plan was set. I'd let him rip into me for two more questions and then I'd stumble to my right and collapse in a heap. At least, there'd be no shortage of witnesses to see what happened, I thought.

'He's a member of Al-Qaida isn't he? And you know all about it.'

'No, that's absurd.'

This was the one. As soon as Hammond opened his mouth I'd be out for the count. I did not deserve this kind of obscene interrogation. Hammond looked down at his papers and then looked up at me.

'No more questions, M'Lady.'

The jolt in my chest was severe. I held onto the

side of the witness box. I should have shown these bastards that this was no way to treat a sick, old man; a man who had laid his body on the line, literally, for his town and his community; a man who had rescued his grandson from annihilation. I still wanted to go down but saw Nadia from the corner of my eye. She had suffered enough and another traumatic, worrying episode – particularly one that was manufactured – would be downright unfair.

'Mr Rafeeq, you can step down now,' said M'Lady.

I hesitated and fantasised how a tumble right in the middle of the courtroom would go down with the jury. I looked directly at the 12 solemn faces sat beyond the wig merchants. They were all – to a man and a woman – staring directly at me. Their faces indicated to me that the sympathy was already there: no need to push things too far. I realised there had been enough drama in my life since Wasim's letter dropped on our doormat at Edmund Street. Now I needed some peace.

# 19.

The jury had been deliberating for four hours. Nadia, who was with Elisha in court, phoned me with an update. She wanted to come home but knowing her luck, she said, they'd deliver the verdict while she was driving down Manchester Road. Once I got off the phone to her, there was a restlessness and hyperactivity about me that was unusual. It was late afternoon and I started wandering around the house: upstairs, downstairs, in the bathroom, in the kitchen, in the back garden and, finally, in the cellar where I started to rummage through my belongings from Maple Street, some of which were still boxed up. I explored a dusty cardboard box and knew exactly what I was looking for, although I had to get past a green cagoule, a couple of Bollywood LPs and a pair of knitting needles to find it. The tartan drawstring bag was in better shape than I expected. I blew away the cobwebs and looked inside it: the tiffin carrier and flask were both in there, nice and compact; unused for God knows how many years. I placed them both on the floor and checked my trouser pocket for my six pebbles. As I got up, I also noticed a crumpled leather wallet inside the drawstring bag. I picked it up and zipped it open. Inside there was a back door key from Maple Street, a few till receipts, a folded up town map of Rochdale and a tiny, black and white picture of Fareeda. Her eyes shone so bright that I looked at the photo for much longer than necessary. I slipped the photo into my pocket and walked out of the cellar. In the kitchen, I began preparing items to put in the tiffin carrier: an apple, fruit yoghurt and a sandwich. Tuna salad would be fine, I thought, but slicing the cucumbers, tomatoes and onions into decent sizes was a bigger challenge than expected. The onions didn't make it. I looked at the clock above the fridge and hoped I could get there for the start. I hadn't been to the cricket club as a spectator for at least 27 years but somehow Wasim's fate co–incided with a midweek Under 11's game and it was too good an opportunity to miss. Put simply, there was no other way to relax.

I took a deep breath and placed the sandwich, apple and fruit yoghurt carefully in the tiffin carrier. The cardamom tea was nicely brewed and poured into the flask. I raised the drawstring bag over my shoulder and walked to the front door. I checked behind me to ensure I hadn't left the keys in the lock. As I walked down Edmund Street, I could hear my hushed, hurried breath accompanying each stride. I wondered whose heart was beating faster: Wasim's or mine? It was no contest. Five minutes later, I was in Spotland Road. The bag felt heavier on my shoulder than it used to. A grey mist hovered over Spotland Bridge but as long as it didn't rain I didn't care. I looked across the other side of the road and imagined both pavements packed with exhausted

323

workers, head down, hunched, streaming back from the factory: their thoughts extinguished by the slog of a 12–hour shift. They were strong, resolute and resourceful. They knew what mattered: to provide and be responsible. So how had that come to this? How did a boy from this town get involved in the dead–end of jihad? Nadia said he wasn't immersed in the host culture but I didn't agree. Hundreds of taxi drivers weren't immersed in football, pop music, politics or even the English language yet they were still well adjusted and weren't interested in 'saving' their 'brothers and sisters' around the world by force. They knew where their bread was buttered. They knew that struggle was about working hard and securing a future for your family not parachuting into a conflict zone thousands of miles away where every living being becomes the enemy. There'll always be too many enemies so why not make some friends closer to home?

This raw, irritable line of thinking subsided once I reached Spotland Bridge and prepared to cross into Bridgefold Road. I looked to my right towards Rooley Moor Road and couldn't stop my hands from adopting a cup–like, prayer motion: one for Bernie's venture which I hoped would create hundreds of jobs in the town and wipe away the legacy of Turner's forever, and the other for Wasim, the little boy with a cause on the brink of throwing it all away. But who would pray for me now? Wasn't I to blame for placing the lad where he is now, with the state scenting blood? Of course, I was to blame for the chain of events that lead up to his arrest and trial. If I hadn't gone to Iraq, none of this would have happened. But I had a sentence too: my decaying lungs without Fareeda's hand to soothe them. As I crossed the road, I cupped my hands for longer than necessary. An elderly woman walking her dog saw me and eventually said 'hello' after a short pause. I nodded politely and responded with a 'good afternoon'. Would Wasim have responded in the same manner? I wasn't sure. Live life where you're at or you'll live no life at all.

I had to cling onto the seat to catch my breath. The match was already in play but I could hardly see that far: I wasn't used to being so far away from the action. My breathing was now fast and heavy rather than the hushed and deep tones I had when I left Edmund Street. The journey to the ground, on foot, was hardly marathon standard – in fact, it was comfortably less than a mile – but I had been naïve to think it would be so easy, the Iraq adventure seemed a long time ago.

I threw my bag down and held my painful shoulder. I sat down on the cold green seat and was thankful the few people already in there had their eyes attuned to the game. I couldn't see any of the staff I knew, which was a relief: it wasn't a day for small talk. It took me about 15 minutes to clear the razor–blade viciousness in my throat. I spat most of it beneath my seat and immediately felt guilty about staining a playful sanctuary that had been so good to me. I settled down and picked up my bag. I opened it and pulled out my sandwich and flask. I looked out at the pitch and started eating my sandwich. It was a glorious sight: young boys looking so calm and considered, talking about field placings, easing into forward defensives, clapping a new batsman in. Whether it was the boys in front of me or the food I was eating, I was feeling better by the minute.

An hour and half must have passed and we were well into the second innings. I had drunk most of my cardamom tea from my flask and wished I'd made some more; there had certainly been room for it. A light drizzle had started but the boys were still giving it their all. I had started counting some of the overs with my six pebbles to ensure the umpires got it right. One of the fielders, on the boundary, was very close to me, about 20 yards away. He looked older than 11 – he must have been 14 at least – and wasn't as enthusiastic as the other players. He had been on the boundary fence since the innings started and I wished he'd get more involved. He looked over his shoulder and glanced at me a couple of times – and I offered a nod of encouragement – but it didn't make any difference. I wondered how well he was integrated into the team: where he went to school, what his family were like, who he hung around with. Suddenly, I got a tap on the shoulder. I turned and saw Nadia with a stern look on her face.

'Where the fuck were you?' she asked. 'I rang home about 10 times.'

'Needed to get out. What happened? What's the verdict?'

Nadia sat down beside me. She picked up my bag and rummaged through the items, shaking her head. She put the bag down and looked out on the pitch. She said nothing as a batsman ran four after a comical overthrow. Then, without looking at me, she slowly raised her index finger. I closed my eyes and tried to take the deepest breath possible but only managed a strained, pathetic one.

'How many years?'

She didn't answer. She looked down at my hand and noticed the pebbles. She stretched out my hand and took the pebbles one by one. ONE, TWO, THREE, FOUR, FIVE…She took the last one and closed her hand.

'Six years?'

She looked at me and didn't answer again. She clenched her fist and then laid out the pebbles in her palm. She pushed her hand right under my nose.

'Add six,' she said.

There was a moment's silence as I absorbed the gravity of Nadia's equation.

'Twelve!'

'He's got a lot of time to watch Countdown now.'

'Twelve bastard years! How? We had a woman judge…'

'We're cold bitches sometimes.'

'But he made a silly little mistake. We've got to appeal.'

Nadia didn't answer and handed back the pebbles. I took them but my hand was shaking. I looked down at the open flask and the tiffin carrier which were resting on top of the tartan drawstring bag. I put my hand on my throat to stem the soldering–iron sensation ripping into it. The asbestos fibres from the flask, bag and tiffin carrier had surely entered my being again and, this time, the body felt weaker than ever to resist them. Of course the items had been washed but why did I go into that cold cellar to bring them back to life once more? I tried to swallow but my tongue kept getting in the way. I felt dizzy and the heart was beating faster. This couldn't be happening now: Dr Howarth said I was doing well. I was desperate to swallow the torrent of saliva gathered in my mouth but it was beginning to escape. Nadia hadn't noticed – and I couldn't bear to burden her again now. She would have that beautiful black hat on her head this summer at university and I'd be the proudest father in the world. In the World.

'Nadia, please…'

'Shit, Daddy, watch your head!'

I ducked as the ball somehow leaped off the boundary rope towards my face. It was as if it came in all the way from Iraq. My neck twisted to the right. A deep, crushing sensation was choking my windpipe. My head lopped foward and hit the plastic seat in front. Bad, bad light. Blinking. Wasim's dark night of the soul at Strangeways. I fell to the right and my face pouched into Nadia's lap. Double vision and tingling. The smell of burning grass and the sickly taste of willow. Her palms were on my cheek but as she mouthed some words down at me, I couldn't respond – a savage ringing in my ears had erupted to make me almost deaf. She called someone on her mobile – it was too late for help now. I looked into her eyes and dreamed of clutching her degree in my hands. She bent down and kissed me on the forehead. A sweet kiss of lifelessness. The twelve pebbles fell from my hand and most of them fell into the flask of cardamom tea. Some escaped. A few years off for good behaviour, I thought. Hope for Wasim – if not for me.

There was only one martyr in this family.

# ACKNOWLEDGEMENTS

*The Author wishes to thank:*

Neville Fletcher, Umpires Secretary of the Central Lancashire Cricket League.

The Rochdale Observer.

The team at Troubador.

Dad for his Turner Brothers' recollections.

The cool delights of Hollingworth Lake.

The street sellers of Kurdistan.

The stoic and patient people of Sadr City.

The lost memories of Redbrook Middle School.

The roaming fields of Lenny Barn and the tireless campaigners of Save Spodden Valley.

Less thanks to Tony Blair, Saddam Hussein and George Bush Jr – but this novel wouldn't have been possible without them.

Finally, a special thanks to all the families, deceased victims and current sufferers of the Turner Brothers menace, particularly in the town of my birth, Rochdale.

# RESEARCH MATERIAL (selected)

*Magic Mineral to Killer Dust* by Geoffrey Tweedale, Oxford University Press

*Empire* by Dennis Judd, Fontana Press

Dispatches: Iraq – The Reckoning, Peter Oborne, Channel 4

*Sing As We Go, Her Autobiography*, Gracie Fields, Frederick Muller Ltd

*Three Kings*, directed by David O Russell

*Dickie Bird, My Autobiography*, Hodder & Stoughton

*Strangeways*, ITV documentary, first broadcast 2011